DEAD LUCKY

DEAD LUCKY

Glenis Wilson

SEVERN
HOUSE

First world edition published in Great Britain and the USA in 2022
by Severn House, an imprint of Canongate Books Ltd,
14 High Street, Edinburgh EH1 1TE.

Trade paperback edition first published in Great Britain and the USA in 2022
by Severn House, an imprint of Canongate Books Ltd.

severnhouse.com

British Library Cataloguing-in-Publication Data
A CIP catalogue record for this title is available from the British Library.

ISBN-13: 978-1-4483-0681-7 (cased)
ISBN-13: 978-1-4483-0683-1 (trade paper)
ISBN-13: 978-1-4483-0682-4 (e-book)

All Severn House titles are printed on acid-free paper.

MIX
Paper from
responsible sources
FSC® C013056

Typeset by Palimpsest Book Production Ltd.,
Falkirk, Stirlingshire, Scotland.
Printed and bound in Great Britain by
TJ Books, Padstow, Cornwall.

ONE

BANG!

The loud noise brought me to instant awareness. I'd been dozing – no, let's have it straight, I'd been sprawled out on the horsebox bench seat, dead to the world, no doubt snoring – the result of staying up too late last night. It had been a good party, although I'm no party animal.

Away from work I prefer the quiet life – when I can get it. But the engagement celebration party in Market Harborough had been enjoyable and I was glad I'd said yes and made the effort. The decision to go had been motivated, if I'm honest, as a tiny thank-you to Keith. No amount of thank-yous could ever express my gratitude to him.

Keith Whellan, horsebox driver, was a decent man, one who always did the right thing. And boy, had he done the right thing by me some months back. I'd be in his debt until they nailed down my coffin – or his.

'Come on, Harry,' he'd urged. 'Holly will be tickled pink if you turn up, I mean, you being champion jockey an' all.'

Holly was Keith's sister and tickling her pink wasn't really a priority; I'd leave that to her newly betrothed. However, doing a favour for Keith was a priority. He could ask any amount of favours he liked of me – and get them, if I possibly could. And with nothing in my diary for that evening, I could.

The loud bang had not only awoken me, but also seemed to continue to ricochet inside the horsebox that was now slowing down and veering to the right.

The windscreen, a metre in front of my face, was a convoluted spider's web, crazed and shattered.

'Bloody hell, Keith!' I exclaimed. 'That was some stone.' I felt the whistle of cold air brush against my right cheek before I noticed the small circular hole, like an eye looking back at me, and the splatter of red drops clinging to the wrecked screen.

We'd been travelling around twenty miles an hour down the country lane, but now the box continued to veer slowly right towards what looked like a deep ditch running along the opposite side, bordered by a hedge inset with some large trees.

I shot a quick glance at Keith, who was driving. Shot was a pretty good descriptive word but not in the best of taste right now. The bullet that had penetrated the windscreen – it was certainly not a stone – had not only gone through the windscreen but had also traced a groove down the side of Keith's head and blood was now flowing copiously down, soaking his hair, pooling on to his shoulders.

Instinctively, I snatched for the wheel and dragged the big vehicle out of the opposite lane, taking with it some foliage from the overhanging tree growing in the boundary hedge. The heavy branch snapped and smacked down against the wrecked screen, scraped the side of the scuttle panel and landed on the bonnet. What with the shattered glass and the dense leafy canopy, visibility was practically nil. I couldn't see a bloody thing.

But Keith's foot must have slipped away from the accelerator when he was shot, because the horsebox was really slowing down. I turned the key and cut off the engine. Manoeuvring my right leg into the footwell, I found the brake pedal and applied pressure. We eased to a stop. At least we were now on our own side of the road. I yanked on the handbrake.

Then I gave my full attention to Keith. He was out cold. I pressed two shaky fingers against the side of his neck and felt, with a rush of relief, that his pulse was still beating.

The lane stretching out in front was empty of traffic. Whether Keith had seen the vehicle from which the gun had been fired was an unknown but now was not the time for an inquest. I tapped in the three numbers and convinced a sceptical operator that, yes, an ambulance was certainly needed – adding the magic words 'victim losing blood'. I was told to stay with the person until the ambulance arrived. Given that we were out in the sticks with no other means of transport, there was nowhere else I *could* go.

I found a box of tissues in the dash, balled up a handful and pressed the wadding against the wound which ran from Keith's temple across the side of his head. How deep the bullet had penetrated, I didn't want to know right now. It was enough to try and stem the flow of blood. Shrugging off my jacket, I covered Keith's upper body. His face was a grey hue and his breathing ragged.

I did the only other thing I could: I kept up an inane line of patter telling him to hang on.

TWO

P en dipped her wooden spoon into the saucepan and topped my toast with a generous helping of scrambled egg. She was the live-in partner of my best mate and boss, Mike Grantley, one of the most successful racehorse trainers in the Midlands, indeed in the country. Breakfast, in a racing yard, was a meal to look forward to, one that had been hard earned by the preceding three hours of graft. Mike was already digging into his mountain of egg protein.

Pen eased her bulk down on to the chair. She was eight months gone and a perfect example of the blooming radiance some pregnant women exuded.

'You were lucky, Harry,' she said gravely.

I was telling them about the shooting – and about Keith copping it.

'Dead lucky,' I agreed.

'And Keith's unconscious in hospital, is he?' Mike queried.

'Yeah, I'm afraid so.'

'Are you *sure* it wasn't just a stone that got thrown up?'

'A stone wouldn't have penetrated the windscreen of a horsebox, my love,' Mike said.

'But who would have done that?'

'Or, more to the point, Pen, who was it meant for?'

'You mean, who was in the firing line – Keith . . . or you, Harry?'

'That's right, Mike. I've been awake most of the night going over it. I've still not come up with the answer.'

'Maybe when he comes round, Keith can enlighten you.'

I met Mike's gaze. '*If* he comes round.'

'That bad?'

I shook my head. 'I don't know. The hospital weren't very forthcoming. He's in intensive care. Told me to call tomorrow.'

'Wouldn't it be better to go and see him?'

'I intend to, Pen. But it will have to be this evening. I'm racing at Towcester this afternoon – four rides.'

'What happened to the horsebox? Did the police impound it?'

'Yes. Looking for the bullet, as far as I know.'

'Not in Keith's body, then?'

'Seems not.'

'I'd say that's a good sign. I mean, if the bullet skimmed his head, it might be just a surface wound.'

Mike waved his fork at her. 'Good thinking, Pen. I agree, a damn sight better than being buried in the poor bloke's head.'

'Does his family know?'

'Oh yes, mother's the next of kin. Dottie Whellan. Then there's his sister, Holly, the one who got engaged.'

'Not married?' Pen asked.

'Divorced.'

'And his father?'

'Ran off years ago, apparently.'

Mike finished his meal and laid down his knife and fork. 'Is there anything you want to tell us, Harry?'

I looked up in surprise. 'Like what?'

'Like are you on a case again?'

'Absolutely not. No more cases for me.'

'Says you,' Pen murmured.

'Look, Pen, I was damned lucky to retain the champion jump jockey title again this year. I lost so many rides due to being dragged into chasing murderers. OK, yes, I was over the proverbial barrel and when family is at risk there's no other option. But the last case was just that – the last. If it hadn't been for two or three of the other jocks having bad falls and being sidelined, I probably wouldn't have held on to the title.'

'Bullshit,' Mike put in. 'You were awarded it because you are the most successful, the best.'

I waved a dismissive hand. 'Honestly, I'm not investigating any cases. I'm not looking for any more. And I don't intend to.'

'Hmm, but then you never did, Harry. They came looking for you.'

I stared at Pen. She stared back. We both knew she was right.

It was a long trawl back from Towcester races that afternoon. There'd been a crash on the A1 and traffic had backed up and was just crawling. Plenty of time to mull over all the comments I'd heard at the racecourse. Email was given a run for its money when up against the racing community's grapevine. The word about the shooting had got around and I'd been quizzed all afternoon.

Keith was a likeable guy and everybody in racing's extended family wanted to know how he was. There had been more than one probing question along the lines of Pen's comments regarding whether I was investigating anyone right now. And several more asking if I thought the bullet had got my name on it, not Keith's. It left me with the uncomfortable feeling that Keith had somehow become my patsy.

Despite not actually working on a case, it didn't rule out an aggrieved party looking for revenge from one of my previous investigations. I was definitely going to visit Keith at the Queen's Hospital in Nottingham tonight. Everything depended on whether Keith had regained consciousness or not. Until he did, all the questions were going to remain unanswered.

I took a left at Saxondale Island and, three miles further on, drove down the country lane that led to Harlequin Cottage, my bolthole from the world. Crunching the tyres over gravel I drew up outside the back door. Predictably, sitting on the doorstep was an enormous ginger tom. His radar was working perfectly. My cat, Leo, knew I was coming home. He gave me time to switch off and lock the car before launching himself, clawing his way up on to my shoulder. His bellow of greeting down my right ear was deafening.

I scrubbed my knuckles along his furry chin. 'Yeah, I'm glad to see you too, mate.'

And I was. His presence alleviated the silence and loneliness of coming back to an empty home. When my wife, Annabel, couldn't stand the ever-present threat of injury I faced daily, she departed, leaving Leo with me. But he didn't hold that against her. We both adored Annabel and her visits were joyful occasions.

As I slid the key in the back door I heard the landline start

ringing. And I felt Leo's muscles tense up, claws digging in that
little bit harder as his ears brushed my cheek on their way back
to lie flat against his skull. He was giving a cat equivalent of a
scowl. Leo hated the telephone. The kitchen extension was situated
on the wall above the worktop. It was also right above Leo's
basket. The telephone frequently woke him up and he viewed it
as the enemy. I pushed open the back door and he leapt down
from my shoulders on to the red quarries. He stood, tail lashing,
emerald eyes glaring up at the source of his annoyance. I lifted
the phone, stilling the noise.

'Hello.'

Leo immediately leapt up and commandeered his basket,
curling himself into a tight ball.

'Harry, it's me.'

A broad grin widened my mouth; I could feel it even if I didn't
see it. The sound of her voice did it to me every time.

'Annabel, lovely to hear you. Everything OK?'

'Fine, thanks. It's *you* I'm concerned about. Victor's just rung
me to tell me about the shooting. Are you sure you're not hurt?'

'I'm not hurt. But Keith was injured. How badly we don't know
yet. He's in the Queen's and unconscious.'

'Oh the poor man! And after what he did for you . . . Life is
so unfair.'

'Yes, I know, absolutely gutting. I'm visiting the hospital tonight,
see if he's making progress.'

'You will let me know, won't you? If there's anything I can do
to help, just ask.'

I knew she was referring to her ability to give spiritual healing.
I'd had first-hand experience and could vouch for the efficacy of
it. Without Annabel's help, my constant falls and injuries would
never have healed so quickly. It was my driving desire to race and
also the one thing that, finally, she couldn't accept. The fact that
she put aside her own feelings in order to help me when I needed
it or, indeed, was grounded in hospital after a bad fall, spoke
volumes about her caring nature. She earned her living as a prac-
tising psychotherapist. The spiritual healing, which had taken her
three years' training to achieve the qualification, was a second
string to her bow – some string. The power that radiated from her
palms when she was focused on a healing had to be experienced

before you were converted to the truth of it. I had experienced it
– I knew.

'Will do. And if he's regained consciousness, I'll pass on your
love.'

'Oh yes, Harry, please. We owe him so much.'

I was still smiling at her choice of words after I put the phone
down. *We* owe him . . . not simply . . . you owe him, kept the
smile on my face. Even though we were no longer living together,
the bond between us had survived despite all the pain, the pres-
sures and extreme dangers we had gone through. That bond was
unbreakable – always would be. But the same history had come
between us. Whether we would ever be together again . . . I didn't
know . . . but I hoped. And would go on hoping.

The smile had gone however when much later than I'd
expected – it had been a pig of a journey back from Towcester
Racecourse – I finally drove down the A52 into Nottingham.

Away to my right stretched the sprawl that was the collective
buildings of the Queen's University Hospital, known to people of
the East Midlands simply as the Queen's. I swung off the A52
that morphed into the Nottingham ring road and followed the
parking signs.

Predictably, given that it was visiting time, vehicles were
practically stacked on top of each other. Driving around in circles
looking for a parking space, and just before I disappeared up
my own end, I saw an old red Ford pulling out and being gunned
savagely away towards the exit. For a split second I caught sight
of the driver, a woman, somehow familiar, but there was no time
to dwell on who it might be with other drivers queuing up behind
me. I spun the Mazda's wheel and claimed the space.

Walking back to the hospital's main entrance, I went straight
through the main reception area. There were staff behind the long
curving desk but I didn't trouble them for directions. I'd been here
too many times before – I knew the way.

Outside the intensive care unit, waiting to see if I would be
admitted, I dutifully applied hand sanitiser and waited, and waited
some more. They were busy; I wasn't – no problem.

'Keith Whellan,' I said when the nurse finally opened the door.
'Has he regained consciousness yet? I'm Harry Radcliffe,' I added

quickly as her brows drew together suspiciously. 'I was in the horsebox when he was shot. You told me to ring today but I thought I'd come instead.'

The ward sister shook her head briefly. 'No change. I'm afraid it's family visitors only.'

I nodded. I'd rather expected that would be the case. But if Keith was still out of it, there was nothing further to be gained.

'Ring again, Mr Radcliffe.'

'Thank you, nurse. Yes, I will.'

The door closed in front of me, leaving me to retrace my steps back through what most visitors acknowledged was an ant heap, a mystifying one that left most of them totally lost. I, on the other hand, had a long-standing up-close-and-very-personal relationship with the hospital and had almost reached the corridor leading to the main reception when a woman rushed round the corner, cannoning into me.

'Steady.' I grabbed her arm.

'Oh! Sorry, I'm sorry.'

'That's OK.'

She seemed in a highly distressed state.

'Look, are you all right?'

'Yes, yes,' she gulped. 'I'm visiting someone in intensive care . . . He's . . . he's been shot.'

She reached into her pocket for a tissue and blew her nose.

What were the chances of anyone else being a gunshot victim? Slim to none. Nottingham, as gun city, was a thing of the past.

'Wait a minute, this man, he wouldn't be Keith Whellan?'

THREE

The woman stared at me as she screwed up the tissue before thrusting it into her coat pocket.

'Are you . . . y'know, Harry Radcliffe? You are, aren't you?'

'That's right.'

Emotion chased across her face. 'You're here visiting him yourself, aren't you?'

'Well, I was trying to, but the nurse told me it was family only.'

She nodded slowly. 'That means they won't let me in either, I mean, not now.'

'And you are?'

'Mrs Cutler, Ginnie Cutler. I'm a friend of Dottie's. Y'know, Keith's mother?'

'Yes. But why did you say "not now"?'

'Keith was married to my daughter, Rosy. They got divorced last year. So, that says I'm not family any more.'

'I see. But obviously it hasn't affected your friendship with Dottie. And you seem to be concerned about Keith.'

'You always stand by your children. But I think my Rosy was wrong to divorce him. He's a decent bloke. And, in my experience, there aren't many decent ones.'

'I hope you don't include me.' I smiled down at her – barely five foot and maybe seven stone wet through. She was worn down by life, the stress of struggling showing clearly in every line on her face. 'Look, you could use a cup of tea, I'm sure. Let's see if the cafeteria is still open. What do you say?'

She nodded. 'Sounds good to me. And no, I don't include you. According to Keith, you can be trusted, OK. You're one of the good guys.'

'Thank you. But I'd add that it takes one to know one.'

She nodded ruefully. 'Exactly. My Rosy's too impetuous. Maybe she'll realize one of these days. Just hope it isn't too late when she does. But you can't live life for them, can you?'

We walked back to the main foyer. There was no hope of tea: the cafeteria was closed.

'How did you get here – by car?'

'No. The parking is a nightmare. And it's so expensive. On my wages, you can't afford to splash out.'

'Well, look.' I thought quickly. 'If you don't have a vehicle to worry about, let me give you a lift home. Whereabouts do you live?'

'Out at Redmile, y'know, near Belvoir.'

'Hmm, not too far from my neck of the woods.'

'Oh, I wouldn't want to trouble you—'

'No trouble. Tell you what, let's skip tea and we'll call in at the Dirty Duck on the way. It will be much more comfortable.'

The pub was in Woolsthorpe village, sited by the side of the Grantham Canal overshadowed by the famous Belvoir Castle. As a watering hole it was pretty good. Add to that it was in the next village to Redmile. Maybe it was my chivalrous side coming into its own, but my instincts were telling me Mrs Cutler was concealing the main reason for her dash to the Queen's. It was a long, wearisome route by public transport from where she lived and she had already admitted she didn't think she would have been allowed in when she got there. The level of her distress said something else had prompted her urgency to see Keith.

The Mazda lapped up the miles down the A52 dual carriageway and on along the Bingham bypass. A sharp right led us into Belvoir Vale and we bumped gently down the approach to the Dirty Duck. A welcoming warmth embraced us as I opened the heavy door and ushered Mrs Cutler inside. The brightly burning fire at the far end of the room drew her like a cat to spilt cream.

'Sit down; I'll fetch us a couple of drinks. What's your preference? Tea, coffee or maybe something stronger?'

'To be honest, I could do with a drop of brandy . . .' She ran her hands up and down her arms as though she was cold although the Mazda boasted a superb heater and, having noted her shivers – agitation or chill – I'd put it on full blast.

'Brandy it is then.'

At the bar I bought her a double along with a half of lager for myself.

She'd left her seat and was standing in front of the roaring fire. The flames were halfway up the chimney, reflecting off all the scores of highly polished copper and brass pans that hung all around the pub walls. She took the chunky glass I held out to her.

'Very kind of you, Mr Radcliffe.' She took a grateful gulp.

'Harry, please. Tell me, how did you know about Keith? About him being grounded in intensive care at the Queen's?'

'Dottie rang to tell me. She said she was going earlier.'

I recalled the old red car being gunned out of the car park. 'Does she drive a Ford?'

'Yes, a red one.'

I nodded. 'I saw her drive away. I parked in the space she'd just vacated.'

'Yes, she said she'd be going in this afternoon. She offered me a lift but I was working, see.'

'And your daughter, Rosy? Does she know about Keith?'

Ginnie sipped her brandy. 'I told her.'

'And is she thinking of going to see Keith?'

'Got the little 'un to look after, hasn't she?'

Ginnie was avoiding answering. I tried again.

'I'm sure he'd be made up if Rosy went to visit him. Later, of course, when he regains consciousness.'

Ginnie looked sideways at me. 'How bad is he, Harry?'

I shook my head and downed some lager. 'I don't know, wish I did. And even more, I wish I knew why someone took a shot at the horsebox.'

'You were coming back from Holly's engagement party, weren't you?'

'That's right.'

She looked down at her glass on the table and began turning it round and round on the beer mat. I kept my attention on my own drink. Silence was potent. If I didn't break it, sooner or later Ginnie would and I knew there was a reason behind her words, something she maybe wanted to tell me but was unsure how to put it.

Finally, she said, 'Maybe they thought you'd overheard something . . . found out . . . and they were warning you off.'

'Hang on, Ginnie, who are *they*?'

She shrugged, her gaze still riveted on the now-empty glass.

'Do you know something about the shooting?'

Ginnie shook her head. 'No. But you've got a reputation, Keith said so. Said you never gave up on a chase. Not until you'd caught them. Could be they're scared you might get involved.'

'Involved in what?'

She shrugged again and didn't answer. The silence stretched and I let it. But when it reached the uncomfortable, painful stage, I reached for her empty glass.

'Another drink?'

'No, no thanks. Well, yes, a coffee would be nice. A bit of caffeine . . . you know . . .'

I did know. The woman looked nearly out on her feet. I brought two coffees and set one down in front of her.

'You're very kind, Mr Radcliffe, Harry.'

'When did you last eat?'

'Don't know. Don't feel much like eating right now.' She sipped the scalding coffee, clutching the cup in both hands.

'Why don't you tell me what's bothering you?' I said gently. 'I'll help, if I can.'

She carefully set down the cup but retained her grip on it. 'I'm in a mess, a real big mess. I could use some help. But I've no money. I couldn't pay you, Harry.'

'Forget about money. The amount I owe Keith for what he did, well, I will never be able to repay it. But you're his mother-in-law—'

'Not since the divorce.'

'A technicality. Come on, Ginnie, tell me what the problem is.'

Her jerky gaze darted around the room, noting people, checking who was there but lingering on no one.

'I was in the right place,' she began hesitatingly. 'The right time to hear . . . but I'm not the right person to know . . .' Her words dried up. The coffee cup rattled in the saucer. I nodded encouragement and placed my hand on top of hers, stilling the chinking china.

'Did you hear about Lenny Backhouse being found dead?'

'The police pulled him out of the Smite, didn't they?' The Smite was a stream that liked to think of itself as a river running through the Vale of Belvoir. In summer it was definitely a stream, but through the cold months it could run fast and deep.

'That's right. Thought he'd had a skinful and fallen in – well, I say fallen in, I mean come on, the water's only a few inches deep. You don't drown in that depth, do you?'

'You do if you've been knocked out first and then dropped in. And especially at this time of the year,' I said.

'You don't think it was an accident then?'

My turn to shrug. 'I don't know anything about the man, wouldn't have a clue. Did Keith know him?'

'I *think* so . . . No.' She shook her head. 'He *must* have done. They both played darts, y'know, on pub darts teams.'

'What's Lenny Backhouse's death got to do with someone taking a shot at our horsebox?'

'Lenny knew what I know . . . more than I know.'

'And you were going to ask Keith if he knew whatever this was as well?'

'Yeah, I was, if he'd regained consciousness.'

'So you think the shot was aimed at Keith rather than me?'

'Hmm. But then if Keith knew, it was more than likely he'd have told you, so I don't really know.'

'OK, Ginnie, so what was it you overheard?'

She took a gulp of the hot coffee but it didn't seem to help steady her shivers. 'I work as a cleaner for a company with contracts in the racing industry. I get sent to different venues around the Midlands. And it was at one of those venues when I was working that I overheard part of a conversation that I shouldn't have heard. Cleaners are pretty well invisible, you know. Like a piece of furniture. I get to hear an awful lot of pretty scandalous things.' She took another gulp of coffee and gave me a weak smile. 'If I had any criminal intent, I could make a fortune with blackmail.'

'I'm sure.'

'It was nearly two weeks ago. I overhead two men talking – well, one man speaking, giving orders, like.' She took a deep breath before adding quickly, 'And before you ask, I don't know who they were.'

I knew she did but no way was I going to stop the flow of her words.

'The boss one said something like, "Lenny's passed on the orders, OK? It'll get the job done. What I need *you* to do is break the link in the chain. For your own sake I don't want the stopping traced back to me. You do understand what I'm saying, don't you?" And the other man said, "Count on it."'

'You're sure he said "the stopping"?'

'Oh yes, I'm sure.'

And I knew she was. She worked in racing industry venues. She would have heard the word before – she would know what it meant.

'Did the men know you had heard them?'

She nodded miserably. 'Oh yes. I was cleaning the cloakroom. Well, I was actually inside one of the three toilets when they came in. That's why they thought they were safe to talk, I suppose, because they didn't see me to begin with when they came in.'

'What happened when they realized you'd heard them?'

Her hands went back to rubbing her upper arms in agitation. 'They threatened me.' She began to rock backwards and forwards, drawing in little snatches of air, only just managing to get the next words out. 'They said . . . if I didn't . . . if I didn't keep schtum . . . the little one would get it.'

Just telling me seemed to have all but flipped her over the edge. I didn't want to push her for more details, but there was precious little to go on and I needed to know.

'Tell me where you were working, Ginnie.'

But she shot another fearful glance around, shaking her head vigorously. 'No, no. I shouldn't have told you in the first place. If anything happens . . . it will be my fault, all my fault.'

'But you need help, Ginnie.'

'What I need is a lift home, back to Redmile. Please, Harry, just take me home, now, *please*!'

FOUR

'It gives a whole new meaning to "sleeping with the fishes".' Mike shook his head in disbelief. 'The Mafia is alive and well and living in Leicestershire.'

'Yeah, that might be funny if it wasn't tragic.'

'The only tragic thing about the situation is the threat to Ginnie and her granddaughter.'

'I think you could safely say Lenny Backhouse would view it as tragic.' I took a pull of my coffee.

'If he was involved, which it seems he was, then he knew the risks. But an innocent toddler being targeted, well . . .' Mike snorted his disgust. 'You're going to have to help, Harry.'

We were sitting in the bar at Newbury Racecourse. With just the one runner, Baccus, owned by Lord Edgware, a win was, if not assured, at least expected. Baccus was a magnificent piece of horseflesh 16 hands high, with a glossy bay coat, a phenomenal turn of speed, and his jumping was every jockey's dream. Cat-like, he never over-extended by leaving fresh air between himself and the top of the brushwood, tucking up his front legs and usually gaining ground on landing.

There was only one other horse in today's race that also stood out and posed a threat: Bayard Boy. He was from Tal Hunter's yard. Tal had picked up Baccus and his lad, Darren, from Mike's stables in her horsebox. Trainers often shared boxes; it cut costs. And today, with just the one runner, it made economic sense to share.

Tal and I went back a long way. John Wayne may have had the words 'true grit' associated with him, but for me they applied perfectly to Tal – real name Albertine. I used to ride for her father, Jack, before his death – no, let's have it straight, his murder. After his interment, Tal, having immediately applied for and been granted a trainer's licence, had successfully carried on the family tradition. We'd been friends for years – if her horse won today, we'd still be friends.

But friends or not, on the racecourse it was winning that mattered. Coming second – for me, for any jockey – wasn't an option. Nobody remembered who came second. Winning was what the game was all about. It was a philosophy I needed to focus on. As champion jump jockey, to retain the title, I had to have winners. Maybe I was counting chickens, but in my mind the coming race had already taken place and the win had upped my total for the season.

'After what Keith did, you haven't an option, have you?'

I drained the black liquid energy and set down the cup.

'I mean,' Mike persisted, 'I *know* how much you detest getting into these situations and you'd rather be out on the racecourse riding winners, but come on, you can't duck this one.' He eyed me expectantly.

'Mike,' I said, sighing heavily at the inevitability of my reply, 'you don't have to remind me about loyalty, gratitude, and all the rest. Keith's not expecting anything from me because he's a good bloke. But he will be getting my hundred per cent on this. I've already promised Ginnie Cutler I'll help her.'

'Good man.' Mike smiled with satisfaction. 'Count me in as shotgun, eh?'

'No. Not this time. You're soon to become a father, remember?'

'Yeah,' he smirked. 'I am, aren't I?'

'There's no need to look so smug. Your part in the game was minuscule and pure pleasure compared to what Pen's contributing.'

'Oh, I didn't mean to belittle her, Harry. I mean, she's

everything, really everything, to me. And I know it hasn't been easy for her, this pregnancy. The morning sickness was a right bugger for her. And then there's her age, of course. Don't think she'll mind me telling you, she's edging towards thirty-eight. It's no small consideration when she's never had a baby before.'

'And that's why she needs you around – and in one piece. If you commit yourself to shotgun back-up for me, straight away you're at risk. And Pen wouldn't appreciate it. She's vulnerable, Mike. She's a lady who needs reassuring that you're putting her first.'

'But I do,' he protested. 'I know she thinks I was deeply in love with Monica, and I was, but Monica's dead. You've got to move forward, Harry, haven't you?' He looked at me pleadingly.

I nodded. He'd been madly in love with Monica, his wife, I could testify to that. And her death, caused by an avalanche while on holiday in Switzerland, had devastated him. He'd withdrawn into himself, built a thick emotional wall to block out the pain – until three years later he'd met Pen.

That meeting had been a traumatic one. Her brother, Paul Wentworth, had been driving their car through the village when White Lace, one of Mike's mares, had been spooked while out on the gallops and bolted. The mare and the car had met on a blind corner near the church wall. Thank God the injury had only been a small one – a rip down her shoulder that had been swiftly stitched by our visiting vet.

The wound had healed remarkably quickly because she'd received spiritual healing as well. This had been given courtesy of my estranged wife, Annabel. I could vouch for the power of spiritual healing. I'd been on the receiving end of it myself. But like other things in life, once Mike and Pen had met, that was virtually that. They'd been together ever since.

'You have to do the right thing, Mike, even if it's a tough call. You have to go on now, not only for yourself but also for Pen and Mike junior.'

His face transformed from anxious to joyful. 'Hey, did she tell you it's going to be a boy, then?'

'Steady on, mate. Don't get me in her bad books. No, I don't know what the sex will be. That's up to you two, OK?'

'Just wondered.' The wattage on his smile toned down a little.

'I take it you'd prefer a boy?'

'Don't mention it to Pen, for God's sake, Harry, but yes, a son would be great. Carry on the family business and all that.'

'She could do as a girl,' I said dryly. 'Don't be sexist.' And I pointed to a familiar figure coming over to us, drink in hand.

'Hey, you two. Good to see you.'

'Hello, Tal,' we chorused, as Tal Hunter flopped down in a chair beside us.

'Any news about Keith?'

I shook my head. 'Hospital not giving away any details. I tried visiting but got turned away, family only.'

'Tried asking Mrs Whellan?'

'Sometimes, Tal, your take on a situation is blinding. I never thought of it. She was driving away just as I arrived at the Queen's. In fact, it was her parking space I collared.'

'Ah, but she'd been inside, *and* got the full SP; you didn't.' Tal grinned. 'Genius, aren't I?'

Thinking back to her handling of our fabulous trip to watch the snow racing in Switzerland last February, I could only agree.

FIVE

Having finished my black, sugarless coffee, I rose from the chair, left Mike and Tally still chatting, and made my way across to the weighing room. They would shortly need to go to the saddling boxes and saddle Baccus and Bayard Boy ready for the 1.30 race.

Inside the jockeys' changing room it was, as usual, full of banter and leg-pulling combined with good-natured mickey-taking – and noisy. I went to find my peg but was waylaid almost immediately.

'What's the latest, Harry?' Hector, a tall wiry man, ex-jockey from way back, collared me first. He'd been a decent journeyman in his younger days, but now earned his crust as a valet.

I shook my head. 'Don't know, I'm afraid.'

'Word is Keith's in hospital, right?'

'Oh, yes, he is. In intensive care.'

He pursed his lips, nodding sagely, 'An' that tells us quite a bit, don't it?'

I had to agree that, yes, it did tell us the state of play right now.

'Was it just the one bullet that was fired?' Sam Whiting, Bayard Boy's jockey, came up through the crush behind me carrying his saddle.

'Yes.'

'Do you reckon it was meant for Keith? I mean, it might have been intended for you, Harry.'

'True enough, Sam. And I can't tell you the answer.'

'More likely it had your name on it, Harry.' One of the other jockeys, his voice muffled as he bent over, pulling on his boot, put in. 'I mean, with all your *extra manoeuvres* off the course, you're bound to have made a few enemies, aren't you?'

And again, as I eased myself through bodies towards my peg further down the room, I had to agree that I'd certainly more than ruffled a few feathers in the past couple of years. One set of ruffled feathers was still languishing in gaol right now.

'My money's on it having your name on it, writ large,' said a voice behind me that I recognized. 'Keith's straight, OK?'

I swung round to face Rawlson. He shrugged his shoulders and carried on zipping up his body protector.

'And you mean I'm not?'

'Tek no notice on him,' Sam growled, his Nottinghamshire accent thickening with annoyance. 'We all know we could use you as a plumb bob.'

'Thanks for the confidence.'

I reached my peg that held the silks with Lord Edgware's bright green colours and began to strip off. Rawlson's comments didn't bother me in the slightest; we'd crossed swords before over rides he erroneously thought I'd taken from him when it had been the owner's insistence that I ride her horses. And you didn't argue with Lady Branshawe's wishes. But he was a man who hung on to grudges. However, the overall mood in the changing room was that it was very odd that Keith had been the one to get the bullet.

Coming on top of the previous comments made at Towcester races, it left me with a distinctively sour taste in the mouth. If someone thought they had an outstanding score to settle with me, that was one thing. But for Keith to get caught, literally, in the crossfire was something else. It was disquieting but, by the time the jockeys made their way out into the autumn sunshine towards the parade ring, I'd pushed it out of my mind. Jump racing was a damn sight too dangerous a sport to let attention wander. In race riding you had to be totally focussed.

Out in the parade ring, Mike was standing with Lord Edgware by the side of Baccus. The horse was stamping a hoof and tossing his head up and down. He knew exactly why he was here and couldn't wait to start galloping. In all racehorses, it was pure instinct, racing bred into their genes – their delight and reason for living.

I touched the peak of my green silk coloured cap in deference. 'M'Lord.'

'Enjoy your ride, Harry,' he said, smiling broadly. 'I certainly intend to. And by the look of Baccus, so does he.' I nodded agreement. 'Just bring him back safely. And yourself, of course.'

'Do my best, Your Lordship.'

The familiar 'Jockeys please mount' was called out and Mike gave me a leg-up and I adjusted the stirrup leathers. Darren, the stable lad, took hold of the leading rein and led Baccus around the parade ring.

It was thick with racegoers crowding the rail to watch the horses walking round. The knowledgeable rubbed shoulders with the average mug punters, who, out for the day solely to enjoy themselves, were less focussed on each horse's form than the colour of their coats and, even more importantly, certainly in the case of the ladies, the horse's name. An attractive name that found a resonance for whatever reason with the punters was a sure way to have them placing a bet – and, nine out of ten times, losing it. But their intent was simply the pleasure of a day out at the races, which included taking part in the betting, meeting up with pals and downing pints.

Baccus, jig-jogging on his toes and continuing to toss his head up and down, was giving Darren a hard time, but the buzz running through him told me he was eager to get out on to the course and run.

Darren looked up at me. 'He's keen.' His face was one beaming smile. Like all the stable lads, he loved race days when he got to take 'his' horse and show it off to the public. Maybe even stand a chance of winning 'Best turned out', a prize awarded to the most perfectly groomed and presented horse in the race. It also carried a small cash bonus which for the mostly impoverished stable lads was very welcome. But he'd love it even more if Baccus won.

'Had a bit on?'

'Me . . . and the rest of 'em.'

'Let's hope we win then.'

'Sure thing.'

And from where I was sitting in the horse's saddle, feeling all the power and energy surging through the superb racehorse, I was inclined to agree with him. The only horse to touch him would be Bayard Boy.

The rest of the jockeys were all mounted now, their horses stepping out around the ring. We did a further complete turn and then the horse in front peeled off, away from the parade ring. Darren followed and led us on to the actual racecourse.

At a collected canter, I set off down to the start way off in the distance where the tape waited for us. The race was over two and a half miles with a total of twelve fences to jump. The starter was a strict, experienced man who exacted his own high standards. When a couple of over-keen jockeys allowed their mounts to come proud of the line-up, he immediately called them to order. So, some half a minute later than scheduled, he dropped his yellow flag, the tape flew high and the race was on.

High Jinx, from a stable in the West Country, delighted in forcing the pace. A front runner that fairly flew at the start of a race, he was putting on a grand show and was soon several lengths ahead of the pack. But it was an exacting pace, one that couldn't be maintained for the whole of the race and he was bound to ease back for a breather at some point.

I sat, one from the back, and let High Jinx throw himself enthusiastically forward knowing that in racing winning was all about pacing. Out of the seven runners following High Jinx, four were content to bunch up half a dozen lengths behind his flying hooves and I nudged Baccus up into sixth place, leaving the two behind me fighting it out for back marker.

We continued in this format for most of the first circuit, meeting each of the six fences and landing safely. The going was good and the horses appeared pretty evenly matched. However on the second circuit, predictably, High Jinx began to fall back and the four horses following overtook him.

Two jumped clear over the next fence but Bayard Boy, Tal Hunter's horse – our main rival – stumbled on the approach, put in an extra half-stride and all but dragged himself through the brushwood, sending broken pieces flying. It was such an unexpected performance, so unlike his usual surefootedness. But I knew then, as Baccus jumped clear, also gaining a length up on the next horse, that barring a fall, the race was ours for the taking.

The two horses behind me were still behind, and would remain so, both labouring and unable to find another gear. That left just two horses in front, one already hanging left, definitely tiring as we closed on the two-furlong marker. But I'd been holding Baccus in and knew he still had plenty in the tank. We cleared the last fence and I booted for home. He surged forward, went past the remaining two horses like a fired rocket, and we raced over the line a clear winner.

Mike and Lord Edgware were waiting in the winners' enclosure as a triumphant Darren led Baccus in from the course.

I slid from the saddle and patted the horse's sweating neck and gently pulled an ear. 'Well done,' I praised him. But the horse already knew he'd done well, that he'd beaten the other horses and won. Snorting and vigorously throwing his head up and down, he was full of himself.

'Well done to you, too, Harry.' Lord Edgware beamed. 'And he looks like he could go round again, he's so fresh.'

'Certainly fit, isn't he?' Mike, justifiably proudly, slapped the horse down the shoulder.

'And that's solely down to your management and training, Mike.'

He accepted the compliment with a smile. Mike loved his horses, loved training them to perfection and happily worked a twelve-hour day when needed. He was one of the most successful trainers in the country and, as his stable jockey, I was in a much sought-after position of being given rides that for the most part produced winners. It was this relationship that made it possible for me to successfully pursue the title of champion jump jockey every year. Of course, I was offered rides by other trainers – and accepted them – but both

Mike and I knew that it was a combined effort which enabled me to win the championship title. And I was very pleased whenever Mike received compliments, because he certainly deserved them.

I undid the buckles holding the girths and drew the saddle down from the horse's steaming side. Looping the girths over my arm I took my leave of the two men and went to get weighed in.

Darren, when he heard the Tannoy stating 'Horses away', would lead Baccus over to the racecourse stables. As a winner, Baccus needed to undergo a standard procedure dope test. This was also requested of any horse which raised a flag of doubt about its expected performance.

I showered, changed and met up with Mike and Lord Edgware in the owners' and trainers' bar where I was plied with a flute of champagne to celebrate our combined win. For me, it was never simply my win, or indeed the horse's win. Behind us both was an army of workers: valets, stable lads, box drivers, the trainer, the owner . . . the list went on. And I also, mentally, said a word of thanks to the man upstairs for my continuing ability to race ride. It had become almost a ritual now, especially pertinent after the bad fall at Huntingdon Racecourse a couple of years ago when I shattered my patella and was hospitalized for some weeks.

My healing had not only been down to the care and skill of many doctors and nurses, but also to the unselfish care of my estranged wife, Annabel. She'd flown in from abroad, cutting short a holiday with her new man, Sir Jeffrey, in order to help me get well so I could continue to race ride – the very reason why she had found it necessary to leave me in the first place. I owed her a great deal, in all ways, and always would.

It was some time later, as Mike and I were preparing to make the journey back home, that Darren came to find us, his triumphant smile now replaced by a serious expression.

'Everything OK, Darren?' Mike asked.

'Well, yes . . . for us.'

'But?'

'But Bayard Boy got pulled in for a dope test as well.'

'Hmm . . .' I said wryly. 'I did wonder why his performance was so bad, considering he was the only other horse in the race likely to win.'

'And what was the result?' Mike was scowling now. 'Surely they didn't find anything amiss, did they?'

Darren nodded miserably. 'They reckon so.'

SIX

M ike and I were talking it through in the car as we travelled back up the motorway to Leicestershire.

'It's utterly ridiculous to think Tal Hunter had anything to do with it. She's arrow straight, as her father was.'

I nodded. I'd liked Jack Hunter, admired him for his principles in business. And Tal was out of the same mould.

'Well, it wasn't the simple "bucket of water" job. They definitely had grounds for pointing a finger, must have.'

'True enough, Mike, and we both know that even a hint of doping is enough to hang a question mark over Tal's stables.'

He struck the steering wheel. 'It's so damn unfair. I don't see how the horse *could* have been got at.'

'Was it OK when the box arrived in our yard? Got to admit, I didn't even see Bayard Boy until we got to Newbury.'

'It appeared to be fine.' Mike swore. 'But I'm going to grill Darren when he gets back tonight. See if he noticed anything – *anything*. She could go to the wall over this, y'know. Something like a doping charge hanging over her business. Doesn't take much to put owners off.'

I knew he was right. Owners, as a breed themselves, were as cautious as a nun in a monastery. The slightest whiff of corruption and they would be swiftly taking their horses away. No yard could stand a mass withdrawal – and to come back after something like that would probably take a miracle. Even if the charges were dropped, the very fact the horse had tested positive would smack of a lack of security and control in the yard. And it was certainly not true. Mike was quite right, it was damn unfair, especially after all the years and years of being above suspicion.

'Don't be too hard on Darren, though. I'm quite sure it's nothing he's been involved in.'

Mike didn't comment, merely grunted. I knew he was wearing his trainer's hat right now and seeing it from Tal's perspective. I didn't blame him. In his position it was what I would have done too. It was a swine of a thing to have happened. And if it came to a doping inquiry, nothing could alter the result of the test – that was rooted in scientific fact.

When we reached Mike's yard on the Leicestershire/ Nottinghamshire border, he switched off the engine and jerked the hand brake. Then simply sat, silently staring out of the window. I waited. From the look on his face he was about to say something I didn't want to hear.

I leaned forward, reached for the door handle, made to get out of the car. His hand shot out, gripping my arm hard.

'If it gets naughty, Harry, you'll have to do something. You know that, don't you?'

'Look, Mike,' I protested. 'I've already agreed I'll look into this business of Keith taking a bullet and I most certainly will – plus the threat against his ex-mother-in-law and his little daughter. But if I'm going to carry on race-riding, chasing winners, I can't take on anything else. You must see that.'

'What I see, Harry, is our mutual friend, Tal Hunter, being set up for a fall. She didn't dope the horse, someone else did – *if it's proven*. And that could take a long time. *But* you may very well be the only person who can help her.'

Mike's words were playing around in my head all the way home to Nottinghamshire, to Harlequin Cottage. If he was correct, and I *was* the only person who *could* help Tal, I didn't even have a choice.

I crunched the car over the gravel outside the back door, got out and, irritation gaining control, slammed the door. Like a reflex action, the cottage door in front of me swung open. I gaped. A woman stood there, slim, beautiful and blonde. And my irritation melted away.

Annabel stood in the doorway, smiling a welcome and nursing a besotted ginger cat. The big beast lay placidly upside down in her arms and, even before I'd closed the gap between us, I could hear Leo purring for England. A pneumatic road drill would have had trouble being heard above those reverberating tiger-loud purrs.

'I see he got first claim on you, as usual.' A stupid grin plastered itself across my face. OK, I couldn't actually see it, but I could feel the smile stretching my lips. And an exquisite drift of perfume brought past memories instantly to mind. I breathed in deeply. The memories were beautiful, sensual, precious and everlasting. 'But, you know what?' I said.

She shook her head. 'Tell me.'

'If it was just Leo you've come to see, as long as you're here, I'll go along with that.'

She met my gaze and you could have powered London with the charge of electricity that zipped between us. For several seconds it bonded us together.

Then she had to go and ruin it. 'Of course I've come to spoil Leo. And if I don't give him his treat soon, that sardine will create a very nasty pong in the kitchen.'

She retreated indoors and, shaking my head but still grinning, I followed her inside and closed the door behind us.

Her visit was such an unexpected surprise. It immeasurably increased my delight and pleasure, her being here. Normally, she would just give me a quick ring. It always left me yearning for more of her. I leaned against the Rayburn rail and watched as she took a saucer from the cupboard, unwrapped the said smelly fish and placed it, intact, on the saucer.

Leo, having jumped down from her arms in gleeful anticipation, was weaving in and out between her ankles, giving little chirrups of encouragement.

'There you are, my beautiful boy. Knock yourself out.' She put his treat down on the red quarry tiles and stepped back to watch. He was instantly on it, grabbing the fish, twisting his jaw sideways as he chewed away.

'You could have cut it up. Make things easier for him.'

'Yes,' she said, 'I *could.* But then, it would be gone all too soon. Small amounts don't last very long, do they? This way, although he has to work for it, the payoff is that it extends his pleasure.'

'We are talking about Leo, aren't we?'

'But of course. You see, I *know* his favourite nibble is a pilchard and I would have cut that up, it's bigger, and I wouldn't want him to struggle. However, I didn't have one on me.'

'Course you didn't,' I agreed, smiling at her, still shaking my head. This was my Annabel, the woman I was crazily, hopelessly in love with, even though we no longer lived together as man and wife. And I strongly suspected I was in serious danger of falling even deeper in love with her – if that were possible.

Leo finished his fish, backed away flicking a fastidious paw, then in a ginger flash he leapt on to the worktop and sat down in his basket. Coiling his thick, furry tail round tidily, he settled to the job of meticulously washing his whiskers, extracting every last taste of sardine.

I never tired of seeing him perform this routine of arranging his tail. There had been a point a year or so back when a midnight intruder, having broken in to the cottage with the intention of seeing me off, had tried to set Harlequin Cottage on fire. It was only Leo's intervention that had saved me being burnt to a crisp. But because of that he nearly had to have his beautiful furry tail amputated. It resulted in an emergency middle-of-the-night dash to the vets to try and save it.

Now, I gloried in the sight of him and his furry ginger banner. That night he'd saved my life. And it wasn't the only time, either. I most certainly owed that cat. Annabel also knew all about his exploits on my behalf and Leo now had two fully committed slaves.

She retrieved the saucer from the tiles and stuck it under the hot tap.

'I've put our supper in the fridge, by the way.'

'Really?'

'Hmm . . . nothing much, just a salmon concoction.'

I grinned. 'Keep your voice down, Leo might hear you and I'm sure he'd like a bit of that.'

'Well, right now, I'd like a nice mug of tea.'

I took the saucer from her as she finished drying it on the tea towel, putting it back in the cupboard. Then I placed my hands on her shoulders and guided her out of the kitchen through to the lounge and gently pushed her down on the settee.

'Sit, and relax. Your tea is coming up, ma'am.'

'How very dominating.' But she was smiling.

Leo, having completed his ablutions, trotted in and jumped up on to her knee. She scooped him up, buried her face in his ginger fur and proceeded to pour loving murmurs in his ear. The deep purrs resumed.

'I know when I'm not wanted,' I said.

And went to make tea.

The salmon concoction was delicious. I'd had no doubts that it would be. Annabel was an excellent cook.

'So, what prompted you to come today?'

'Two successive clients – both cancelled. That left my diary clear from three this afternoon.'

'Sorry about your loss of business.'

'Don't be, doesn't happen often. But when it does I try to make the most of my time.'

'Then I'm honoured you're here.'

She shrugged. 'Like you said, I came to see Leo.'

'Course you did. Like you made that lovely supper for him . . . not for me.'

A slow smile spread across her face. 'I could have brought you a sardine, I suppose . . .'

'But you didn't.' I let my hand slide across the table and placed it on top of hers. 'Stay overnight?'

She turned her hand over so that our palms met. Her eyes then met mine. My heart beat increased and I squeezed her hand. '*Please?*'

Slowly she shook her head. 'I'm not ready . . . yet, Harry. One day, maybe, but not now.'

'Still because of the racing, the risks?'

'You don't ever need to ask that, do you? It hasn't gone away, Harry. You can't give it up. I can't take it. It hurts you when you have a fall. But it hurts me too, each time you ride – even when you *don't* have an injury.'

I stroked her hand. 'I know . . . And I know it's because you love me, I don't even need to ask you that question.'

'No, you don't. It's what brings me back, keeps on bringing me back.'

'Couldn't you stay?' I said softly.

'Harry, if I stayed, if we slept together, I couldn't go home again. I'm not strong enough to fight it. Don't ask me to.'

I bent my head, hiding my disappointment.

'If you'd rather I didn't come round any more, please . . . tell me to stay away.'

'Annabel, my darling, I'm not that strong either.'

'Then don't spoil what we have.'

'One day, and I can't say when that day will come, racing will give me up. It can't be the other way round. On that day, don't ask if you can come. Just come. Unless you find another man in the meantime.'

She shook her head. 'Darling, Harry. I've *tried* that. It doesn't work, does it?' Her voice was barely above a whisper. 'Second best is not good enough – for anyone. And that's what Sir Jeffrey realized. Oh yes, he was in love with me. And I really thought I cared enough for him to make it work. But it wasn't enough, was it? Not in the end. It's never enough.'

'You and I, we have the real thing, Annabel. Beyond questioning.'

'Yes.'

'When we get rid of the risk, there'll be nothing to keep us apart.'

'Even now, you're like a magnet for me, Harry. I *can't* keep away. But the thing is, I can't stay either.'

I went to her, put my arms around her and simply hugged her whilst she clung to me. Like Leo and his sardine, we stayed that way for some time – extending our embrace, embracing our closeness.

SEVEN

At my knock, Dottie Whellan opened the back door of the terraced cottage. The facial resemblance between herself and Keith immediately stamped them as mother and son.

'Oh, hello, Mr Radcliffe.'

'Harry, please.'

She nodded. 'Of course. Come on in. Sorry the place is a mess, I've only just got back from the hospital.'

The introduction to why I was standing on her doorstep couldn't have been orchestrated any better. 'Thanks.' I stepped into the tiny kitchen and she immediately showed me through to the equally small sitting room.

'Take a pew. I'll just switch on the fire, it's parky in here, isn't it?'

'If it's not convenient right now—'

'Aw, don't be silly. Anyways, I was wanting to speak to you, *privately*, like. Just sit yoursen down and I'll mash a cup of tea.'

She bustled away and within minutes I could hear the kettle getting up steam. My first question had to be to ask how Keith was, but although it seemed sensible enough, if he had suffered a setback and was worse, my query could spark off an attack of upsetting anxiety.

I listened to the approaching rattle of pots and decided I'd let her make the opening remark. She set the tray of tea down, lifted one of the mugs and handed it to me. 'Didn't think you took sugar.' I shook my head.

'As I said, I've just been up the Queen's to see how Keith's going on.' She took a long, restoring gulp of tea. How she swallowed it I'd no idea; it was scalding hot.

'Ha, that's better, you can deal with anything, can't you, when you've had a drink of tea. It's got to be hot, mind.' I nodded – and waited. 'He's no better.' Her fingers gripped the handle of the mug more tightly.

'Still unconscious, then?'

'Yes.'

'I'm really sorry. Is there anything I can do?'

'Yes, there is.'

'Tell me.'

'I want to know if that bullet was meant for Keith – or did it have *your* name on it?'

It was the question a dozen other people had asked me. I shook my head helplessly. 'Dottie, if I knew the answer to that, I'd tell you. But I don't. Just wish I did.'

'Well.' She drank deeply from her mug. 'You're supposed to be a whiz at solving mysteries, murders . . . I mean, you *are,* aren't you? You've got murderers banged up . . .'

She let the silence stretch between us and I was forced to agree that, yes, I had been instrumental in bringing criminals to justice.

'I know you're not one to brag about what you've done, Harry. I understand that.' She buried her face in the mug and finished her tea. When she looked up at me again, there were tears running down her cheeks. 'After what my Keith did for *you*, I'd have thought you'd help us now.'

I reached across and took her hand. 'Dottie, I've already agreed I'm on the case. That's why I've come to see you.'

'Who did you tell that to?' She bridled. 'I'm his mother. You should have told me first.'

'Wait, now before you get upset, let me fill you in. I went over to the Queen's the night before last. They wouldn't let me in.'

'Family only, is what they told me when I went.'

'Yes. And as you drove off out of the car park, I took your parking spot. However, they wouldn't let me see Keith.' She nodded. 'But there was someone else trying to see him. And they wouldn't let her in either.'

'Who?'

'A friend of yours, well, a short while back she would have been classed as family—'

'Y'mean Ginnie?'

'Yes. I gather that she thinks a lot of Keith, wishes her daughter hadn't divorced him.'

'That's right, she does, tried to talk Rosy out of it, but that girl's headstrong, y'know. Alus lookin' for greener grass.'

'Anyway, I promised Ginnie that I'd do my best for Keith – and I will. There's nothing to go on at the moment. I'm hoping that when Keith regains consciousness, he may be able to remember those few seconds just before that shot came through the horsebox windscreen.'

'But what about you? Didn't you see anything?'

'No,' I said ruefully. 'I'm afraid Holly's party the night before was a bit too good. I'd fallen asleep in the cab. It was the shot that woke me up.'

'I see.' Her voice was flat, hope draining out of her. 'Well, if you was asleep, an' you didn't see owt . . . that's it then. Yer can't help. Even if you want to.'

'Now hold on, Dottie. Let's wait until Keith gets a bit better, when he's able to talk to us, eh?'

She sat, hands clasped together, tears trickling down. '*If he gets better . . .*'

'Hmm.' Mike frowned. 'Dottie could be right. We don't know any details about Keith's condition apart from the fact he remains unconscious. I suppose it depends how much damage was done by the bullet.'

'I can't help feeling responsible. I mean, which is the most likely? Someone wants to kill me – or wants to kill Keith?'

Mike and I were sitting in the office at his racing stables. He'd rung me late last night. I'd just got in from seeing Dottie Whellan and reached for the kitchen wall phone across a recumbent – and cross – Leo who had been unceremoniously woken up.

'Been thinking it over, Harry,' Mike had said, diving in as he usually did. 'This grilling of Darren, I've held off having a word with him until I'd spoken to you because I want you to sit in. You've never had a doping job to look into before, but it can't be much different from your usual investigations, can it? Tracking down what actually happened? Anyway, I want you in right at the start.'

'Mike, I *am* in right from the start.' And I'd told him of my visit to see Keith's mother.

Now, this morning, stirring a spoonful of honey into my coffee mug, I put forward a tentative theory that had been keeping me awake in the night. 'Whichever one of us was the target – and if I *were* allowed a bet, I'd have to say it was me they were aiming for – I'd say these two situations are linked. No way of telling how, of course, just a gut instinct.'

'Knowing the results of some of your previous gut instincts, Harry, I'd say you may be right. Question is, how do you start? Which person is in most need?' Mike spread his hands. 'There's Keith, of course, but his needs are being met by the hospital. And Dottie's needs are tied up with the nursing care he's receiving. She can't do anything for him personally right now. Then there's Keith's little girl, Sophie. She's been threatened.'

'Don't forget Ginnie Cutler,' I put in.

'Yes, of course,' Mike said irritably, 'and Ginnie. Then after that part of the puzzle, we have poor old Darren—'

'Who we don't think was in any way to blame.'

Mike glared at me for interrupting his thought pattern. '*Then* we have Tal and the hell of a mess *she's* in.' He paused to draw in a deep breath. 'That makes six – that we know about. There could well be others that are caught in the fall-out—'

'Whoa, hold it. OK, Mike, OK. You've made yourself clear.

And six people in need are way more than enough. Whatever I can do, I will.'

'So, when you finish racing today, you'll come back here, yes? Better make it at the close of afternoon stables.'

'Right,' I said, suppressing a sigh. There was still half of my column to finish writing for the newspaper – deadline nine p.m. Sometimes, like now, I really resented having to start writing after a day's race riding. But then I had to remind myself it was only the income from my writing that had seen me through after the horrific fall at Huntingdon Racecourse had shattered my left kneecap and kept me out of the saddle. It had proved remarkably fruitful in that, in addition to my newspaper column, I'd also been commissioned to write a biography for a retiring trainer.

And not only was I grateful for the income I received from the subsequent sales of the biography, what had happened afterwards – causing owners to take their horses away from Elspeth Maudsley's stables – had resulted in one of the owners, Samuel Simpson, sending his horses to Mike's stables instead. That in turn had led to my increase in rides as Sam requested I ride for him. Very much a win-win all round.

It was Sam I was riding for today. The first mare, White Lace, actually belonged to his daughter, Chloe. He'd bought the filly as a thirtieth-birthday present for her. I'd ridden out White Lace first lot the previous morning. She was a sure, cat-footed jumper and usually gained a length on landing.

The other was a gelding Samuel had bought at the Newmarket sales. He'd twisted my arm to accompany him and run an eye over the horses on sale. Today would be Black Ice's first race for our stable and we were all quietly hoping for great things.

You could track a horse's history, go into all the details of his breeding, but until you'd had a race with him, you couldn't be sure of his performance. His temperament, however, was wonderful and I doubted if we would find any hidden faults with him. He belonged to Samuel – no giving this one away. I knew Samuel had big plans for the horse's future.

However, a horse might be beautifully bred with a sire who had won Group 1's and on paper was very tempting, plus your outlay – which was a substantial amount – seemed to uphold this, only to find that the horse itself actually proved a big disappointment.

So today's race was the important one. Would Black Ice uphold all the promise? Until he'd been raced against the other promising four-year-olds, nobody could be certain. All else could only be planned once we'd seen him in action on the racecourse.

'Dottie going to let you know how Keith's doing then, is she?'

I dragged my attention back to the present. 'Sorry, Mike, I was in front already thinking about Black Ice's race.'

'Don't apologize. You're quite right.' He jumped to his feet. 'Let's get on with the job.'

'I expect she'll let me know as soon as she hears anything, but I'll give the hospital a call later, this evening, probably. At the very least they can say "No change".'

We walked out into the stable yard. It was as usual a bustling place, full of activity, the lads going about their normal routine but the atmosphere edged with expectation – unseen but definitely there. This was a race day and that meant the probability of bringing home a winner later. Nothing like a winner to increase the feel-good factor in a stable yard.

I was motoring down to Uttoxeter Racecourse in my own vehicle but the two horses were going in the small horsebox. It would be driven by the box-driver and, because the horses were in consecutive races, it meant two other lads were also needed.

'Now make sure you're back at the end of evening stables,' Mike cautioned. 'And for God's sake bring Black Ice back in one piece. I couldn't cope with Samuel going to pieces.'

I grinned. 'He'll be ecstatic. That horse is going to win.'

'Wish I could be as optimistic.'

EIGHT

Chloe and Samuel were standing talking to Mike in the centre of the parade ring in the mellow autumn sunshine. Chloe fluttered her fingers towards me as I came across from the weighing room. Fashionably dressed as usual, this time in a scarlet trouser suit, tiny black hat perched at a raunchy angle on her head, she turned male heads all around the white perimeter rail.

I'd taken Chloe out more than once and knew she was intelligent and bubbly. It occurred to me, as I entered the parade ring and made my way over to where they were all standing in a smiling, chattering group, that it wouldn't be a bad idea to ask her out again. Total work wasn't good for anyone. And I'd gained a fair lead in the jockeys' table so far – that could change, of course, if I had a bad fall and was laid up for any length of time. However, maybe a night out was just what I needed. I couldn't remember the last time.

Then I remembered those six people Mike had been painstakingly persistent in counting off on his fingers. I groaned silently and filed the idea for later.

'Here he is,' Chloe said, laughing up at her father before turning to me. 'I picked you out as you left the weighing room.'

'Well.' I smiled back at her. 'You couldn't very well miss me in these colours.' I was decked out in bright purple and emerald silks – Samuel's racing colours.

'True enough.' Samuel beamed. 'And I shall like seeing them even more when you flash past the finishing post – in front, of course.'

'But of course,' Mike agreed. He was enjoying himself – there was nothing he liked more than keeping his owners happy. 'I never forget they're paying the bills, keeping my stables going, Harry,' he was often given to say. 'Without happy owners, it's the start of the end for a stable.' And we both knew that the one thing guaranteed to keep the owners in a good mood was to win races on their horses.

Owners paid out handsomely for the privilege of owning a racehorse. The payback in prize money from winning a race helped, of course, but what brought joy to them was watching their horse actually race. If it also went on to win, well, that really was a bonus. And since most of the time it didn't win, we had to be grateful for their ongoing optimism.

'Keep the owners happy.' It was Mike's mantra, his fool-proof method of running his business. And his business was very successful. He was one of the leading trainers in the country. As his retained jockey, I was in a very enviable position, from the point of view of the other jockeys. Retaining my champion jockey status was down in no small part to continuing to ride Mike's horses.

'Jockeys please mount,' was called and Mike gave me a leg-up into White Lace's saddle. Darren held the lead rein and we walked round in front of the wall of racegoers. Earlier, he had triumphantly won 'Best turned out' and was in a very happy mood. The cash payment would make a real difference to his weekly pay packet. White Lace certainly looked superb. A grey, she had an almost-white flowing mane and tail and her coat shone in the sunshine, a tribute to all Darren's efforts earlier today.

'Looks good, dun't she?' he said and turned a beaming face up at me as we approached the entrance to the course.

At that moment I knew with a blaze of certainty that Darren had nothing whatsoever to do with the doping – if that was what it turned out to be. He was committed to the horses, revelled in them winning. He would never do anything to cause them harm. He had no inkling that Mike intended to grill him later this after-noon and was genuinely enjoying his race day.

'Oh, yes.' I leaned forward and gently tugged one of the mare's ears. 'It takes a team to get a result, Darren, and you've done your part well.'

His ears grew red with the praise. 'Thanks.'

'Now, let's see if we can get you another bonus to go with it.'

It was general practice that a winning owner would show his monetary appreciation to the stable lad who looked after his horse.

He released the lead rein and I squeezed the mare forwards on to the racecourse. White Lace knew what was required of her and her ears were pricked forward in anticipation.

She'd already proved herself a worthy winner on the flat and over jumps. And today was a hurdle race. The way she blew down her nostrils said she considered the race hers. Knowing the horse and, as the bookies' odds-on favourite, I thought so too.

I put all thoughts of the unwelcome situation coming down the track tonight from my mind. Right now, it was a distraction – and I could do without one. I needed to focus on the coming race. White Lace and I needed to work in harmony to bring off a win. She would give her best, and she deserved the same commitment from me.

And we didn't let each other down, or the scores of jubilant racegoers gathered expectantly around the winners' enclosure as we made our way back from the course to the number-one spot.

White Lace flicked her ears back and forth, taking in all the noise and laughter, her eyes bright with the satisfaction of a race well won. Horses knew when they had done well and certainly White Lace, tossing her head up and down vigorously, surveying the doting crowd round the edge of the winners' enclosure, accepted their praise gracefully as her rightful due.

I leaned forward, gently pulled her ear, and told her what a good job she'd made of the race.

'Made-up, in't she?' Darren's face was crimson with pride.

'A credit to you, Darren.' It wasn't simply the two lots of cash coming his way – if he'd had a bet on as well, which could be depended on, White Lace had repaid all his efforts handsomely today. And he deserved it. A stable lad's life was hard, grafting all hours with little time off, winter frozen and summer baked. The emotional upside was a day like today when 'his horse' made it to the winning post ahead of all the other horses. And for Darren today, his additional reward for 'Best turned out' was a further fillip. Plus, I knew Samuel would slip him a bonus. A good owner recognized the care poured out to their horse by his lad.

'Keep the owners happy' might well be Mike's mantra; for myself, I believed a happy horse won races, willingly giving their best effort, recognizing the mutual partnership and appreciating the care and affection given to them by their stable lad. I gave the mare a last couple of pats down the neck before raising a hand and touching the peak of my jockey crash cap before sliding down from the saddle. White Lace might like to win races, accept her congratulations regally, but I liked to acknowledge the applause of the punters. Without racegoers, my job was dead in the water. Like owners, racing also needed the crowds that flocked to the different race meetings, often travelling many miles to see their favourite horses in action. Their entrance fees kept the courses open and ongoing. I tried never to forget it.

But it was a two-way job; the money had to be earned, and I undid the girths, let the saddle slip down the mare's sweaty, steaming sides into my arms, releasing the intoxicating smell of hot horse, and made my way to the weighing room. I needed to weigh-in to have the race confirmed. I also needed to wear Samuel's green and purple silks again for the next race, which would be run in around twenty minutes' time. Depending on the number of rides a jockey had over the afternoon, it could be – and often was – a physically punishing schedule.

White Lace wasn't the only horse who knew what was expected of them; Black Ice was full of himself as Mike legged me up into the saddle. He was raring to go and I was glad of the Chifney bit he was wearing. I'd be earning my jockey's fee this time all right. His lad, not Darren, led me out on to the approach to the course and I knew I had to settle Black Ice before he had a chance to try and bolt.

Turning his head sideways towards the rails, I managed to prevent him tanking away, but it was proving a real battle. However, halfway down to the start he gradually eased off fighting for his head and finally cantered smoothly down to join the other horses waiting for the starter's orders.

And he was amazing – a powerhouse of energy.

Leaping forward as the yellow flag dropped, he took me four lengths in front of the pack before I could steady him. However, his jumping ability was peerless. My confidence in the decision to purchase Black Ice soared as the horse effortlessly leapt over each of the hurdles before us.

The crucial test was how he would perform in the last couple of furlongs. Would there still be enough petrol in the tank to hold on to his lead where it mattered most? The horse delighted in giving me the answer. I asked him for a last effort at the one-furlong marker. Black Ice dug deeper, his will to win equalling my own, and produced a fantastic finishing burst of speed as we sped away to sweep past the finishing post in first place.

'Marvellous result, marvellous, Harry.' Samuel slapped me on the shoulder.

I'd gone into the owners' and trainers' bar afterwards to update Mike and Samuel on the gelding's performance. I didn't expect any adverse comments in view of the run. And I didn't get any. Both men were in great spirits having watched the race and knew they had seen a very good performance.

'I don't think you're going to regret buying him,' I said, accepting a flute of champagne.

'Most certainly not,' Samuel said emphatically. 'I'd like to find two or three more just like him.'

'Well, we can't guarantee being able to do that,' Mike said, 'but what we need to do now, having seen his potential, is plan his future races and his training programme.'

'I'm more than happy to leave that to you, Mike. I'm confident in your expertise, that's why I place my horses with your stables – and also why I pay you.' He burst out laughing.

Mike shot a quick glance at me and we both joined in. I could practically see a bubble form above his head containing his mantra, written in capital letters.

We spent an enjoyable hour and a half in the racecourse hospitality suite with Samuel before parting company, the mood still high and positive.

Darren had received his monetary reward for 'Best turned out' and I knew Samuel had discreetly handed him a generous bonus for White Lace's earlier win. He'd returned in the horsebox to get on with the usual afternoon stable work whistling loudly.

The ebullient atmosphere also prevailed when we arrived back at the stables. With two wins in one afternoon, the mood of the yard was one of jubilation. Mike had driven me back to the stables where, in preparation for speaking with Darren later, I'd left my own car parked up beside his office.

'OK,' Mike said, fishing the house keys from his pocket, 'let's get some coffee on.'

I made myself comfortable in the lounge scanning today's *Racing Post*, while he disappeared into the kitchen, returning shortly carrying a tray of delicious-smelling coffee.

'I've asked the head lad to send Darren across when he finishes work around six o'clock, so we can relax for a while.'

'For my money, Darren's got nothing to do with anything dodgy.'

'Probably not. But somebody knows something. And we're involved simply because our horse travelled with Tal's in her horsebox.'

I inclined my head in agreement. 'I take it you've not heard anything further from Tal?'

'Nothing. But you can bet on her sweating right now. I know I would be. I mean, the whole future of her stables could be in jeopardy.'

We sat sipping our coffee in silence, mulling over his words.

'I think whatever Darren tells us, we need to speak with Tal, get her take on the situation. See if she has any ideas what's happened.'

Mike got up and refilled our coffees. 'I don't *like* having to do this, but you have to agree, Harry, Darren must have a bit of pressure put on, try and find out if he knows something – anything.' He shook his head. 'OK. No, I don't think it would be his handiwork, but we need to find out if he's covering up for somebody else – possibly even unaware of what's actually happened.'

'In which case, he's the innocent party.'

'He may well be, but . . .' He spread his hands.

We finished off the delicious coffee and the clock moved around to six o'clock. On cue, the back doorbell jangled. Mike got up and went to let Darren in.

His demeanour from earlier this afternoon had drastically changed. Long gone the bright, beaming smile; in its place a seriously worried frown lined his young forehead. 'You wanted a word, Guv?'

'Yes, Darren. It's regarding yesterday at Newbury.'

'I don't know anythin' about it, honest.'

'We want you to tell us every single thing that happened, right from the start when the horsebox arrived in our yard.'

I nodded encouragement. 'We're not accusing you of anything, Darren,' I said. 'Just tell us what you know.'

'But that's just it, Mr Radcliffe,' he insisted. 'I don't *know* anythin'.'

NINE

I drove away from Mike's stables with Darren's words still echoing in my mind. The lad had become increasingly agitated during that next half-hour, but never altered his phrase: 'I don't know anything.' It left both Mike and me frustrated but unable to get him to say more. Now, I made my way back to Harlequin Cottage without a lead in any direction. It meant I couldn't do a bloody thing to help Tal.

Despite Darren's mulish refusal to tell us what had happened, I hadn't changed my opinion that he'd had nothing to do with why Bayard Boy behaved so badly. And it had been this gut instinct that helped me keep my temper. But I knew Mike's was fraying. He'd begun pacing the room, and I knew Darren was seriously worried about hanging on to his job.

In the end, when it seemed Mike was about to blow up at Darren's obstinacy, he'd stopped suddenly, swung round to face the lad, index finger jabbed towards him. 'OK, what you *are* saying is, in effect, "No comment."' There was still no response. 'Very well.' Mike dropped his hand. 'I can't make you talk, and I'm not going to try.' He jerked his head towards the door. 'I'll see you in the yard tomorrow morning, six o'clock.'

Darren, tapping his forehead with one finger, managed to say, 'Yes, Guv,' before he fled. I know if Mike hadn't thought highly of the lad, by now he'd have been down the road. And I was nearly as relieved as Darren must have been that he still had his job. But it was a bloody shame his successful and enjoyable day had ended this way.

I cast a glance in my rear-view mirror just as I turned left. A minute or two later another car did the same. It had been behind me for several miles. Such was the nature of my lifestyle now that I automatically clocked cars that took the same route as I did. I'd been tailed too many times not to be careful.

This car seemed innocuous, harmless – it was an old Ford Fiesta, much battered and an indistinguishable shade of grey. There seemed to be just the driver, no passengers on board. But it was too far behind for me to see what the driver looked like. It was still behind me, no nearer, no farther away, when I approached the right-hand turn off the A52 into Oatfield Lane.

There was more than one way of getting back home but, for safety's sake, I chose this one. I'd used it before when I was being chased and had been very glad afterwards that I'd done so. Very aptly named, Oatfield Lane ran across the whole width of the lower village, cutting its way between the fields, boasting passing places here and there because of its narrowness, culminating finally at a three-junction crossroads leading to my own village and the other two, Shelford and Newton.

But within yards of the turn-off from the main road, the lane wound its way up a sharp incline over a hump-backed bridge spanning the Nottingham–Grantham railway line. On the very top of the bridge it angled sharply, creating a blind spot, and it was wise to sound your horn to warn anybody else driving up the other side that you were on your way down.

I knew on the other side there was a passing place near the bottom of the incline and considerate drivers, warned by a sharp blast from the horn, usually did the sensible thing and got out of the way. I dutifully gave the Mazda's horn a work-out and cruised on up and over the bridge. There were no oncoming cars in sight.

At the first passing place on my side, I indicated and pulled off the road. It was an insult to simply call it a passing place. There was a small wood running alongside the road and the start of the wide entrance path formed part of the curving passing place. I drew in further along the tree-lined path before stopping. Then I turned in my seat, sat and waited. Two or three minutes later, the old grey Ford appeared over the top of the hump-backed bridge – with no blast of horn. That immediately told me whoever was driving wasn't a local.

Having negotiated the bridge, and before the Ford picked up speed, I had time to catch a swift glimpse of a sideways profile, eyes resolutely fixed on the road in front, before it barrelled past. The car dwindled away down the lane between the fields and out of sight. I sat and let it go.

Then I turned the Mazda, nosed it back over the bridge, and drove the last couple of miles or so to my home. I knew he would find me. Just that one swift glance had told me who it was. He'd been to Harlequin Cottage before, but I'd rather meet him on my own turf than down the lane. Now I wanted to get back, get the kettle on ready and think this through before he actually arrived at my door.

There was nobody waiting for me at the cottage, not even Leo. He'd already set off on a foraging expedition for food and females and he'd be back later. I stuck the kettle on, took two mugs from the cupboard and dropped in a couple of tea bags. Then I sat down in the old armchair by the Rayburn and waited some more. It didn't take long. I heard the car engine coming up the lane well before the crunching of gravel beneath tyres said the car had turned into my drive. Seconds later, the horseshoe knocker sounded loudly and I went to open the back door.

'Come in, Darren, kettle's just boiled . . .'

He sat down at the kitchen table and I made us both some tea.

'I had to come, have a word, like . . .' He squirmed with embarrassment. 'You understand, don't you, Mr Radcliffe? He's the Guvnor . . . and I . . .'

'And you're one of the stable lads, right?'

'Yes.' He nodded, visibly relieved that I understood.

'Sort of a "him and us" situation, eh? And you don't want to let your side down.'

'That's right,' Darren said miserably. He sat hunched apprehensively over his mug of builders' strength brew.

'So, if you can't snitch to Mike, can you tell me?'

'But I was *tellin'* you . . . an' it *was* the truth. I don't know *anythin'*.'

'Maybe not, but just tell me everything you can remember, just as it happened that day. Leave me to puzzle it out.'

He'd taken a big gulp of tea to bolster his confidence and now relayed the work pattern for that day at Newbury races. It was disappointing.

He hadn't heard anything, or seen anything.

'I *told* you, Mr Radcliffe . . . there weren't nothin' out of the ordinary. The whole trip were, well, just . . . normal.'

'OK, Darren, now did you stop to pick anyone up? Maybe another stable lad? Did anybody have access to the horses that shouldn't have?'

He shook his head gloomily. 'No, nobody. Just the three of us, like I said. Me, Rob and Paul the box driver.'

'Was Paul the usual driver?'

'No, no he weren't. He's second travelling head lad.'

'And the main travelling head lad was away at one of the other courses that day?'

'Yeah. Well, y'see, there were just the two horses, Baccus an' Bayard Boy – one from our yard an' one from theirs.'

'Now, I'm going to ask you a tricky question, Darren. All I

want is the facts – I'm not going to drop you in it. But I do want the facts, OK?'

He gulped. 'OK.'

'Right, now somewhere between Tal's stables and Newbury Racecourse, Bayard Boy was given something. I don't know exactly what. That's what they're testing the urine for. So, if the horse was OK when he left her stables, and duffed up at Newbury, it must have happened on the journey.'

He nodded, staring down into his empty mug and turning it round and round in his hands.

'Did you actually stop the horsebox on the journey?'

'We never picked anybody up, Mr Radcliffe, honest.'

'I didn't ask you that, Darren. Did you at any time stop the horsebox?'

His shoulder slumped lower. I waited.

'Yeah,' he finally mumbled.

'Now we're getting somewhere. Where did you stop?'

'Don't know exactly. Some petrol station, not far off Newbury.'

'Describe what happened, every detail. It could be very important.'

He gave an exaggerated sigh and then gave me the facts. 'Paul was drivin', I told you that. An' he said there was a petrol station comin' up. Not long after he indicated and turned in on the fore-court. He cut the engine and fished some money out of his pocket. Then he told me and Rob to go inside and get us three hot steak pasties. Don't get cold ones, he was firm about that, must be hot. They were on him.'

I nodded. 'And you were both delighted.'

'Yeah, well, it were a free meal, weren't it? Saved us getting something at the races.'

'Go on.'

'Anyroad, we took the money and went into the petrol station cafe. We ordered three lots, hot ones, and waited whilst the girl served us. Then paid her and took them back to the horsebox.'

'Did you two stay together all the time?'

'Yes, I reckon so. Oh, no, Rob said he could do with a slash.'

'And he left you queuing?'

'Yeah. But he weren't long, three or four minutes, somethin' like that, I suppose.'

'And you left Paul in the horsebox?'

'Yeah. He was just going to wait until we brought the dinner back.'

'Hmm . . . So, both Rob and Paul weren't in sight all the time?'

'No.'

'What happened then?'

'We ate the pasties.'

'And . . .?'

'Then Paul fired up the box and we carried on to Newbury.'

'And neither you nor Rob went to check on the horses in the back before you carried on the journey?'

He squirmed around on his chair. 'No. There weren't no need. Paul said he'd checked. Both horses were quiet.'

I let it go for a minute. I needed him on my side. 'And then you drove on to Newbury?'

'Yes.'

'And you didn't stop again until you reached the box park at the racecourse?'

'Yes.'

'And the reason you didn't want to tell Mike was because you, personally, didn't check Baccus?'

'Hmm.'

'And that's all, no other reason?'

He shook his head. 'No. I'm tellin' you the truth. I didn't check meself.'

'Well, it's not a hanging offence.'

'But I should've, shouldn't I? If I had checked . . .'

'Baccus was fine. There wasn't anything you could have done, Darren. Most probably you wouldn't have noticed anything wrong with the other horse.'

'But I *should've*.'

I didn't say anything else. The lad was beating himself up enough for both of us.

TEN

I saw the chastened, yet also relieved Darren out, waving away the lad's thanks. I followed the car over the gravel to the gateway, raised a hand in farewell and then closed both gates securely with chain and padlock. The cottage was in an isolated spot. After unwanted things had begun to happen, like bizarrely finding a pair of false teeth on the doorstep for instance – and look what happened after that! – it made sense to secure the garden as well as the cottage. Before I had reached the kitchen door a ginger flash had zipped across from the shrubbery and Leo, tail raised high in greeting, was waiting on the doorstep.

'Antisocial you are, mate.'

Leo sprang up to my shoulder, grappling the last foot or so with cruel claws that penetrated my shirt. 'Ow!' I bellowed and he flattened his ears in annoyance. But he'd gained his favourite perch and was content now to withdraw the claws while I carried him into the cottage. I knew there was a tin of pilchards lurking on the pantry shelf – Leo was especially partial to pilchards – and I went across and took the tin down. Waving it in front of him I said, 'Do you think you deserve some?'

What a damn fool question. After all Leo had done for me, just little things like saving my life, more than once, like my debt to Keith Whellan, it could never be repaid.

He responded with a bellow that outstripped the one I'd given, and jumped down on to the quarries, weaving in and out between my legs, threatening to trip me up while urging on my efforts to find the tin opener and his dish. I heaped out a generous helping of fish and placed the dish on the tiles. Not being as hard on him as Annabel, I'd smashed the fish up into cat-bite sizes. Leo might not care for other people's company but, right now, I was most definitely his favourite person.

I left him indulging himself and went through to my sitting room. The laptop sat on the desk. I selected the file with my current copy for the racing paper partway written, and concentrated on producing a decent script.

I'd written about half my column already, deliberately omitting the events at Newbury races, and followed it on now with happier events from Towcester. Reading it through in its entirety, I was reasonably satisfied and sent it off to the editor. I was well within time – nine o'clock was the deadline and it was only eight-thirty.

It was then I heard *The Great Escape* tones issuing from my mobile. I'd left it in the kitchen. Hurrying through, noting the flattened ears and green glare Leo was giving me for waking him up, I snatched the mobile from the worktop beside his basket. 'Yes?'

'Harry. Tal Hunter here . . .'

'Ah, yes. Hello, Tal. Sod of a business for you. Any developments?'

'The development I need is to find the bastard trying to drop me in it.'

'We all do, Tal. Everybody's on your side. You're way above suspicion.'

She sighed heavily. 'Thanks, Harry. Tell that to the authorities. I need all the support I can get.'

The way she said it immediately alerted me. Before she could say anything further, I jumped in. 'You want me to get to the bottom of this for you?'

'I do, Harry. And I know what you're going to say. You have a championship title to win, you don't have the time . . .' She left the sentence hanging and I knew right then just how desperate she was feeling. A lady given to understatement, was Tal.

'You're so right, I don't have time – but I'm going to make time. I'm already involved in that shooting incident when Keith Whellan was driving the horsebox and some bastard took a shot at us. The bullet went straight through the windscreen, missed me – it was sheer luck because at that time, I was sprawled out on the bench seat fast asleep – but it KO'd Keith.'

'I know. Have you heard anything? How is he? Any idea?'

'The hospital's being tight-lipped. They aren't giving out any information. I'll try them again tomorrow, see if there's any change. It's possible he may have come round by then.'

'Still unconscious, then?'

'Hmm.'

'One of the body's healing mechanisms, sleep. With no energy being wasted on life, it can concentrate on repairing itself. You've been knocked out with concussion, Harry. You know first-hand how beneficial completely resting the body – and the brain – is.'

'I'm not arguing, Tal, but I'm really banking on Keith remembering what happened just before the shot was fired. As I said, I was out cold, no damn use whatsoever.'

'I wouldn't say that. You took control of the horsebox, contacted the emergency services.'

'Anybody would've.'

'You attended the engagement party, though, didn't you? Oh yes, the racing grapevine is very efficient. And, knowing you, I think that you probably didn't want to go. I bet you only went for Keith's sake, yes?'

'And look how that turned out. Keith could be at death's door for all we know. And that bullet, Tal, may have been fired at me. It could be *my* fault he's lying in the Queen's right now.'

'Yes, well, the bullet could have found the wrong target, but until you don your deerstalker, we shan't know.'

'Except that right now, I have nothing to go on.' I slammed my fist down on the worktop in frustration.

She snorted down the phone. 'You've been here before, on your other cases. And you've gone on to get the sods banged up where they belong. I've got faith in you, Harry.'

'In that case, help me out. Tell me how I can get to speak to one of your lads, without making it too apparent. Yes, I know, pretty bloody impossible. Even so . . .'

'Which one?'

'Your box driver, Paul.'

She snorted again. 'That's easy enough. Most nights the lads, including him, are down the village in the Flying Fox, well, for happy hour they are.'

'When's that?'

'Six to seven.'

She ended the call exhorting me to do my best, and I glanced up at the kitchen clock. It was well past happy hour, long past; it was edging towards bedtime. Speaking to the box driver was going to have to wait until the end of afternoon stables tomorrow evening.

Five a.m., cold, bright and blowy, and I awoke with a jerk as a heavy ginger cat landed on top of my duvet. Leo gained access from the top of the conservatory roof and thence through the open bedroom window. He proceeded to burrow down beneath the cover and to enquire whether I was going to bother getting up, miaowing in a very loud and demanding bass down my left ear. There was no chance of a further ten minutes' gentle snooze. He was well aware of my routine and was making sure of getting fed before I burnt rubber and disappeared down the lane.

However, before I succumbed and pushed back the duvet, I reached up, tugged him down beside me and tickled his furry chin. The insistent miaows changed instantly to his characteristic impression of a road drill as the purrs reverberated against my chest. We had a bonding few minutes and then I released him and got out of my warm bed. Tail raised, he stalked in front all the way down the stairs and into the kitchen.

With a tinge of conscience, because I knew I'd be back late tonight, I tipped the rest of the pilchards from yesterday into his dish.

'Fill your boots,' I instructed and made myself a large mug of tea.

It was Leicester races today – I had five rides. Considering my chances as I drove down the lanes to Mike's stables on the Nottinghamshire/Leicestershire border, there were at least two odds-on favourites that I was hoping to add to my score. To be honest, I wasn't doing half badly – I was fourteen ahead of my nearest rival in the championship race. But it was a dire mistake to feel even a little complacent. As a jockey I knew – we all knew – that a fall was out there on the green turf waiting to claim its own victory. And it could be anything from a minor bruised hip through a broken collar bone to a broken neck. *That* was the reason Annabel couldn't hack it. As a jump jockey, it wasn't a scenario I dwelt on, I couldn't afford to, but even so I couldn't ignore the statistics that said out of every ten or twelve rides, you were going to come crashing down.

Then it was a case of taking sufficient time off to recover, which in itself was an unknown depending on how you landed, what got bruised or broken. And if the following horses found they couldn't avoid kicking you as they thundered by and you got a second injury on top of the first one. Plus I was of an age now when whatever injury I suffered took longer to heal, to recover from. One day, not too distant, I knew that racing would impose its own restriction. Even though I knew that day was coming, I also knew I'd never be ready to welcome it.

Arriving at the stables, I determinedly pushed that pessimistic thought from my mind and made my way round to the kitchen. Of Pen there was no sign, but Mike sat in front of an open laptop, a mug of coffee steaming away at his side.

'Morning, Mike.'

He grunted, nodding towards the coffee jug. 'Help yourself.'

'Like that, is it?'

'Hmm, sorry, didn't get a lot of sleep.'

'Oh?'

'Pen's been up a lot in the night and that means I've been up a lot too. Not her fault, the dear girl's such a size now, she can't get comfortable in bed, plus she needs the loo seems like every half-hour.'

'Don't exaggerate.' I grinned. 'Anyway, it's all good practice. The baby will be here soon, *then* you certainly won't get any sleep. Can't think how your staff will cope with your grumps.'

'Huh. I can do without your wisecracks.'

While I was getting a dig in, I'd also poured myself a strong coffee. Leaning over the table, I loaded in a spoonful of honey – my usual preference. 'Cheer up, Mike, we're likely to get at least a couple of winners this afternoon.'

He shoved the laptop to one side and reached for his drink. 'Yeah, must admit, it is looking good for today. It's really helped the stables since Lady Branshawe decided to swap stables and have her horses trained here.'

'Yes.' It was my turn to look pensive. 'That could account for Rawlson's comments down at Newbury. He's never forgiven me for getting what he considered his rides.'

'Yes, but that was while her horses were being trained at Mousey Brown's stables. Now, having them trained here should have shut him up, I would have thought.'

'Regretfully, no.'

'Sour grapes, Harry. Let it go. You need your mental focus firmly on today's races. It could give you an even further lead. What is it now?'

'Fourteen.'

'That's damn good this early in the season. But with today's possible wins you could draw away beautifully, give you a cushion . . .'

He didn't finish his sentence, didn't need to. We both knew he meant *should I have a bad fall*. I decided to change the subject. Falls were something I didn't want to consider.

'Had a telephone call from Tal last night.'

'Oh, how is she?'

'Well, she's all right, but I could tell she was in need of some support. So . . . I promised her I'd make time and look into what happened at Newbury.'

'Good man.' Mike drained his coffee and stood up, slapping a hand down on my shoulder. '*Knew* I could rely on you,' he chuckled.

'Oh, sure,' I said, 'and perhaps you could extend the usual twenty-four hours in a day to, say, maybe thirty? *Then* I might just be able to pull everything in.'

He was still in a high good humour later as I made my way across the Leicester races parade ring to be legged up. Ode to Joy, one of Lady Branshawe's horses, was skittering around while Darren was struggling to hang on to the mare. She was the first of my five rides today. I'd ridden her out at the stables a couple of mornings ago. Mike had brought her to a peak in training and she was filled with enthusiasm. She was also one of the two odds-on favourites that I expected to win. Just the sight of her, ears pricked, neck arched, justified my conviction that this race would be a walk-over. I dutifully touched the peak of my crash cap silks – turquoise and black diamonds, they were Lady Branshawe's colours – and wished Her Ladyship a good day.

Lady Willamina beamed at me. 'In the bag, Harry, don't you think?'

'Certainly hope so.'

She chuckled. 'No hoping about it. This mare's one classy girl.' And she was right. But Ode to Joy wasn't the only classy girl: Lady

Branshawe, a widow, dressed in a short-skirted, perfectly fitted turquoise suit, topped off with a bit of black nonsense perched on her auburn hair, could out-class any other female at the course.

Mike legged me up and then Ode to Joy was led out on to the course and we cantered down to the start.

And the win was easy, very easy. Ode to Joy's jumping was pitch-perfect, sailing over each fence with confidence coming out of her ears, I, a mere passenger.

Some minutes later, Lady Branshawe came forward in the winners' enclosure, hand outstretched, to greet me. 'I told you she was a beauty, Harry.'

'You did,' I agreed, and was about to excuse myself to go and weigh-in but she forestalled me.

'I'd like to invite you to a party I'm giving at the hall. I've given the actual invitation card with the details to Mike. I know you can't take it now.' Her wide smile encompassed the winners' enclosure. 'He says he'll let you have it later. But I wanted to ask you personally, as a small appreciation from me. Do say you'll come.'

'Thank you, I will, if I can.'

She pouted sexily. 'Do try.'

If I didn't bother sleeping for the next week or two, I might just be able to fit everything in.

ELEVEN

I drove straight from Leicester races to the Flying Fox pub. It was already nearly half past six when I drew up in the car park and locked the Mazda. Mike, when I'd asked him this morning, had given me a slim chance of blagging it.

'Gary Butt, he's one of my stable lads – you know his older brother, Ciggie, don't you?' I agreed that we'd met before. 'Well, Gary is a member of the local darts team. Why not tack on to him tonight? I know he's intending playing at the Flying Fox. He's a big fan of yours, watches most of your races. Fancies being a jump jockey himself. He'd be made-up to chat to you.'

It wasn't a great deal of cover, but it was better than no cover.

I pushed open the pub door and went into the bar. A wall of warmth and raucous good humour hit me. The noise level was unbelievable. How anybody made themselves heard, let alone carried on a conversation, was a miracle. I weaved my way through the mass of bodies at the bar and ordered a drink.

For once, thanks to the general melee, nobody noticed me initially and I gratefully took my glass over to one of the tables where there were a couple of spare seats. Fortunately, it was in an alcove and the seats faced away from the bar. I sat down, buried my face in my beer and surreptitiously scanned the room. Tal's description of Paul Oats had been concise – tall, ginger hair gelled up. However, right now I couldn't see him.

Gary was on his way back from the far end of the bar. I recognized him because he was the spit image of his big brother, Ciggie – so obviously named for his surname – and because I'd noticed him on previous mornings among the many lads beavering around like ants in Mike's stable yard. Gary was concentrating on not spilling his beer and didn't notice me until he'd drawn level.

'Hey.' He nodded towards me, his face split into a wide grin. 'Good to see you.'

I smiled back. 'Hello, Gary.'

'Do you play darts, then?'

I shook my head. 'No. But I didn't fancy a boring night in on my own tonight. Thought I'd try a different pub, see some new faces. Mike told me there was a match on here tonight. And one of his lads was playing, if I wanted to give it a go.'

'Me?'

'You.'

His face went a bit pink.

'Said you were a cracking player. So . . .' I spread my hands.

'Well, that's great.' His face flushed a deeper pink. He took a long slurp of his lager. 'Course, the Flying Fox lads are first rate. We'll have a tough match on our hands.'

'Do I know any of their players?'

'Might do. There're three Polish lads – Mariusz is their star player. Honestly, they're good.' And he ticked off on his fingers the names of several others, including Paul Oats, the box driver. 'Course, Paul's only been here for the past three weeks. He was at another stable down in Leicestershire. He played for their darts team – red hot, he is.' I sat nodding – and slowly drinking my beer. But really I was quartering the room trying to see where Paul was. Finally I spotted him in a huddle with, presumably, the lads Gary had been naming.

It seemed all the lads in the pub were delaying the start of the match until the end of happy hour – during which they were intent on downing as much liquor as possible at the reduced prices.

'Get you another, Mr Radcliffe?' Gary enquired and finished the remains of his drink in a long swallow.

'No, no thanks.' I lifted a restraining hand. 'Still OK with this one.' I fished in my wallet and drew out a twenty-pound note. 'Here, get yourselves drinks on me.'

The other three at our table whooped and banged the table in appreciation. It crossed my mind that it was a good job happy hour only lasted an hour. They were certainly all on the way to being well-oiled before a dart had been thrown.

However, on the other side of the room their opponents were in a similarly happy state judging by the ribald laughter and shouts. Paul appeared to be the ringleader and was posturing and whooping louder than any of them. As far as I was concerned, it was a very fortunate state to be in. I'd found many times before that the amount of information that leaked out was in corresponding ratio to how much my suspect had imbibed.

I'd not thought of any direct questions to put to him: just winging it had proved effective in the past. I decided to let happy hour pass and allow the darts match to get well under way before getting closer. The later it got, the more the alcohol would be consumed which could only be good as far as I was concerned. As to the outcome of the match, I was just a bystander.

But I needed to get a little more involved. Justify in general terms why I'd decided to come tonight. However, before I could question Gary any further than simply asking about their chances of winning, he jumped in, giving me a really good lead.

'Just a pity Lenny Backhouse isn't with us. Now *he* was a good player. Damn good.'

'You mean, the man who fell in the Smite and drowned?'

'Well, don't know about *drowned*.'

'Oh?'

'Hmm . . .' He glanced sideways, slyly, at me, lowering his voice so the others couldn't hear what he said. 'With your reputation, I'm not sure I should tell you.'

'My *reputation*?'

'Best tec in town.'

'Gary, I'm a jump jockey.'

'Sure you are . . . an' that's why that arsehole Jake Smith's banged up doing time.'

I took a small sip of my beer. There was no way I could argue with the lad.

Lowering his voice still further – although with the racket going on, anybody more than a couple of feet away catching what was being said was impossible; conversations had to be conducted almost at a shouting level to be heard – he bent forward closer to my left ear.

'Seems playing darts wasn't the only thing Lenny was good at,' Gary whispered.

I strained to hear what he was saying but I didn't want to stop the flow of information.

'And certain people wanted to make sure it was kept quiet. He was the . . . well, not the weak link in the chain, but the link that could be broken. That way there was no continuous chain to follow, no leading back to other links, more important ones.'

'You're saying his death wasn't an accident?'

'I've seen the results of the post-mortem. Well, I've been *told*.'

I shook my head. 'Now, come on—'

'S'true!' he protested. 'My sister-in-law's related to Lenny's sister.'

I prepared to put my disbelief to one side for now. 'OK then, what did Lenny die from?'

'Well, he wasn't dead when he entered the water, but he'd been given a massive whack on the head. He would have been unconscious for sure.'

'He could have hit his head on a branch or a rock or something—'

'No, no, the post-mortem *did* find water in his lungs, which proved he was still alive when he went into the Smite, but his stomach contents also contained evidence of a drug of some sort, a sedative.'

I stared at him. 'Who else knows about this?'

'Just his family . . . and the police know, it's a suspicious death, isn't it? Bound to be. But it's being hushed up.'

'And the police are investigating?'

'Have to, won't they? I mean, two things *might* be an accident, but three? I don't think so.'

'And you know a lot more than you're telling me, don't you, Gary?'

A bell behind the bar clanged and the entire atmosphere changed as the landlord called time on happy hour.

Still, with half a pint left in my glass of beer, I sat and watched the two teams of lads hustling around, sorting out themselves and their darts and the dart board being uncovered. I hadn't really thought about it before, but I realized that darts matches were taken very seriously. My father had been a whiz at long-alley skittles in his day – and *he'd* taken that very seriously.

Now, I sat and watched each lad line up in his turn to toe the line and aim his dart. The majority of them were good players, one or two from each rival team very good.

Then it was the turn of Paul Oats. Predictably, he strutted forward making a great show of fondling the feathers on the darts and deliberately taking his time in placing his foot dead to the line. He glanced round, smirking at the admiring circle of lads from his team who were whistling and shouting encouragement. His eye met mine. He recognized me and his smirk grew into a wide, unpleasant grin. Dropping a mock bow, he deliberately drew the attention of the whole pub to my presence.

'Hey, look who we have with us.' He shouted the words out, his voice carrying around the bar. 'It's the *top jock*.'

I groaned inside and simply raised my glass a couple of inches in acknowledgement to the others who had raised a somewhat uncertain ragged cheer. So much for extracting any information from Oats without attracting too much attention. My chance of innocently shouldering up to the bar hoping to hear anything had vanished.

But I couldn't just down the dregs of my beer and walk out. Gary was expecting me to watch him play. I owed him that for the interesting information he'd slipped me about Lenny Backhouse.

However, I'd seen enough of Oats to easily recognize him again and to form a pretty fair assumption of his character. He'd have no problem fitting in at Jake Smith's round table of reprobates.

And I knew I'd get nothing from him to further my investigation tonight.

TWELVE

I didn't stay until closing time. Just long enough to see Gary make a pretty good fist of it and for his team to secure a win. Then, timing it right, I said a quick goodbye, well done, and made my exit while Oats was visiting the gents. I intended to speak to Tal as soon as I got home. There was something only she could answer and it could prove decisive.

However, Leo had other ideas. Opening up Harlequin Cottage, I'd got as far as kicking off my shoes when a ginger streak shot through the kitchen door. His irritated bellow was deafening – his total focus was on where his dinner was – and did I realize it was hours after he should have been fed? I scooped up the squirming bundle of irate fur and made peace with him.

'Not good enough, I know,' I cajoled him. 'But don't pack your bag yet; food is on its way.'

I placed him in his basket on the worktop so he could watch as I hastened to open a tin and fill his dish while he kept up a running, complaining commentary about my tardiness in getting back home. Appeased by the sight and smell of his just rights, he also timed it just right and leapt to the floor as I placed the lavishly filled bowl down on the quarries.

Silence fell – and I appreciated it. After four hours stuck in a noisy, heaving pub, I needed some solitude and some peace. I made a black coffee and took it through to the lounge, dropping down on to the settee with a sigh of pleasurable relief. I was knackered – I'd started work at six o'clock this morning and ridden in five races before I'd driven straight to the Flying Fox. All I felt like doing was burrowing underneath the duvet – with or without Leo – and getting some kip.

I allowed myself ten minutes, gulped the coffee, then reached for the phone. The day wasn't over yet.

'Hello, Tal. You OK?'

'Harry. Yes, I'm good, thanks.'

'I need to know something.'

'Fire away.'

'Does Paul Oats live in at the stables?'

'Yes, at the stable lads' hostel.'

'Right. I take it he has his own room?'

'Oh, yes. And he has his own key.'

'That brings me to the nub of what I need to know, Tal.'

'Go on.'

'I take it you also have a key to the rooms?'

'I do, yes.'

'Is it possible you could go in and have a quick look around?'

There was a few seconds of taut silence. 'You mean, if I *thought* I could detect a smell of burning, say, I could go in and check everything was OK?'

'Something like that.'

'And when might this be necessary? Do you have any ideas?'

'Market Rasen races tomorrow. Any chance you're sending Oats to drive the small horsebox?'

'What a coincidence you should think of that, Harry. Yes, he is driving over. I've a runner in the three thirty.'

'And I suppose your other lads in the hostel will be going out to do afternoon stables at . . . four o'clock?'

'Yes, yes, you're spot on there. They'll be busy until six or thereabouts.'

'Perhaps you could give me a ring later tomorrow night, then? Let me know if you find anything?'

Tal chuckled. 'You're a sod, Harry. What is it I'm supposed to be looking for?'

'Oh, I don't really know. A plastic tube maybe, something small like a urine sample.'

'Really?'

It was my turn to laugh. 'No urine.'

'And no needle attached?'

'I certainly hope not. But be careful. Don't handle it at all. I don't want it to get you. I'd come over and do a search myself but it could prove very tricky if I got caught – for both of us. And if you *do* find anything, don't tell anyone. It could be misconstrued as planting evidence.'

'That serious?'

'Oh, yes. One thing I've discovered, Tal, during my impressions of Sherlock Holmes, is don't ever underestimate the police. If you think *I've* got a suspicious mind, believe me, the police are way ahead. They've passed the post before you've even left the stalls.'

'And what if I do find this "object"?'

'Let me know straight away.'

'And if I don't?'

'Keep looking – discreetly, of course.'

'Of course.'

'Thanks, Tal.'

I disconnected and took my empty coffee mug back to the kitchen. Leo's bowl was empty and I washed up both items. He'd gone to ground in his basket, but one emerald eye watched me finish the chore. I suppose he hoped there was just a slim chance I might feel the need to pamper him with more dinner.

I went to the back door. 'Going out to do your duty with the local queens?'

Leo had a perfectly adequate cat flap, but he liked the additional attention of me acting as his personal doorman. After everything he'd done for me, I was more than happy to do the honours. And I also knew my place.

Accepting I was not going to indulge him with more food, he gave a tiny miaow in acknowledgement of the compliment to his manhood, but declined the invitation to sally forth. Tonight, he decided, the queens could go without his favours.

Hopping down from the basket he set sail for my bedroom, tail held high, imperiously beckoning me. Dutifully, I held open the door leading to the staircase and meekly followed his lead as he bounded up each rise.

In his present mood, I knew there was no possibility of hogging the duvet whilst he slept on top. Even before I reached the bedroom, Leo had installed himself very comfortably, burrowing down under the length of the duvet, and all I could see of him was a blurred mound somewhere in the region of where my knees would be in the centre of the bed – obviously where he fully intended to spend the night.

He left me to curl myself around him in whatever space there was left.

I'd set the alarm even earlier for the following morning. I wasn't going over to Mike's. Today I'd promised to ride out a newly acquired mare, Dark Vada, sired by Dark Destroyer, at Barbara Maguire's stables. It was often the case that a foal would be named after the dam or sire, or even a combination of their names. We were both keen to see if the promise showing in the superb pedigree actually proved a fact. I was certainly hoping so. After riding out her sire over several fruitful years, I was hoping that his jumping ability plus staying power had been passed down to his progeny. If it proved the case, the future for me as her rider would ensure wins that I could add to my tally.

Barbara and I went back years – and through some pretty hairy, very dangerous situations, too – and I appreciated her confidence in allowing me first trialling ride. However, Barbara was a businesswoman down to her toes – not a great distance, she was barely five feet tall, built like Barbara Windsor. She was one tough lady; a widow who had come up the hard way and knew that the ends had to meet, if not overlap, in today's competitive world. Barbara trained at stables in Harby, Leicestershire. And gave parties to rival Lady Branshawe's.

I put down the just-boiled kettle – coffee could wait. I'd just remembered. Lady Branshawe had left a card with Mike. In turn he'd slipped it into my jacket pocket before I'd driven off from Leicester Racecourse to the Flying Fox yesterday afternoon. And I'd forgotten all about it. Picking up my discarded jacket from the back of the kitchen chair, I fished in the pockets. It was a very posh affair, stiff, cream-coloured, gold-edged, italic black lettering. 'Lady Branshawe invites Harry Radcliffe and guest to a party at Hempton Hall on 17 October at 8 p.m.'

Mike's words echoed in my ears as I read it. 'Keep the owners happy, Harry.'

I knew what that meant: agree with them, wherever possible – as well as ride their horses to victory. And now, in this instance, be a good boy, take a girlfriend to Lady Willamina's party. I groaned aloud. Further hours lost that could have been spent more productively trying to find answers. But even trickier, who should I ask to go with me?

My immediate thought, of course, was Annabel. But would she? OK, she was no longer living with Sir Jeffrey, but being seen with me at such a prestigious do was bound to be reported, not only on social media but, even more telling, by the local jungle drums. And it was sure to be embellished, bound to be, as it passed around. Annabel herself was still hurting from the break-up and needed time to heal and balance.

As for Sir Jeffery, yes, he'd preferred his live-in nurse as his life partner – that had been a massive shock to Annabel, and to me. But even so, the poor devil was now confined to a wheelchair – for life. He'd drawn the shortest straw that horrendous day of the car crash, but both Annabel and I hadn't come through unscathed. It was agonizing situations like this that bound all three of us with titanium bonds. It was a very strange triumvirate, but they were bonds that would never be broken and each of us knew that we were there for the others – forever, whatever.

Probably oversensitive of me, but if I were to ask Annabel to go to the 'all dancing, all singing, party', which it would be, I'd feel I was hitting Sir Jeffery when he was down. I don't suppose *he* would see it like that; a more generous natured, decent man you'd never find. But I would, *and* I'd feel guilty.

So, I sighed again. Which girl could I ask? It was between two others. Chloe, Samuel Simpson's daughter, was a definite possibility – and I knew if I were to ask her, she'd say yes. I wasn't being big-headed, just recalling what Samuel had said to me once on a racecourse: 'She thinks you walk on water.' His way of warning me off, at that time.

But then again, perhaps the obvious choice was my old friend Georgia. She'd accompanied me to Switzerland in the superb comfort of Lady Branshawe's private jet back at the start of the year when we'd gone over to watch the racing on snow in St Moritz. I'd thought our relationship had a very real possibility of being long-standing. But although we got on extremely well, Georgia was still grieving for her soldier who had died in Afghanistan. Neither of us had realized it until the point of truth when, in the sumptuous suite at the Koselit Hotel in Switzerland, we shared a double bed.

It left me in a quandary right now.

I put the kettle back on again. What I needed was coffee.

THIRTEEN

t was a quick journey. Up the A52, a right turn to Langer and then on towards the village of Harby. I decided to go the back way into Barbara's stables. The narrow farm track was potholed and played hell with the Mazda's suspension, but it wasn't the first time. The car had been down here before in the days leading up to Jake Smith's arrest. Avoiding the deepest and worst of the potholes, I finally nosed the car in to the back of the stable yard. It was an L-shaped run of stables and looked as smart as an advert in one of the 'glossies'. Barbara ran a tight ship.

I got out, locked up and sauntered over the yard to the far wall. Looking up, I could see the dated brick reading 1920 that had played its own important part in bringing about justice.

'Could turn it into a tourist attraction, couldn't I?'

A smile widened my lips and I swung round to face the lady herself. Well, I say face; it was more a case of dropping my gaze by a good foot or more. She was even smaller than the last time I'd seen her. Either that or I'd grown a bit more. She smiled back – seeming to know intuitively what I was thinking.

'No high heels on. Can't muck out in stilettos.'

'Of course you can't,' I replied.

That was a joke. Barbara had a willing army of stable lads to do the heavy work. She just gave the orders. And led by her head stable lad, who also acted as her minder – she needed one with all her feminine attributes and allure – they carried out her wishes implicitly. And not only as stable hands – they had in the recent past adopted the extremely dangerous role of bodyguards, armed only with pitchforks.

However, I think they were delighted to have had the chance of protecting her and were proud to do it. But it had been a taut,

critical situation that could have gone either way – with deadly
results – for both Barbara and me. There weren't many people I'd
trust with my life – just a handful. They included Annabel, Mike,
Sir Jeffrey . . . and Barbara.

Now, remembering the debt I owed her, I swept an arm around
her shoulders, pulled her close and gave her a kiss on the cheek.
'How's the horse, then?'

Her reply was somewhat swamped by the whoop of joy and
jealousy from the lads, who were watching with interest. 'The
mare's settled in well, eaten up last night, looks as though she's
always lived here.' Barbara patted the handle of a convenient
nearby wheelbarrow with satisfaction. 'All good. So, are you
ready to ride her, see if Dark Destroyer has left his legacy to his
filly?'

'Oh yes, looking forward to it.'

'Want a coffee first, with honey?' She knew my preferences.

'No.' I shook my head. 'Work comes first.'

She led me to a separate stable away from the others. It paid
to be cautious when taking in a new horse. Until Barbara was sure
the mare was 'clean', scoped clean and had nothing contagious,
she would be stabled separately.

The mare heard our footsteps and swung a grey head over the
half-door. I stroked her nose and she blew into my hand. In
the cold morning air, it felt like a fan heater.

Barbara told Mickey, the mare's stable lad, to tack her up and a
few minutes later I was trotting Dark Vada out of the yard and up
on to the gallops. Barbara, mounted on her hack, followed on behind.
I was to canter on for two furlongs but finish the last part at a half-
speed gallop. By this time, Barbara would have reached a suitable
vantage point from which she could watch my return. No half speed
now – a full gallop. It would give both of us a good idea of the
mare's capabilities.

I followed Barbara's wishes to the letter and pulled up Dark
Vada, who was showing her pleasure in the work with much
snorting and head-tossing. My hopes that she would have inherited
the qualities of her sire were, at this point, justified.

'Now, Harry, I want you to pop her over, say, three jumps and
canter her back. OK?'

'Sure thing, ma'am,' I said, in what I hoped was a fair rendition of a Texas cowboy, and flicked my hand up to what would have been the peak of my crash cap had I been wearing any silks.

'Oh, get on with the job.' Barbara shook her head, laughing.

But I knew, when I returned from working the mare over fences, that Barbara was going to be even more pleased in the future than she was right now. The mare had shown a keenness and style that had carried us over the fences cleanly with no loss of ground on landing.

Things were looking good, and if Barbara allowed me the rides in Dark Vada's races, I'd be very pleased too.

She was a cracker.

Sliding off the mare's back, I tossed the reins over her head to Mickey who, all smiles when he saw my satisfied grin, was waiting in the stable yard.

'Take good care of her,' I said, 'you've got a good one to look after.'

'And do y'reckon you'll be riding her, Mr Radcliffe?' he replied chirpily.

'I certainly hope so.'

I tugged off my crash cap and was about to follow Barbara across the yard to the house when I realized this was a really good opportunity to perhaps find out a bit more about Paul Oats. Gary had said Oats was working in a Leicestershire stables prior to coming into Tal Hunter's yard. The stable lads' knowledge of the racing family – who worked where, for how long and which yard they might be going to next – was a brilliant network, far outstripping social media.

'Mickey, could I ask you, have you come across a lad called Paul Oats?'

'Yeah, I have. He used to box drive for O'Brady. Good darts player. He's on the circuit. Patty Doyle, a mate of mine, knows him. He came over from Ireland with Oats about a year ago.'

'I see.' I nodded. 'And is your mate Patty a friend of Oats?'

'Nah, not really, except for the darts matches. 'Tween you and me, Mr Radcliffe, Oats is a bit more than a bit . . . dodgy.'

'In what way?'

'Aw, well now, I can't—'

'Of *course* you can't say, Mickey, I understand. But if I were to say, maybe, into . . . drugs?'

I let the word float in the air between us.

'I'm not ratting on him.'

'And I'm not asking you to. But it is important. Do you think I might be on the right track here?'

'I told you, I can't say, but I reckon there's a fair chance you might be, yeah.' He gave a massive sniff.

As a breed, stable lads seemed to have developed 'the sniff'. And it covered an awful lot of things, answered a lot of things without anything else being spoken. It certainly told me my oblique guess was correct.

'Thanks, Mickey.' With my back to the rest of the yard, I slid a discreet tenner from my wallet and passed it to him. 'Can I have your mate's contact number? I'd really like to meet him. Just to ask him one or two questions. Nothing heavy. Just a bit of background, you know?'

'Don't see why not. He's at Rasen with Brighouse today. But you want to ask him about darts matches, don't you?' He drooped an eyelid as one of the other lads marched past with a saddle over his arm.

I raised my voice just a tad. 'Yes, it's about the next darts match.'

I took out my smart phone and Mickey quickly fired off the eleven numbers.

'Appreciate it, thanks Mickey. Now, don't forget, take real good care of this mare. She's going to make you some money.'

The broad grin was back. 'Sure she is,' he said.

I left him happily dreaming of all the races she was going to win – and all the back-handers he would receive from her owners – and strode off towards the house to find Barbara.

She had busied herself making coffee and was now pouring out a couple of mugs.

'Came up trumps, then, did she?'

'Oh yes, gave me a really good feeling. Her jumping reminds me of the way Dark Destroyer took his fences. He judged the height perfectly, tucked up as he went over, never wasted energy in allowing space, *and* he used to gain ground on landing. She does the same.'

Barbara nodded her agreement. 'I could see that. What about her speed?'

'Well, she certainly pulls hard enough, still strides out when I'm trying to pull up, so yes, I think she'll also be OK for stamina as well.'

'Excellent.' Barbara set down a mug of coffee and a jar of honey in front of me. 'I think we're in business, then, Harry. Do you want to have her rides? Well, subject to her owner's approval, of course. What do you think?'

I dug a spoon into the jar and stirred honey into my coffee.

'Can't wait to ride work on her, get her used to me.'

She nodded with satisfaction. 'Leave the owner to me. I'm sure we will make a good team.'

'I *know* we will,' I said, drinking the excellent coffee. 'Could I ask who Dark Vada's owners are?'

'Not owners, Harry. Just owner.'

'Right, and his name?'

She laughed. 'He's a she. You may have heard of her. Dame Isabella Pullbright.'

'Wow. The actress?'

'Spot on.'

'She's just got a film out – a film that includes some horse racing. It's called *Ride For Me*. And she does do some riding in it. Unless it's some clever camera trick and there's a substitute.'

'As far as I know, Harry, there're no camera tricks. Dame Isabella is quite an accomplished rider.'

'And a looker.'

'You men.' Barbara sighed. 'Always after one thing.'

'With your looks, and your own minder, you should know.'

She burst out laughing. 'Anyway, I have already run it past her that you might be interested in riding Dark Vada.'

'And?'

'And she's very happy with that.'

'Then so am I,' I said. 'However, I'm off to get a couple of lots in for Mike.' I glanced at my watch. 'Well, maybe only one lot now.'

'Thanks for coming over, Harry. I'll be in touch.'

I walked back outside, raised a hand to the stable lads, and drove away.

It wasn't far cross country to Mike's and I arrived after second lot had just pulled back in, nicely timed for breakfast. I went into the kitchen. Pen was busy cooking eggs and toasting bread.

She saw me before Mike did and waved her wooden spoon. 'Hello, Harry.'

I went over and received an affectionate peck on the cheek. 'Thanks. What a nice welcome for someone who's not your husband—'

'Nor yet her lover,' Mike growled from behind his copy of the *Racing Post*.

'Uh-oh, feeling touchy, are we, this morning?'

He picked up the knife waiting beside his plate and tapped it on the table in front of the empty chair. 'Sit.' Grinning, I exchanged a raised eyebrow with Pen. 'Timed it right, didn't you, you jammy bugger?'

'I can always go,' I said and sat.

'Usual, Harry?' Pen asked.

'Please.'

'So, give us the SP on this mare of Barbara's. Is she any good? Could she pose a threat? What's her name?'

'Phew, give a chap chance to breathe.'

Pen placed a steaming mug in front of me. The honey was already on the table, she'd seen to that.

'Come on, Harry, what's her name?'

I smiled up at her. 'Well, her sire is Dark Destroyer—'

'Yes, yes, we *know* that,' Mike said tetchily.

'Take no notice, Harry. I don't. Poor lamb, he's been up a lot in the night with me, haven't you, darling?'

'Like I said before, just putting in the practice until Mike Junior arrives.'

Pen exploded with laughter, shoulders shaking with mirth.

'Steady on, sweetie,' Mike protested, giving me a hard look. 'Can't have you going into labour today. Harry and I are due at Rasen at twelve o'clock.'

At his words, Pen convulsed even more. 'I'll tell your offspring to delay entry until tomorrow, then, shall I?' she spluttered.

'It would be more convenient tomorrow—' Mike stopped speaking at the sight of Pen leaning on me for support as we couldn't suppress our laughter.

A grin slowly spread across his face. 'Oh, very funny, you two.' He shook his head. 'The amount you laugh, Pen, it will be born wearing just a grin.'

She abandoned me and flung her arms around his neck, giving him a smacking kiss. 'I'm laughing because I'm happy, you silly man. You make me happy.'

At this point, I cleared my throat loudly. 'Before I feel obliged to leave for decency's sake, I'll answer your questions, Mike. The SP is this mare is seriously good. And yes, she will certainly give our horses a tough race.'

'Her name, Harry?' Pen asked, returning to rescue the pan of scrambled eggs.

'Dark Vada.'

'Hmm, original. Won't give the commentator any problems calling her home,' Mike said. 'And did Barbara offer you the rides?'

I smiled with satisfaction. 'She did.'

'Hmm . . . well, it will help you with notching up the numbers,' Mike said somewhat grudgingly.

'Of course it will. You can't begrudge him winners.' Pen gave the eggs a final stir.

'Don't worry, Mike. I still aim to win on your horses, too.'

'And talking of winning, we need to pull out by ten to declare at Market Rasen.'

'So, here you are.' Pen spooned out the scrambled eggs. 'You'll need some energy. Get stuck in.'

'Just one more thing. You'll never guess who Dark Vada's owner is – so I'd better tell you.'

Mike, having just dug into his mound of protein, hesitated, loaded fork hovering in front of his mouth. 'Well?'

'Dame Isabella Pullbright. The film star.'

His mouth was already open but now Pen's jaw dropped and joined it as well.

FOURTEEN

We set off for Market Rasen just after ten o'clock. But before I left, I went into Mike's bathroom, keyed in Patty Doyle's number and was rewarded by him answering.

'Don't want to keep you, Patty. It's Harry Radcliffe here. I'm riding at Rasen today and your mate Mickey says you'll be there too. Could I buy you a pint, ask you a couple of questions, please?'

Patty chuckled. 'I'm pretty law-abiding these days.'

'Meaning, you weren't always?'

'Ran a bit wild in my youth. But I'm married now, with a baby on the way. So, my wild days are over.'

'What time would suit?'

'I'll be in the bar around twelve thirty, if that's any good?'

'That'd be fine. How will I know you?'

'Doesn't matter, does it?' He laughed. 'I'll know *you*.'

'Yes, fame does have its drawbacks,' I said.

Outside, Mike was waiting impatiently, car engine running. We were travelling up together. Rasen wasn't very far and it made sense to use the one car.

'How long does it take to have a pee?'

'As long as it takes,' I said. 'Calm down, Mike, Pen's not even gone into labour yet. And even if she does, she's not likely to give birth before we get back from the races.'

He bent his head over the steering wheel and took several slow, deep breaths. 'No, you're quite right. I'm getting myself into a real state about her.'

'No need, I'm sure. She seems fine.'

He nodded and gripped the wheel. 'It's just . . . well, she's not in her twenties any more.'

'She'll be fine,' I repeated firmly. 'Now, let's get this show on the road, OK?'

I deliberately didn't want to tell him about using his bathroom to telephone Patty or about the proposed meeting when I got to Market Rasen. Every time in the past – except the last time, because I'd blocked him – he'd been right in there with me, in the thick of danger and riding shotgun. And I'd had good cause to be grateful.

But last time, Pen had been told she was pregnant and I'd had to remind Mike that his loyalty was most definitely to her, not to me. He hadn't liked it, had fretted about my safety and had been greatly relieved, at the end of the case, to visit me in hospital and find me still alive.

This time, I intended to keep him in the dark as much as I

could, not distract him from taking care of Pen and Mike Junior. So, I didn't tell him.

Mike parked in the owners' and trainers' car park at Market Rasen Racecourse and we parted company to get on with our usual routines. My first race was at one thirty. Once I'd taken my saddle over to the weighing room, signed in and handed it over to the valet, there was plenty of time to slip around to the bar. I knew Mike would be in very shortly, but with luck Patty would already be ensconced, and we could have a brief chat first. I bought a sugarless black coffee and found a spare table. I'd barely sat down when a young chap approached me.

'Hello there. My name's Patty.'

'Thanks for coming. I appreciate it. Hope you didn't mind Mickey giving me your mobile number.'

'Nah, he's a good mate. Not one to drop you in it. We do each other favours.' He dropped down heavily into the chair beside me. 'You wanted to ask me something?'

'I did, yes.'

Patty took a deep draft from his glass and sighed with satisfaction. 'Come on, then, what is it?'

'You know a chap called Oats, Paul Oats, yes?'

'Ha.' He tensed, cast a quick glance around the bar. 'If it's about what I think it is, then . . . here's not the best place to talk.'

'Fair enough.' I backed off.

'Look.' Patty winced. 'How about I come round your place? That way we can talk private like, eh?'

'Suits me. When do you suggest?'

'Tonight? I've nothing on.'

I nodded and took out one of my business cards. 'Any time will do. I'm home all evening.'

Patty palmed the card with all the speed and dexterity of a seasoned poker player. 'I'll be there.' He drained his lager.

'Look, let me buy you another—'

'No, best I'm not seen to linger.'

And I was left staring after his fast-retreating figure. Seconds later a cup of coffee was placed down on the table and Patty's vacated chair was filled by Mike.

'Who's your friend? He went off a bit quick. Doesn't he want to speak to me?'

'Oh, he's just Brighouse's stable lad.'

Mike looked at me quizzically. 'Have you got a lead?'

'On what?'

'Tal's little problem.'

'Wish I had.'

'Hmm. I know you, Harry. You've got that look in your eye.'

'And what look is that?'

'The one that reminds me of a bloodhound just before it's let off the lead. Like, y'know, it's picked up a scent. It's a look you get, Harry, when you're on a case.'

'Oh, give over.'

'You are going to keep me in the frame, aren't you?'

'Look, Mike, if you *need* to know, then, yes, I'll certainly keep you updated.'

He snorted. 'That confirms what I'm thinking. You *do* know something, but you're not telling me.'

'Now would I do that?'

'Yes, you bloody well would.'

I finished my black coffee and stood up. 'Got to go. Got a date with a horse.'

I left him grumbling to himself, but I caught his last few words: 'Just make sure you win.'

Putting all thoughts of Tal and her problems out of my mind, I concentrated on those words. A single-minded approach was needed and all the time I was in the weighing room, getting dressed in Samuel's green and purple silks, I found myself repeating them. Horses needed a calm, confident jockey if they were to give their best and I certainly needed to win, again and again, if I were to retain the championship title.

Mike had picked Market Rasen deliberately with Blueberry in mind. The horse naturally ran right-handed and this course, being a ten-furlong, right-handed track, should suit him perfectly. The punters were also aware of these facts – the horse was odds-on favourite.

Blueberry belonged to Samuel and, trooping out to the parade ring for the one thirty race with all the other jockeys, I spotted him and made my way over. He was chatting to Mike and, when he saw me approach, his smile was full-on.

'Looking great, isn't he, Harry? Your boss here certainly knows how to prepare horses for courses.'

I agreed that, yes, Mike did know his job – backwards.

'So, now it's all up to you, Harry. He's odds-on favourite, y'know. I'm expecting a win.'

I could feel my smile getting fixed, but Samuel was a friend as well as a paying owner and he was entitled to want his horse to be first past the post, so I nodded and assured him I'd do my best.

But horses were not machines. And I couldn't guarantee Blueberry's motivation. They definitely had their off days, just like humans, days when they felt less enthusiastic about expending energy, putting themselves through massive effort, and more about getting back to their warm stable. It was very understandable if they were tired, or possibly in pain. But as soon as Mike legged me up into the saddle, I knew it wasn't the case today.

Blueberry felt my weight on his back and it seemed to activate all his bloodline genes. He knew he was expected to act, to extend himself today – and he was up for it. So much so that I had to remove my boots from the stirrups and ride long-legged as we circled the parade ring as I tried to calm him down. There would be no need to coax him once the race was underway.

And so it proved as the starter's yellow flag dropped and we galloped away towards the first fence. He cleared it cleanly and we were in total accord in our elation. It was fabulous. I could feel his enjoyment travelling along the reins into my hands and when we'd jumped the last fence a good seven lengths in front of the field, I urged him with just hands and heels to finish his job.

And he did. Samuel had got his winner – he'd be pleased. I was pleased, and so was Blueberry. He deserved his warm stable and his dinner tonight.

I leant forward, patted his neck and pulled his ear gently. 'You were brilliant,' I told him. But the arch of his neck and his pacing hooves told me the horse already knew he was. As for myself, as the stable lad caught hold of Blueberry's leading rein and led us into the number-one spot in the winners' enclosure, I relished every second of the win, storing it up in memory to be relived in later life, a sadly depleted life that didn't contain rides or wins. And I gave thanks to the boss upstairs for the opportunity I had of being fit and strong enough to ride races right now. Every race, a win or lose, was a bonus to be enjoyed to the full. There would come a time, and not too long in the future, when racing would end.

It was a thought I tried not to dwell on.

I had three more rides this afternoon – two I won; the third one on Bombardier, a massive seventeen-and-a-half hands high, bright chestnut bay, built like the proverbial, put in an extra half-stride at the fifth fence and I left the saddle in an awkward arc. Despite rolling on impact, the ground was no softer to land on than my last fall.

It banged every bit of air from my body and I was left gasping like a landed cod whilst paramedics leapt from their following vehicle and descended on me as, unable to get up, I lay flat on the grass.

They carried out a frighteningly efficient examination and I assured them, when I could actually speak, that I had no broken bones – I'd broken enough to know what that felt like. They agreed that I'd been lucky and was still holding together, although badly bruised. I hadn't blacked out, as I was at pains to tell them. However, they were well used to attending fallen jockeys and didn't take my word for it.

Had I lost consciousness, even for a few seconds, it would have been a red-card job and meant I'd be stood down. These days, they took no chances with head injuries. But their initial inspection, however, proved there were no visible signs and I was allowed to walk back to the medical officer's room. He repeated the checks and finally I was given the all clear – not the red card, thankfully – and allowed to limp off to the weighing room.

A hot shower, along with commiserations from the other physically intact jockeys, eased my aggrieved left hip and I re-joined Mike in the owners' and trainers' bar.

'Get this down.' He thrust a small brandy into my hand. Of the owner of Bombardier, there was no sign. 'Very disgusted,' Mike said. 'Soon as he saw you weren't a coffin case, he buggered off. Owners like that, who needs 'em?'

I downed the brandy in one go, feeling the steadying, burning warmth go right through me, and suggested that it seemed like a good idea if we hit the road. He chortled and slapped me on what I *hoped* he'd thought was my good shoulder, but actually wasn't! 'I thought you'd already gone down and hit the hard stuff.'

'Not funny, Mike,' I said, wincing and clutching my left arm. 'And if you were thinking of giving me another slap down the shoulder, don't. Or if you must, make it the right one.'

'Sorry,' he said, biting his lip to control his chuckles. There was no hope of any sympathy from him. 'Come on. Let's get home, then.'

Back at his stables, I swapped from his vehicle to mine. I toed the Mazda back to Nottinghamshire and Harlequin Cottage, hobbled painfully across the gravel drive and gratefully went inside. For once, Leo was away on private cat business and I went straight upstairs.

In the bathroom, I stripped off my gear and took stock of my battered body. It was a stock-taking job that happened too frequently for my liking, but went with the territory. OK, the sight in the mirror wasn't pretty, and by tomorrow it would look a damn sight worse, but I'd had worse, a great deal worse.

Sticking the plug in the bath, I ran the hot tap, pouring in a substantial amount of foaming muscle relaxant, and at the same time poured myself a glass of water from the cold tap.

Fishing in the medicine cabinet on the wall, I found three strong painkillers and swallowed them. Then I eased myself, with considerable swearing, into the exceedingly hot water and prepared to simmer gently until relief arrived.

Closing my eyes, I thought about the possibility of Annabel giving me some spiritual healing to help speed recovery. And regretfully decided I wasn't hurt sufficiently to bother her this time. It was the only thing that made coming off a horse at over thirty miles an hour worth it – the chance of Annabel coming round. But not this time.

A long hot soak would have to do. Still, if I concentrated on her beautiful face it would take my mind off the intense discomfort of being immersed in near-scalding water, as long as I kept completely still and didn't attempt to move.

Right then, there was a loud banging on the horseshoe door knocker that hung on the back door.

FIFTEEN

I was groaning softly anyway, but I put in a big one. Who the hell was it? The horseshoe banged against the door again. I wasn't expecting anyone. They could take themselves off. The thought of more agony when I tried to get out of the bath was not welcome. They'd have to come back again.

This time, it wasn't so much of a knock as a battering down job, insistent and continuing. Ignoring the racket, I sat motionless for several minutes, eyes closed. The noise had eventually stopped: whoever had been knocking had obviously got tired and gone away. Already it seemed my nerve endings had gone into shock because after the first hardly bearable level of heat in the bath water, now it was simply hot. And it was starting to soothe the bruises – that or a combination of the heat and the three painkillers was taking effect.

I slid down a little further, foam lapping against my chest. Whatever was helping, I was quite happy to allow it to continue and I began to doze. It had been a long day.

Then, strangely, I heard a tap being turned on and felt a fresh gush of hot water.

'Would you look at that, now?' said an Irish voice.

I opened one eye, very slowly. Through the swirling clouds of steam, I saw Patty Doyle's face swim into focus. He was grinning widely.

'Can't have you catching your death, sitting in cold water.'

Already the temperature in the bath was escalating – and the water level rising.

'Turn the bloody tap off, Patty,' I bellowed.

'Can't hear you.' He was doubled up with laughter. 'Just like you with the door knocker.'

Then relenting, before the bath overflowed, he leaned over and turned off the hot tap.

'How the hell did you get in? And what the hell do you want?'

'Aw, now. We had a gentlemen's agreement to meet tonight, so we did.'

I clapped a hand to my head. 'Indeed we did. Sorry, Patty, I'd completely forgotten.'

'Ah, well, you did come off . . . I'll make allowances.'

'I didn't actually hit my head, so, no, it's my fault.' As I spoke I stood up and reached for a towel.

He winced and whistled. 'Some come off, so it was.'

Wiping the mirror free of steam, I had to agree, a good chunk of my anatomy was a most interesting purple colour, enhanced, of course, by the boiled lobster red of my skin. I wrapped the towel around my waist and added a further one round my shoulders.

'Anyway, how did you get in? I'm sure I locked the door, didn't slide the bolt though.'

'Good job about that.' He shook his head. 'If y'had done, these little treasures wouldn't have been much good.' He took a set of slender keys from his pocket and slid a finger through the retaining split ring they were hanging from, twirling them around.

I knew what they were. I'd actually got a set of my own: skeleton keys, very useful, very illegal. 'Put them away, Patty. I'm not even going to ask why you've got them. I don't want to know.'

He chuckled and replaced them inside his inner pocket.

'The last time someone broke into my cottage whilst I was in the bath – and came right up into the bathroom – I ended up in a very dangerous situation.'

'Not this time.' His mood altered. 'How about we go downstairs, have a drop of the hard stuff, eh?'

'Why not?' I said, dragged on a pair of loose jogging bottoms and winced my way inside a baggy sweater. The worst of the pain had diminished but it wasn't giving up the fight just yet.

However, stretched out on the lounge sofa, the electric fire on full bore, and a small whisky clutched in my fist, life seemed a reasonable prospect once more. 'So, what couldn't you tell me in the pub?'

'Anything I'm about to say now.' He took a sip of the excellent whisky, raised both eyebrows, gave a slight nod of acknowledgement to its quality, and began to fill me in on Paul Oats' background – and his own.

He'd been born in Ireland on a farm where his parents had scraped a living but had seen the light regarding the future and escaped at the earliest opportunity. Both he and Oats had come over on the same boat, got taken on at a racing stables in the north of England and rubbed off their rougher edges in hell-raising and devilment, boozing, nicking cars and joyriding.

'But then Oats decided his wallet wasn't getting thick enough quick enough and got into the drugs scene.'

'And what about you?' I put in. I wanted to see the whole picture here.

'Oh, I was tempted, so I was. There was big money to be made, easier than shovelling shit, but . . .' He swallowed some more of his whisky. 'I didn't fancy being the bloke who supplied stuff that could fry your brain cells. Yeah, maybe it wouldn't do it straight away. I know that, but it was still the start to getting hooked, getting in deeper and deeper, having to take more and more . . . ending up turning into a zombie.' His face twisted with pain and distaste. He stopped talking, twirled the near-empty tumbler round and round, staring down into the glass.

I didn't hurry him, just waited. This was coming from deep within the man and it wasn't easy for him. But his next words hit me like being double-barrelled by a horse – right in the solar plexus.

'I *know* all about your little sister, Silvie.'

I was so shocked I felt my own glass slipping through my trembling fingers. Taking a grip, I drained it in one swallow, stood it down safely on a coaster on the coffee table. He didn't move but his gaze lifted from his own drink and fixed on my face.

'I can't see where this is going,' I said, 'but carry on.'

'She was in the nursing home, near Newark, wasn't it?'

I nodded silently.

'Hmm . . . so was my sister's little girl, my niece, Maeve.'

Desperately trying to regain my equilibrium, I searched my memory for any recollection of that name. But if the memory existed, it eluded me. I shook my head slowly, emotion choking me. 'Sorry, but I don't remember—'

'Ah, don't be giving yourself a hard time, now. Our little Maeve was only there for a few weeks after your Silvie was admitted. But she loved the smell of the flowers you brought for her. They were white freesias, weren't they? Every time the same, white freesias.'

I nodded, suddenly unable to speak, the massive lump in my throat threatening to choke me. They had indeed been Silvie's favourites.

'The flowers gave her a lot of pleasure, just smelling them. The nurses used to wheel her chair down the corridor past Silvie's room – they often had the door propped open – that's when she first smelled the freesias. They thought her sense of smell had increased, y'know, as her other ones . . . faded.

'When their wheelchairs were taken into the community room they were placed side by side. Our Maeve was blind as well as severely disabled. So it was the smell, you see, that's how Maeve knew who was sitting near her. Silvie used to have a blossom twined into her plait.

'We brought her some after that, had a lovely spray of them made when she died, laid it on top of Maeve's coffin. That was white as well . . .' He was getting emotional now himself.

I stood up abruptly. 'Give me your glass. We both need a refill.'

He handed it to me without meeting my eyes, head bowed over, hands dangling loosely between his knees. Standing with my back to him, I poured the drinks, giving him time to get a grip.

I'd thought that nobody could be as badly disabled and restricted as Silvie had been – had raged against God, life . . . the injustice and unfairness of it. She had drawn the shortest of short straws.

Silvie was actually my half-sister. She was the outcome of my mother's need for comfort as she grieved for my dead father, and a man seizing his chance because of her vulnerability. But both my mother and I had loved Silvie very much. The doctors warned us she wouldn't survive into adulthood. A grim prospect and I could only be relieved when, many years later, my mother died first and would never have to suffer the loss of her daughter. It left me with sole responsibility for Silvie's welfare.

Yes, I'd thought nobody could be as disabled as Silvie. I was wrong. She hadn't been blind, thank God, like Maeve. And because I knew what a heavy emotional burden it had been, I could empathize with Patty Doyle.

'You're taking your time with that hard stuff . . .'

I braced myself and turned to give him his glass of whisky.

'I'm sorry, sorry I can't remember your niece . . .'

He flapped a hand and took the glass from me. 'Don't worry about it. But I owe you one. There was so little Maeve could take any pleasure from. Yes, I know, *she* didn't realize what she was missing, and Jesus be praised for that, but we did. And those flowers were one of the very few pleasures she could appreciate. They made her world a bit brighter.'

He sighed heavily and lowered the whisky level in his glass. 'So, ask me what you'd like to know about Paul Oats.'

I dragged my thoughts back from the dark path they were going down. 'Am I right in thinking Oats is into drugs – drugs for horses?'

Patty took a swig of whisky. 'Yes, for both.'

I frowned, 'Both?'

'People and horses.'

'Do you have any proof?'

'I know where the handovers take place. I can take you so you can see for yourself.'

I took a drink of my own whisky and gave myself a few seconds of thinking time. It wasn't that I distrusted Patty, but what he was suggesting was a dangerous game to be playing. I changed tack a little. 'Do you know anything about the horse that was possibly doped the other day, Bayard Boy? Belongs at Tal Hunter's stables.'

'Hmm, not the sharpest tool, Oats. Got the wrong one, didn't he?'

I tried very hard to control my amazement. 'He did?'

'It was meant for your horse, Harry, Baccus.'

I stared at him. 'But the man worked for Tal, he'd surely know which one was Bayard Boy.'

'Not been there long, has he? And those two horses look pretty much alike, the same height, same colouring – bays, aren't they? Difficult to see which is which sometimes, you have to admit, especially if you're working in a small space with dim light – and under time pressure.'

'Come on, Patty, level up here. Are you saying that the wrong horse got the drug – *and* it was probably administered inside the horsebox, maybe during a quick pit-stop?'

Patty drained his whisky, stood up. 'You've got it, Harry. Yes, that's exactly what I'm saying.'

He moved quickly for the door, but I moved quicker. Placing my hand on his arm, I said, 'Where might he keep the drug, do you have any idea?'

'I think maybe I've said too much already.'

'Just give me something to go on, Patty. You don't approve of drugs, I can see that. So, where might Oats hide the stuff?'

He hesitated, hand already turning the door handle for a swift exit. 'Look, we're equal now, mate, OK?' Then, looking at me slyly, he added cryptically, 'Soap gets things clean.'

And before I could question him further, he was gone, through the kitchen and out of the back door.

SIXTEEN

I felt I'd been sandbagged. First, there had been the shot fired at the horsebox that could have been meant for either Keith or me. Now, the horse that had been drugged had been Tal's, but the drug had been meant for Baccus, my horse.

As I thought about the two separate events, I experienced the prickle at the back of my neck that I'd learnt to trust over the last two or three years – since I'd been forced to try and save other people and track down vengeful criminals. It was almost like experiencing a sixth sense, not clear cut like the normal five, but still I was aware of it. Almost like a throwback to eons ago when primitive man had to rely on himself to remain alive. It was a sharpening of all the senses. Like guidance and a warning from deep within, the prickle alerted me to unseen, unknown danger – and so much more. No way was I going to discount it.

And just as I'd learnt not to question it but to pay attention, it forewarned me of answers to questions I didn't know I was asking. Which sounded fanciful in the extreme, certainly not rational, and yet by not discounting the prompting, or whatever it was, I seemed to intuitively know more than was apparent on a conscious level.

The sensation didn't last for more than a few seconds, but it was enough. I'd had cause in the past to be thankful for the warning it gave. I'd be a fool to dismiss it. And I didn't. Somehow, and as yet I didn't know how, these two events were linked – discovering the answer to one would also give me the answer to the other. There was nothing to prove this and yet I just knew it to be the truth.

I started to feel hungry – the whisky on its own was not cutting it. The physical body was demanding food. I'd had very little all day. But I also felt nauseous. Still, I'd had two shocks, one physical, the other emotional. Some sustenance was definitely required.

Getting up stiffly from the sofa, I hobbled to the kitchen and put a pan of tomato soup on the cooker. Whilst I was waiting for it to heat up, I ran through everything Patty had told me. Even cudgelling my brain some more to try and recall the child named Maeve, nothing gelled. And until I'd come to a concrete acceptance of all he had said, there would remain the flicker of distrust that somehow, he'd made it up.

But I'd liked the man. Yes, he had faults – didn't we all? – but as he'd admitted, his youth had been wild – wilfully ill-spent from what I could gather – and I was willing to bet there was an awful lot more he hadn't disclosed. Like, where had he acquired the set of skeleton keys in the first place and why continue to carry them around with him? That alone raised doubts.

The soup began to spit tiny globules of scarlet. I dragged my attention back and poured it into a mug. I collected up my mobile on the way back to the fire and sofa, and having taken a sip of the burning hot soup, put it down for a minute or two in favour of making a telephone call.

I felt the accustomed rise of happy anticipation as I tapped in her number.

She answered on the third ring. 'Harry.'

The one word carried warmth and pleasure. My heart did its usual crazy flip and went into overdrive simply at the sound of her beloved voice.

'Hello, is everything well in your world?'

'Yes, all is very well. And yourself?'

'Hmm . . . to be truthful—'

'The only way,' she said firmly. 'Am I right to assume you've had a fall?'

'Well, yes, but—'

'No buts, Harry. Are you hurting? Be truthful, now.'

'Yes. But it's mainly bruises, very superficial.'

'Would you like some absent healing?'

'You're an angel, you know. But I wasn't going to ask. However, what I'd really like is for you to come over. Or are you busy? It's some information I'm after. About the times we spent visiting Silvie in the nursing home. There's only yourself that I could ask.'

She gave a sharp gasp. 'Oh, Harry, whatever's happened?'

'I don't want to talk about it over the phone.'

'OK. What time do you want me to come over?'

I risked it. 'Now?'

'I could do. What about supper? Have you eaten at all today?'

How well she knew me. But after living together as husband and wife before the ship hit the rocks, foundered and sank, of course she did. 'No,' I said, 'but I've just heated up some tomato soup.'

'Hmm . . .' It was all she commented but the disapproval was evident.

'Come on, there's nothing wrong with a drop of soup.'

'You said it, Harry. A drop of soup . . . after a day of fasting and racing, plus with what seems to be two good shocks to the system. You need something solid. Your body's crying out to be fed. Why don't you listen to it?'

I had to concede she was right. In fact, Annabel was scarcely wrong. It was damned annoying, really.

'Pan-fried sea bass with tartare sauce suit?'

Her words conjured up a picture of delicious, crisp-skinned, succulent fish and my stomach immediately responded with a groaning rumble. 'Sounds marvellous.'

'Sit down, sip your hot soup and just relax, get over whatever life's thrown at you today and I'll be there soonest. OK?'

'Yes ma'am,' I said, and followed her instructions to the letter.

And I felt a warm glow spread through my whole body. It could have been the bright fire, or the hot soup – or then again, it was simply so nice to feel someone cared. I fell asleep, of course. Which was precisely the result she had been aiming for and the next thing I was conscious of was her voice, calling me.

As I muzzily came back to life, she appeared by my side, deposited one enormous ginger tomcat – who was purring for England and no doubt anticipating a handout of sea bass – on to my recumbent lap and enquired after my state of health. 'All the better, et cetera, et cetera.'

'Hmm . . .' She stood, frowning down at me. 'A bloody stupid thing to do, coming off.'

'Bloody stupid,' I agreed, nodding.

'I've put the fish in the fridge, safe from my gorgeous boy, here . . .' She smiled adoringly at Leo. 'So, I'll make some tea and you can carry on where you left off.'

She disappeared in the direction of the kitchen to reappear a few minutes later with a couple of steaming mugs.

'Wrap around that.'

I reached across Leo and took the one she was offering me. 'Thank you.'

'Don't mention it.' She plumped down on the end of the sofa and immediately Leo swapped his allegiance and draped his furry body languidly across her chest. Jammy sod. *And* she allowed him to. That cat got away with murder. But since he had once saved me from being murdered – being burnt to death, actually – I allowed him to monopolize Annabel, and her beautiful body.

'Now, come on, Harry.' She took a gulp of her tea and sighed with satisfaction. 'Tell me all about it.'

I followed her example with the tea and then told her. 'So,' I concluded, 'do you remember a young girl called Maeve at the nursing home?'

Annabel had listened silently whilst I updated her. Now she frowned. 'I can't say I do.'

I groaned, disappointed at her non-recollection of the girl. I'd been banking on her being able to confirm Patty's story.

'But,' she continued, still frowning, 'I *do* remember Silvie loved the smell of freesias.'

I nodded. 'So do I. It's not the freesias that are the relevant thing here.'

'Ha, wait, Harry.' She wagged a forefinger. 'I think it's more important than you think.'

'Go on.'

'Patty told you this other girl, Maeve, was blind.'

'Yes, that's right.'

'Then, if she couldn't see it, how did Maeve know Silvie wore a single bloom woven into her plait?'

'By the perfume from the flower.'

'No, no.' She wagged her finger more vigorously. 'How did she *know* it was in Silvie's plait?'

'Patty said the nurse used to position her wheelchair next to Silvie's in the community room. And Maeve could smell the flower, which is why she knew it was Silvie sitting next to her.'

'I get *that*. But the position of the freesia is what I'm trying to get you to understand.'

'Well . . . I don't know . . . probably the nurse told her.'

'And you need definite clarification that what Patty has said is the truth?'

'Yes, I do. If I can't prove it, I can't fully trust the man. And I need to if I want to go forward in this investigation.'

'Hmm, yes, I see that.'

'Bit of a dead end then, isn't it? And I've dragged you over here on a wild-goose chase.'

'No, you haven't. At the very least, I get to cook us both a lovely meal to eat together – always tastes better with two – and I can give you some healing, if you want me to. Plus of course, whilst not quite being the cherry on top, because I didn't bring any cake, the very best bit is . . .'

'Go on.'

She grinned cheekily at me. 'I get to see—'

'My gorgeous boy,' we chorused.

She collapsed laughing across the sofa and kissed me.

'Whoa,' I said, widening my eyes and twinkling at her, 'can I hope that this might also actually refer to . . . me?'

She sat back in her seat and hugged the disgruntled Leo who, having got caught in the crossfire, had stopped purring, and was fully aggrieved. 'Of course not, Harry, you silly man.' She buried her face in Leo's long ginger fur. 'I've only got one gorgeous boy.'

I'll swear that cat shot a one-upmanship glance at me and smirked.

'Drink your tea, woman,' I ordered, and proceeded to drink my own.

We spent a wonderful evening doing nothing – just talking, after we'd polished off a superb seafood creation that Leo also got to sample. It was just like old times – beautiful old times. And I could have wept when it was time for her to go. Then I remembered she hadn't as yet given me any spiritual healing and I gently reminded her about it; anything at all that might delay her leaving.

'But I don't think you're in any pain now, Harry, are you?'

And I had to admit that, no, I was remarkably pain-free right now.

'That's because I sent you some absent healing before I left home.'

'So that's why you told me to lie back, sup soup and think of England?'

'Something like that, yes,' she admitted. 'And I'm sorry, but I really do have to get back.'

'No, I'm sorry. I'm just greedy where you're concerned.'

She fished in her handbag, making sure of her house and car keys, plucked her coat from the back of the kitchen door and was about to go out into the cold evening when she gave an exclamation. 'Would you believe it? I'd forgotten.'

'What?'

'I think, after all, that Patty *was* telling you the truth. I remember before we used to leave Silvie, I'd take one of her flowers and secure it in her plait. So she could take it with her in the wheelchair. Then.' Annabel gulped. 'Poor Silvie tried to say "smell", but of course, she couldn't. And she'd lift my hand and her plait to my nose, so I could smell the beautiful perfume.' Annabel stopped talking and stared at me. 'I bet you anything, Harry, that's what she did with Maeve. And if so, that other little girl would have been able to feel the plaited hair *and* smell the flower.'

I stared back at her. 'Do you know, I'd forgotten, but you're quite right. Silvie did do that. And, yes, I think Patty was telling me the truth. It had the right ring to it.'

She leaned towards me, giving me a quick kiss on the cheek as she opened the back door. 'Glad I've helped. Must go. Goodnight, Harry. God bless.'

SEVENTEEN

I went to bed a very happy man, slept soundly, and when I awoke the following morning, decided I wasn't going to go racing. Yes, I could have said I wasn't fit enough – and it would probably have been the truth, although I'd been racing with far worse injuries – but Patty had sent an email late last night saying that the business we'd been discussing was taking place later tomorrow afternoon – which meant today. Was I interested?

You bet I was.

After I'd read the email, I rang Mike. 'Sorry it's late, Mike, but I've just had a message.'

'Oh yes. Do I get to know who sent you it?'

'You surely do. Patty Doyle. Giving me the heads-up that I might be in for a breakthrough tomorrow afternoon.'

There was a moment or two of silence. 'Do I take it you're not racing, then?'

'Afraid not, Mike. It's a good chance of possibly nicking whoever is supplying the drugs.'

'Watch your back, Harry. And I'll see you when you're ready.'

'Thanks.' I put the phone down. I didn't like skiving off racing. It was something I abhorred. But there were other people's lives at risk here and I had to weigh that against being up at a race-course. It was a non-starter. I'd had to do it before, not often, but always when other people's safety was in the balance. There was never any question of what was the right thing to do.

However, my conscience usually gave me a difficult time later. It was hard-wired from an early age that it was unprofessional to put other things in front of my rides. But as long as it didn't become a habit – or worse, a get-out – I managed to squash the guilt. One day, when racing had given me the elbow, perhaps I'd be able to make the choice of helping other people without my conscience giving me a mauling, but that time hadn't arrived yet.

Mike would undoubtedly soothe his owners, probably make my fall the reason – they couldn't argue with injuries – but just the thought of that scenario made me feel uncomfortable. Those same owners were people who indirectly paid my wages, and their beautiful horses kept me in the coveted championship top-spot for jump jockeys.

It was rare for them to jock me off, replace me with another jockey. They kept their part of the unspoken bargain and it didn't sit comfortably with me to let them down. But today's chance of cracking a drugs ring was too important to turn down.

There was a strident miaow from downstairs – Leo was back from his seduction of the local queens. He'd got some stamina, I gave him that – there were dozens of little, ginger Leos prowling around the locality. I didn't know the full scope of his range, probably never would, but going into some far-flung farms, I was constantly amazed by coming across a litter of tiny lookalikes. 'Your tomcat's a bloody nuisance,' the farmer would say. 'Time you had him seen to.' It was a well-worn phrase. To which I always replied with a smile and said, 'If they turn out anything like their father, you're a lucky man.' I usually received a grudging grunt in acknowledgment. Leo's exploits were the stuff of legend and everybody for miles around had heard them. Let's face it, he was more famous than I was.

Regretfully, stiffly, I hauled myself out of bed, muscles shrieking in protest, and staggered to the bathroom, ran a hot bath and lowered myself in gingerly. Leo would have to wait for ten minutes. But I'd left the bathroom door open and, sure enough, when the sound of running water alerted him that I was not coming down to the kitchen any time soon, a furry ginger body, green eyes gleaming, oozed around the door frame. Full of himself and fit as a butcher's dog, he leapt straight from there across the room to the top of the wicker linen basket close to the non-tap end of the bath and, on an eyeball to eyeball level, fixed me with an unblinking emerald stare.

'Soon, Leo, soon,' I murmured and closed my eyes, letting the hot water work miracles on my bruises and loosen the knots in my muscles.

He was a forgiving cat, sometimes, some days, and today was one of them. He conceded, settled down to watch, and curled up with front paws neatly folded underneath him and serenaded me with a loud, slate-rattling purr.

'And I love you, too,' I said, sliding down further in the hot water, my thoughts turning to what the coming day might hold.

Patty had suggested picking me up from Harlequin Cottage, but I'd vetoed this. The whole situation was so delicate, not to mention bloody dangerous, that I wanted to keep as far from the main players as possible. The thought of being spied on at the cottage was not an image I fancied. And it was certainly possible. If anyone had got wind of my interest, they only had to keep tabs on Patty and follow him and yours truly was definitely in the frame.

It had happened on a couple of previous occasions when I'd had to get rough to defend myself – another memorable time when Leo had saved me from getting roasted to a crisp, and found himself badly injured in the process. So, no, I didn't want Patty inadvertently leading the black hat boys to my own doorstep.

As an alternative, I'd said I'd catch the train from Redcliffe, .

my local station, and travel east as far as Sleaford. He could pick me up in the marketplace there then drive north towards Newark before joining the A1.

'But it's in Leicestershire, Harry . . .'

I'd calmed him, told him we'd then head south and come off the A1 at Harlaxton on the A607. 'Muddy the waters should anybody have ideas of following us.'

His objection had died instantly as he'd cottoned on, agreeing willingly. 'That'll put them off the trail, so it will.'

'I just hope there won't be anyone trailing us – or rather, you.'

'Nah, there won't be anyone trailing me,' he asserted. 'Bank on it.'

No way was I putting money on it. Working with another person wasn't my usual way of going about solving a crime, and I didn't like it, but in this instance I had no choice.

I'd been shocked when he'd told me where the drugs had come from, and had to shut him up from disclosing any more information. 'Tell me on the way, Patty. It will be a lot safer than over the phone, or by email.'

He'd agreed, so although I knew an approximate destination, I didn't know any further details. As a belt and braces job, however, I'd left a handwritten note for Mike in case I didn't return, telling him I was going to where the man who had stitched up White Lace lived. Nobody else would have a clue what that meant, but when he read it he'd know instantly where I'd gone. But God forbid he would need to. The note would not be found by anyone else. Long ago Mike had suggested it as insurance and after a deal of consideration, I said I'd stick any urgent notes on the underside of Leo's dinner bowl. Mike already had a spare key to the cottage. In the worse scenario, like I'd finally bought it, the cat still needed to be fed. I mean, it would be the height of self-ishness to die and leave him without a new devoted slave.

Mike had always had my back in dodgy situations, but with Pen nine months pregnant, no way was I dragging him in to help, unless it was dire. He was still there, though, in the background. And it was comforting to know.

At this point, I became aware of something and it cut across my thought patterns. Not a noise. But definitely something. I opened my eyes. Silence. Leo had stopped purring for England

and was now standing up on top of the wicker basket and staring balefully down at me. His patience had run out, and he was hungry.

'OK, OK, cut out the glare,' I said and reached for a bath towel. 'I'm on my way.'

Tail erect as a flagpole, he beat me to the kitchen, but when I hobbled through the door and took out his dinner bowl, the purr was back. He loved it when he won. I dropped a piece of kibble on to the floor to keep him going and he was on it in a flash. 'A slave, that's what I am, d'you know that?' I told him as I carried on filling the bowl. Clutching the bath towel around me, I placed his dinner down on the red quarries and stuck the kettle on.

The handover, Patty said, wasn't taking place until late afternoon, so I had a fair bit of time to play with, although I'd have to check on the train times. Steaming mug in hand, I applied myself and discovered there were only two trains that stopped at Redcliffe then travelled directly on to Sleaford; all the others went straight to Grantham station first before, retracing their route, they branched off right up north.

But I wanted a train that went straight there. The first one left just after nine in the morning and the second, and last, at ten past one. I was losing a lot of time anyway, playing cops and robbers, and going all the way to Grantham first was a no-brainer. I opted for the ten past one train. Maybe I was being over cautious by taking a massive loop around the country first, but I'd learned the hard way. Now I eliminated as many risks as possible.

Doing it this way, me catching a train, Patty driving his car, it was certain that anyone keeping tabs would have no idea that Patty and I had joined up. And if by the remotest chance they saw us meet in Sleaford and drive off north, at this point they would surely lose interest. Their business was lower down the country, in darkest Leicestershire.

At half past twelve, after ringing Patty on the landline to confirm pick-up time, I locked the cottage door and set off to walk down to Redcliffe village. With just the two railway tracks – one running east and one west – 'station' was really a grand name for a simple stopping spot. However it did the job, and after walking up the rise and over the bridge spanning both tracks, I walked down the concrete steps on the left-hand side and waited on the platform for the Sleaford train.

I'd downed three painkillers with a coffee before leaving the cottage and that walk had helped loosen up any residual stiffness. Now, reasonably pain free, I stood under the shelter and waited for the train.

The journey took just over an hour. Alighting at Sleaford station, again a one-in-one-out job, I walked down the hill into the market town centre. It was surprisingly busy and I had no trouble weaving unobtrusively in and out of the shoppers, sure now that this had definitely been a good idea and nobody would be following me, and made my way across the thronged square, past all the different colourful stalls of fruit and vegetables, pies and cakes and piled high pyramids of bright knitting wool, pleasurably breathing in the scents of frying onions and hot dogs wafting across from the many cafes. Even if I couldn't indulge and actually eat one, there were no calories gained in sniffing.

Crossing the square, I fetched up against an open shop doorway – a barber's – on the other side. It appeared full indoors and there were already three other men forming a queue on the pavement outside. I simply tacked on to the end and waited for Patty to show up. My luck held and, just as the last man in front of me went through the shop door, Patty appeared. Still walking, he gave the slightest tilt of his head indicating which way he'd parked the car and, without breaking step, went on in front. I followed.

Heading north-west, he drove fast but within speed limits, no sense in drawing attention to ourselves, and we were soon on the A1. Now, he put his foot down and we flew south, destination Leicestershire. We passed the outskirts of Grantham and, after taking a left turn in order to get across the fly-over, he turned right near Harlaxton. From there it was merely minutes before we were approaching the southern boundary of Belvoir Castle woods.

I'd kept a close eye on the traffic behind and was sure that nobody was following us. We'd maintained silence the whole way, but now Patty nudged my right arm. 'Not far. The handover doesn't take place at this bloke's premises.'

I nodded and waited. From the little he'd told me the previous day, and before I'd stopped the flow of information, I'd had serious doubts on this point.

'No,' he went on, 'there's a back entrance, down a long drive.

It leads off close by a wood, and there's a narrow lane outside the wood. That's where I'll be parking up. OK?'

I nodded again, not sure exactly where he meant but prepared to go along with it. But he seemed to know and drove on confidently through the next village and the twists and turns of the following lanes before taking a sharp left at the side of a wood. There was any amount of small woods and coppices around here and it would be easy to get lost.

But I had to trust Patty, because it occurred to me that maybe I hadn't been so clever in deciding the logistics. There were no trains or buses around here. He was the one behind the wheel, and if it all went west, I was sunk. I had no other form of transport to get back home. My own car was enjoying a rest, parked up outside the back door of Harlequin Cottage.

'The bloke's name's Rantby,' Patty reminded me.

He'd told me this before I'd shut him up. And I knew who he meant – had met the man before. And I found it very hard to believe.

Perry Rantby was Mike's veterinary surgeon.

EIGHTEEN

P atty drew in under the overhanging branches of the nearest tree and cut the engine. He took out his mobile and checked the time. 'Might as well have a bit of a kip,' he said. 'There'll be nothing doing for a couple of hours.'

'What time is the handover?'

'Either side of six o'clock. But it depends when the vet finishes.'

I winced and hoped he hadn't noticed. I was finding it difficult to cast Perry Rantby in the role of baddie. As a qualified vet – after at least seven years of tough training – before oaths taken, no doubt, like doctors, and with a good chunk of his working life in front, why would he jeopardize his future? It didn't make any sense. 'Are you *sure,* Patty? I mean, the man's a professional . . .'

Suddenly, I wanted to know the whole story, not a fraction. Yes, I'd stopped him from spilling it all out yesterday but right now, today, was what counted. 'Tell me everything.'

He'd slid down in the driver's seat, tipped his baseball cap over his eyes in preparation for catching a nap. I looked at his profile as he stared straight in front through the windscreen. After what Annabel had said regarding Sylvie and the freesias, I'd changed my opinion from doubting Patty to trusting him. But now, I wasn't so certain.

'This Rantby, he's a vet, right?' I nodded. 'So, he's got access to drugs, probably a whole load of different ones.'

I shrugged. 'It's his job; he needs them.'

'Exactly. And he's keeping them all under lock and key, isn't he? But, not only are the drugs kept locked, so is his surgery door. Double security, you might say.'

'So?'

'So, when he wants the drugs he has to get into the surgery first. And that's where security breaks down. Because Rantby has a nephew, Giles, who comes in to lend a hand, get some experience, right? Most of the time, Giles is studying hard in college. Wants to follow on as a vet. But – *but* – in between terms, he comes over to help out his uncle Perry, doesn't he? And Uncle Perry has given his nephew a key to the premises. You with me?'

'Yes, so far. Go on.'

'Seems Giles has developed a liking for the gee-gees. Bets big, I've been told.'

'Is this on good authority?' I broke in.

'Absolutely. He lives in at college with his mate Alfie. Now Alfie is a gambler as well. He was the one that introduced Giles to the *delights*. And now both of them are in way over.' Patty shook his head slowly. 'Mug punters, the pair of 'em.'

'I get the picture. And they're tight for cash?'

'Tighter than my old ma's washing line. But Alfie knows Paul Oats . . .' He half turned and raised both eyebrows at me. I nodded. He resumed his scrutiny of the windscreen. 'And Oats dreamed up this scam, but needed drugs.'

'Wait a minute, have they done this before? Or is this handover today the first?'

'Oh yes, they've pulled it before. Why do you think Bayard Boy didn't come across in that race against you, Harry?'

'Paul Oats had rigged it?'

'Too right he had. And using some drug he'd got from Rantby's stock cupboard.'

'Did Rantby know he'd had a break-in?'

'No, that's the beauty of this little caper. Giles didn't take enough for it to be noticed. He knew just how much would be needed – and I understand it wasn't a great deal at all. The horse only need to be slowed down, not knocked out.'

'And this drug should have been given to my horse, Baccus, not Bayard Boy?'

'That's right.' Patty nodded. 'Bloody fools, got the wrong horse, didn't they?'

'Seems so,' I said drily, not liking anything I was hearing. 'And I suppose they put a packet on the wrong horse?'

'Yep, they did.'

'Hmm. Which brings us to today's little shenanigans.'

'That's right.'

'No, Patty, that's wrong.'

'What?' He turned away from the windscreen and looked straight at me. 'What you on about? Soon as this bloke Rantby leaves, this pair of tossers lift a bit more of this drug. Detomidine, I reckon, or could be Etorphine, some sort of barbiturate, anyway.'

'And then wait their chance for another go to recoup the money they lost the first time.'

'I reckon so, yeah.'

'But there's more to this than the horse doping.'

'Is there?' His surprise was genuine.

'Oh yes.' But I wasn't going to tell him what. 'You carry on, Patty, grab a nap. I'm going to scout round up the front of the building, check it out before the action begins.'

'If anybody spots you, it's curtains.'

'They won't spot me, I'll be very careful.'

As I said this, I opened the car door and slid out. 'Won't be long. You have your kip. I'll be back before you wake up.'

There were two cars parked up close by the doors into the surgery and another two further away. The first vehicle was a Range Rover, dark red. I knew it belonged to Rantby – I'd seen it parked up in Mike's stable yard. However, I made a note of the registration number. Then working my way around using what bit of cover I could find with the bushes that edged the drive, and keeping well out of sight of any of the windows, I made a note of the make and numbers of the other cars.

Two of them parked side by side were Peugeots and I deduced they probably belonged to the veterinary nurse and the receptionist.

The last car, nearest to the vet's, I guessed belonged to the nephew, Giles. It was an old, clapped-out Vauxhall. But then Giles, as Patty had informed me, was a penniless student. You wouldn't expect him to own a new model. And obviously, Uncle Perry didn't believe in wet-nursing his nephew by helping him out with a newer model. He was a sensible man, Uncle Perry.

I felt the beginnings of anger rising inside me at the thought of Giles and his grubby little friend pulling a fast one when Rantby was giving Giles a sound grounding in the life of a rural vet.

However, these were the only cars – no sign of Paul Oats having arrived in the vicinity as yet. I mulled it over as I weaved my way back through the concealing trees to where Patty was parked up. He was fast asleep, cap tilted over his eyes. I tapped on the driver's side window.

He awoke with credible swiftness and leaned across and released the passenger door. 'How did you make out?'

I slid into the passenger seat. 'Nothing suspicious at all, at the moment.'

'No sign of Oats, then?'

'None.'

'Not time yet. Told you we could have a kip.'

'Something I want to ask you, Patty.'

'Go on, then.'

'This handover, why is it happening here?'

'Should have thought that was obvious.'

'No, it isn't. Surely it would be a hell of a lot safer to hit the road and get away from the crime scene.'

'But that's *why*. Giles said he wants in on this because he's over a barrel for money. At the same time, he's laid it on that no way is he running any risk of being caught with the drugs on *him*. I mean, he's the only one who knows which drugs to take and what quantity. Oh yes, he'll nick them, yes. But that's all he's prepared to do. Any carrying is on someone else's shoulders.'

'I can see his point. That way he's cutting his own risk of getting nicked. If the drugs are then handed over straight away and found on someone else, that's enough proof of carrying and chargeable.

There's no proof Giles nicked them. The chance of being caught *actually* lifting drugs from the surgery is just about nil.'

Patty nodded. 'He gets rid of them immediately. Nobody can prove it was him. Do you see?'

I did see. And what I saw was a broad yellow streak running straight down the middle of Giles's back at the same time as he held out his hand to receive his pay off. There was nothing like a barrel job to make someone do something, even if they didn't like it.

I should know; I'd been in that situation far too often. I was over my own barrel right now. And sure as hell, I didn't like it.

'Now, if you *don't* mind,' Patty said, and pulled his cap down even further, 'I'll finish my beauty sleep.'

I gave it until a quarter to six. Then, extremely cautiously, I left Patty still snoozing and made my way through the trees and bushes to a vantage point I'd picked out earlier. This gave me a good view of the front of the surgery, the entrance doors and a fair part of the approach drive from the connecting road at the bottom running in each direction.

I hadn't climbed a tree for years – I didn't want to think how many years – but as a concealed look-out, it was perfect. This one was a very old ash tree and sported some huge, leopard-bearing branches that would certainly bear my own weight. Like that beautiful big cat, I picked a broad safe one and spread myself out along its length. Placing a hand either side of my face, I rested my chin on the rough bark between them. The ash still retained its leaves, most of them anyhow, and it would be impossible for anyone on the ground to spot me amongst the foliage.

Then I waited, silently and comfortably, confident in my chances of securing some telling images on my phone's camera.

The four cars I'd noted earlier were still in place. But at five past six a Volvo turned in and drove right up to the surgery doors. My hopes of catching Paul Oats on camera died as a big woman clambered out followed by an equally overweight and extremely reluctant boxer dog. Without bothering with a lead, she grasped its collar and marched off through the door into the reception area.

Within minutes, she returned, urged the now-eager animal back into the rear of the car and drove off. There was then a quick exodus from the building as two young women, followed by the vet himself

– I recognized him – left and got into their vehicles. Lastly, they were followed by a young man – Giles? – who produced keys and busied himself locking up. After waving the others off and walking over to the clapped-out Vauxhall, he took his time unlocking it.

By now, the three-car cavalcade had travelled down the drive, reached the road and the cars were busy peeling off in different directions. The man, it had to be Giles, straightened up and, after making sure they had all disappeared out of sight, rushed back to the surgery door and unlocked it, left it swinging open and hurried inside. All of these manoeuvres I captured on camera.

Within minutes, Giles was back, carrying a folded newspaper that he laid down carefully on the passenger seat. What it contained – or concealed – I could make a good guess at, but any security camera would see only an innocent newspaper.

Giles then relocked the surgery door before getting into the Vauxhall and setting off. He drove as far as the junction with the road before turning left out of sight.

I climbed hurriedly down the ash tree, scraping shins and knees, swearing under my breath as I rushed to get down to ground level again. Then I ran, weaving between clutching tree branches and undergrowth, and made my way back to where I'd left Patty and the parked car.

It didn't take long, but even so I was too late: there was no sign of the Vauxhall or any vehicle that might have held Paul Oats. But even more telling, there was no sign of Patty. And no waiting car. He'd done a bunk. Whether a forced one, or he'd simply decided to bugger off, was unknown.

What I *did* know was that I was stranded – miles from home and without transport.

NINETEEN

I t beggared belief.

I hunkered down with my back pressed against a broad tree trunk. For one thing, there was now no danger from the rear, plus it made me a smaller target. For another, the only possible attack could come from the front and it wouldn't take me by surprise. But I wasn't expecting one.

Patty's disappearance was down to one of two things: he'd got cold feet and sodded off, or he'd seen Giles's car, rightly assumed the drugs were still on him and, without risking losing him, had decided to trail his car to wherever the drugs were going.

However, Patty knew I had no transport, plus we were out in the sticks and I would be stranded. Did that mean he intended coming back for me? It was anybody's guess. And I certainly wasn't guessing right now. I took out my mobile and dialled Patty's number. The phone was switched off. Swearing forcibly, I dialled Mike's number.

'Mike. I'm in a spot. How are you fixed right now? Are you free and have you got any transport?'

His voice, clearly concerned, came on the line. 'I take it you're stranded, yes?'

'Damn right, I am.'

'Not a problem.' Mike didn't do problems. As far as he was concerned they were opportunities awaiting solutions. 'Tell me where you are and I'll get over straight away. Not injured, are you? Not in immediate danger?'

'Not injured, but the jury's out about danger, not sure what's happened except Patty's swanned off leaving me stranded – possibly in bandit country.'

'And *where* are you?'

I told him as clearly as I could, although I myself wasn't too sure.

'Just keep your phone on, because I'm leaving the stables now. If I get as far as Rantby's place, you can talk me through the last bit, OK?'

'Yes, and thanks, Mike.'

'Oh, do shut up and let a bloke drive. After all, it was partly my fault for talking you into helping Tal Hunter.' He ended the call and I settled back against the sturdy tree trunk to await developments.

Enough time had elapsed for me to strike up a close and meaningful relationship with the local wildlife; two woodpigeons cooing overhead, a single robin cocking a bright and hopeful eye in case

I had a spare sandwich, and a manic squirrel chattering loudly and angrily that this was *his* tree, before my phone jumped into life. Mike was apparently parked on the lane near the junction with the track into the wood at the back of the surgery.

'Stay right there. I'll get to you, easier that way. Then you won't get picked up by any security cameras, if there are any.' I scrambled up and jogged through the trees until I broke cover on to the lane. Mike's four by four was a welcome sight. I opened the passenger door and swung myself up and in.

'No sign of the bandits, I take it?'

'You take it right, Mike, thanks.'

'Not much fun spending the night on your own out here.' He released the handbrake and motored off smoothly towards home. I waited until we'd gone about five miles, well away from any possible unwanted action, then filled him in on what had happened and what I needed him to do.

'And you've got pictures of this little parasite unlocking the surgery door after the rest of them have all gone off home?'

'Yes.'

'So, where does this leave us?'

'Do you happen to have Rantby's phone number saved on your mobile?'

'Yes, of course. Never know when I might need him urgently.'

I nodded. 'You need him urgently – now.'

'I *do*?'

'Pull in and park where you can. Then give him a ring.'

Mike didn't bother to ask any questions.

'Ringing now,' he said and passed over his mobile.

Rantby answered a few seconds later. 'Yes?'

'Mr Rantby, Harry Radcliffe here. I'm using Mike Grantley's phone.'

'OK.'

'I know you've only left the surgery about forty minutes ago, but can I ask you to get back there? It is urgent, I assure you.'

'I can, but for what purpose?'

'I want you to go in and check your drugs stock cupboard.'

'And what am I checking? I mean, I've a wide range of drugs—'

'Yes, I assume so. But it is very important. The drugs to check on are the ones for sedating horses. I'm sorry I don't know exactly, but if you could check if any are missing, I'd be most obliged. I *do* have good reason to think that there will be some missing.'

'OK . . .' he said slowly. 'But I'd like some more information from you.'

'And if I could ask you to wear gloves, please, it might help.'

'Is this turning into a police matter?'

'I'm sorry, but yes, it very well might do.'

'I see.' His tone changed straight away. 'Yes, well, I'll get over immediately.'

'Could I also ask if you could let Mike know the result, please?'

'Yes, I certainly will. But I do have to insist on knowing what exactly is going on.'

'And I will tell you, I promise. But it's really urgent to do a check as quickly as you can. I don't imagine anybody else will attempt a break-in this evening, but there is always that slim chance. That would certainly muddy the waters considerably.'

'Very well, I'll get there now. Let you know what I find. Goodbye.'

Mike had been listening to all that had been said. 'Harry, shouldn't we just turn around, go back and talk to Perry?'

'No, Mike, we shouldn't.' I shook my head. 'I've never been into his surgery before. OK, I've seen the man in action at your stables, but never at his surgery. There will be no signs of my DNA to be found inside there. And if he comes back and tells us he's discovered some missing drugs, he will certainly need to ring the police. And given my track record with the police, they won't take very kindly to what they'll no doubt see as interference.'

'Hmm. Yes, I see your reasoning.' Mike stroked his chin. 'This could get a bit nasty.'

I smiled at him and handed his phone back. 'As you pointed out to me, it's partly your fault for talking me into helping Tal Hunter.'

Mike grunted and drove off up the gears. 'What beats me,' he said, easing up to negotiate a tight junction, 'is that with all your experience in dealing with wrong 'uns, Harry, what made you trust Patty?'

'My Achilles' heel.'

'Eh?'

'Sylvie, Mike.'

'But . . . Sylvie's dead . . . I don't follow.'

'Patty was levelling a score, *he said.* A score I wasn't even aware he owed me. And because it was about Sylvie, I believed what he told me. Still seems like he was pulling a fast one – gaining my trust with a view to working it in his favour. To what end, I have no idea. I mean, leaving me stranded . . . what or how would that be to his benefit?'

'No idea,' Mike grunted. 'But it does mean, as you've just said, he knew your weak spot was Sylvie.'

'Yes, not a pleasant thought. Using her to manipulate me is well below the belt.'

We travelled on and were within a handful of miles of getting home when my phone suddenly began playing *The Great Escape.* I groaned and grabbed for it.

'Harry, mate, where are you?'

I raised expressive eyebrows at Mike. 'Patty . . .?' Mike raised eyebrows back.

'You still at the same leafy place?'

'No,' I said, equally cagey, 'I'm enjoying a lift.'

'Ah, good. Look, I didn't mean to ditch you, but it was a great chance to find out the . . . destination. You get my drift, yeah?'

'Not sure I do, but carry on.'

'Since there was no sign of you, I followed the car – not the old banger, the other one – when it left the . . . er . . . *Uncle's* place.'

'Can you describe it?'

'A Ford saloon, latest model, a black paint job. Just the driver in it, no passengers. Someone we both know. Thought you'd like me to keep tabs on where the drop-off might be.'

'And did you?'

'Yep. The car didn't make any diversions, just homed in on its destination, like a reliable pigeon. And that's also where I am right now, Harry, old mate.'

'Which is where exactly?'

'Your lady friend's stables.'

'Tal's place?'

'On the nail.'

'So where do we go from here?'

'Thought you could tell me.'

'Hang on, Patty.' I covered the phone with my hand. 'He's at Tal Hunter's, Mike. And so is Oats . . . and the drugs. He wants to know what he's to do next. What do you reckon?'

'Damned if I know. Do you want me to drive you over there?'

'No.' I shook my head. 'I don't see it getting us anywhere, steaming in like the cavalry. We've no jurisdiction, no authority at all to demand a handover of the drugs. And besides, we need to catch him in the act of using the drugs on a horse to have actual proof of doping. Nothing short of that is going to help Tal.'

'But we *do* know that that's where they've pitched up. It confirms that Oats is your man.'

'Hmm . . .' I agreed and uncovered my phone. 'You still there, Patty?'

'Sure, now where else would I be?'

'You've done a good job. Thanks.'

'I would've come back to pick you up if you'd still been in yon leafy glen.'

I laughed. 'I'm sorry I doubted you. Call it quits today, Patty. Get yourself off home. Because that's where I'm headed for right now.'

'Be in touch, so I will.' He ended the call.

I turned to Mike. 'If you could just drop me off at Harlequin Cottage, Mike, that would be good.'

He nodded. 'And will you be hanging up your deerstalker when you get home? You're not going anywhere dangerous tonight?'

'Most certainly not. I've had more than enough travelling the countryside today.'

'Good to know. And do I take it you will be donning your crash cap ready for going racing tomorrow, six a.m. at mine?'

'You do. And thanks again.'

He grinned and turned off the A46 at Saxondale Island on to the A52. 'Well, couldn't leave you in the leafy glen, could I? What sort of a mate would I be?'

'A bloody good one.'

TWENTY

I waved Mike off in the lane outside the cottage and crunched my way over the gravel to the back door.

There was only one thing I needed right now – a scalding hot mug of tea. Everything else could wait. I made the tea and drank it, leaning against the butler's sink, staring out of the kitchen window at the quiet, peaceful garden. The cottage was my bolthole from the raucous and violent outside world and it never failed to restore my equilibrium. It would have been even better had Annabel still lived here with me. But I hadn't given up all hopes of her returning one day. In the meantime, it was just us two chaps who lived here – me and Leo – and we fully appreciated its warmth and shelter.

However, right now, there was no sign of Leo. He was busy, either fully committed to chasing down the local queens, or engaged on a foraging expedition – it was always food or females – and God help anything that he considered fair game. He'd likely already earned his spurs and would no doubt come back as a panther – a black one, probably. He was well on the way to being seriously big and scary.

I finished the drink and made a second. My fluid intake today was well below normal level. There was not much chance of getting a cup of tea when stuck up a tree. Sipping the reviving liquid, I reached across the kitchen worktop – and Leo's basket – lifted the receiver from the wall-mounted phone and dialled Tal Hunter's number.

'Hello, Tal. How're things?'

'Oh, hello, Harry. I haven't rung you because I've nothing to report. I couldn't find anything, I'm afraid. I did look, I assure you, but either I didn't look in the right places or there really wasn't anything *to* find.'

'It was unfair of me to ask you, Tal. I'm sorry. Look, don't worry, I'll come over myself. See if I do any better.'

'I really think that would be best. But we will have to liaise very carefully because you could only do it when that certain *gentleman* is safely out of the way. I don't want you to run any risks on my behalf.'

'That's fine, Tal. We will liaise, but can I just ask you if you're in a position at the moment to see what's going on in your yard? And in particular, is there a black Ford parked up anywhere?'

'You're talking about *his* car, aren't you?'

'Yes.'

'Well, all I can tell you, Harry, is that, yes, he did drive in a short while back. But I didn't take any notice, except for realizing it was a darn good job I'd done a search before he got back.'

'It's possible that what you were looking for wasn't there – which is why you couldn't find it. However, it is now.'

'It doesn't help, Harry. I mean, if he is back, no way can either of us go into his room and do a search.'

'Certainly not, Tal. I didn't mean you to take a massive risk like that. I'm just giving you a heads-up that from what I've discovered today, the . . . er . . . *goods* are now definitely somewhere at your place.'

'That makes me feel decidedly uneasy.'

'It must do,' I said soothingly. 'I'm sorry I can't be of any more help tonight. But look at it this way, racing is over for today. So there won't be any more horses doped until tomorrow at the earliest, if indeed his target is running at one of the racecourses on tomorrow's cards. And it may very well not be. I think it would be too short notice to have collected the items today for using in the next twenty-four hours.'

'Hmm, well . . . yes, I'll go along with that. I'm not sending any horses racing so, selfishly, I suppose that puts me above suspicion – at least for the moment.'

'Not selfish at all, Tal. You're the one in the frame now. *We* all know you're absolutely blameless but, unfortunately, the authorities don't.'

'And I intend to stay blameless, Harry.'

'Just hang in and see what happens. I'm working on it. And we are getting further towards a result.'

'Thanks. Yes, I'm fortunate to have everyone's back-up. Anyway, must go, duty calls . . . my late round of stables, you know.'

'Of course, speak to you again, Tal. Bye.'

Predictably, my tea had got cold so I went to make a fresh mug. However, something Tal had said was niggling away inside my head. Taking my drink, I went through into the conservatory. It was warm and quiet in there. Plus there was an extremely comfortable squashy sofa and lots of squashy cushions. I found it the perfect place to relax and think things through.

I also took my folder of case notes with me. It was something I'd got into the habit of doing from the very first case. It contained not only the complete facts as I knew them, but also when and where I'd visited people during the course of the investigation.

And not only did it contain the relevant facts; I also listed obscure things like odd sounds and smells, things that shouldn't be where they were, my impressions, my feelings and hunches, in fact everything that had come within range of my five senses – and also, sometimes, my sixth – what my instincts were prompting me to do or say. These of course were not facts. But they were just as invaluable in their own way, as had proved the case many times before.

Some of them – and those had nearly always been preceded by that strange prickling down the back of my neck which I now never dared ignore – had been really outlandish yet had proved to be the truth. And without paying heed to them, I wouldn't have been able to solve the cases.

I plumped down on to the deep cushions on the sofa and grabbed a gulp of tea in between thoughts as I jotted down today's strange happenings. The facts, when joined up like dots, turned into a picture, similar to the one on the lid of a jigsaw puzzle. And the even stranger thing about it was that before I had uncovered all the facts of the case, my intuition went into overdrive and supplied me with the complete picture – even if I didn't believe it. And often I didn't, such was the level of my faith. But afterwards, I used to kick myself for doubting it and wasting valuable time.

Yes, it had happened before. But it wasn't something you could coerce. I just hoped it would deign to come to my assistance again this time. So many people's lives were being blighted on this one case, it felt like a heavy yoke across my shoulders and I needed to come up with the answers.

I wrote quickly and logged down everything that had happened. Then I leaned back, swallowed what was left of my tea and gave myself over to thinking about Tal's words. I didn't push it, simply allowed thoughts to slip into my head. At this point, I wasn't in charge – my subconscious was. And it didn't work under pressure. Demanding answers sent it heading for the hills. The trick, if it was a trick, was to totally relax and allow the information, the intuitive insights, to flow unrestricted with no rejection of even the most bizarre ideas.

I came to about half an hour later. Yes, I'd dropped off to sleep, but that often happened, along with being presented with a solution – or even a partial solution – to the problem in my head.

As I returned to awareness, I felt sharp needles rhythmically kneading my thighs, together with the soothing drone of a half-volume purr, both emanating from Leo. As I opened my eyes, he squeezed his brilliant emerald ones tightly shut and positively smirked. If you think cats – or indeed dogs – can't smile, you'd be wrong. Opening those same green orbs, he proceeded to work his way up my jersey until his head butted up hard against my chin.

'Hello, you,' I murmured and stroked the smooth dark marmalade fur.

There we sat enjoying a deeply relaxed time together and my subconscious, delighted with itself for having the ideal conditions, released the answer to my query of what Tal's words had set in motion, albeit not on a conscious level. I'd been concentrating too hard on her side of things when what I should have been doing was stepping back and taking a different view.

Tal's focus, and mine, had been on her situation, her horses and her racing stables. What I ought to have done was reverse that. It wasn't Tal as trainer, nor her horse Bayard Boy, that had been the intended victims, but my horse, Baccus. I'd already found that out and then stupidly ignored the obvious. The stable that had been targeted wasn't Tal Hunter's, it was Mike's. And that altered everything. It also gave me a lead to follow.

Reading through and jotting down all the facts had given my conscious brain a clear picture of events. Armed with this blueprint I had, in effect, handed this over to my subconscious mind with all its superior intuitive and creative capabilities and, by deliberately standing aside and taking myself out of the way, had allowed the solution to come forward as to the correct answer. It was a method

I'd used many times before and it proved invaluable and rarely let me down.

An even better one, which I definitely used towards the end of a difficult case, was to employ the same technique when immersed in the bath. Why this worked even better was something nobody could answer – but it did work – and that was all I was bothered about.

'And you played a part too,' I informed a sleepy Leo. 'Cats are renowned for their relaxing capabilities, did you know that? And I owe you. How about pilchards for breakfast, eh?'

But Leo wasn't interested. He'd gone back to sleep again.

'However,' I said and reluctantly eased him out of the way, 'I'm sorry, but right now I do have to shift you.'

Leo took umbrage and, flattening his ears to his skull to show me his displeasure, he leapt from my knee and disappeared. A few seconds later, I heard the cat flap in the kitchen door open and close as he departed.

Reaching for my mobile, I dialled Mike's number.

'I should have thought you'd be safely tucked up in bed by now,' he growled.

'No, no,' I said soothingly, 'still on the case.'

'Well *I'm* going to bed; don't know how much sleep I'll get though—'

'Very little, I should imagine,' interrupted a woman's voice. 'And it's not for the reason you're thinking of, Harry. It's because this fast-approaching Grantley offspring is determined to ride a great finish and is kicking hard.'

I spluttered. 'There's nothing I can say in answer to that, Pen, except perhaps good luck.'

'OK, stop chatting up my woman. What are you ringing for, Harry?'

'Yes, I'm sorry to disturb you both. Can I just ask if you're sending out a horsebox tomorrow that's accommodating any other trainers' horses, or even one horse? Or are you sending one or more of your horses to the races in another trainer's box?'

Then I waited for the answer that would tell me if my subconscious had got it right.

TWENTY-ONE

I was up early the next morning. Pilchards had been opened and duly despatched by Leo and relations between us were once more harmonious.

There had been a sharp frost overnight and the grass verges down the lane were crisply white. And if the lanes were slippery at my end of the world, it was a sure bet they'd be even worse further north – I was riding at Doncaster this afternoon. It certainly wasn't a morning for a toe-down job. And the cold wasn't helping my sore stiffness. I'd sat and stewed in a very hot bath again last night before crawling into bed. The solid eight hours sleep had, no doubt, helped the healing, but there was still a good way to go.

I poured a strong black coffee – no sugar – swallowed three painkillers and hoped they'd do the job. It was going to be a long day. I'd wanted to catch a word with Mike before diving into the regular work routine in the stables, but the road conditions were as tricky as I'd thought they would be and that reflected in the level of speed I could safely drive.

Work was underway in the yard with a vengeance, stable lads scurrying back and forth with brushes and forks, mucking out, topping up water buckets before carrying armfuls of tack into stables. I knew Mike would be busy in his office prior to driving up on to the gallops to watch the string of horses in the first lot. With a race tomorrow at Huntingdon, I was down to ride out Soulmate, a new mare to Mike's stables, a bright bay with beautifully contrasting dark mane and tail, in order to assess her progress.

I went in search of the head lad. He was in the tack room, sorting out bridles.

'Hello, I think I'm down for first lot on Soulmate.'

He straightened up, gave me a nod. 'That's right, Harry.' He found the correct tack and handed it to me. 'She's in the fourth stable along; should be an interesting ride. She seemed very keen yesterday when I took her out. And Mike wanted your take on her.'

'Does that mean I should watch myself?'

He grinned. 'Not really, no more than usual with a new horse. But you had a fall the other day, didn't you?'

I nodded and grimaced.

His grin widened. 'Still feeling the effects, then?'

'Who me? No way.' It was the right answer to give. Any jockey who was not one hundred per cent fit wasn't allowed to ride in races. But most jockeys usually covered up any pain or discomfort.

I walked over to the fourth stable. Soulmate gave me a strong blow down her flared nostrils, nuzzling her velvety lips against my palm in case I'd brought her a treat. Instead, I patted her neck in return. She might prove to be a skittish ride, but I knew she seemed basically good natured. Her stable had already been mucked out so I carried on and began tacking her up.

It was not the usual thing for a professional jockey to do. They would have quite rightly expected to find the horse tacked up by the horse's lad and ready to ride. However, Mike and I were mates, went back as far as the Ark, and we'd pulled together in our youth when neither of us was successful and at that time it was simply a matter of survival. But our early combined efforts had resulted in where we were today: Mike, one of the most successful flat and jumps trainers in the country, and me champion jump jockey. The partnership had paid off big time for us. I continued to graft at his stables when I could, and Mike continued to persuade his owners to agree to putting me up as jockey. And with horses as good as those in Mike's stables these days, I was being amply rewarded in riding winners.

I began whistling softly as I slid the saddle cloth over Soulmate's neck, down her withers and on down her back, ensuring that her coat lay flat and no hairs were brushed the wrong way to irritate her skin. Then I placed the pad, Witney rug and saddle gently on top and adjusted the girth to hold it in place, knowing that, like most horses, she would probably blow herself up. That would entail re-tightening the girth before I mounted.

I rubbed the solid steel of the bit between my warm palms before sliding it in between her jaws. Daft, I suppose, but I know

I wouldn't take too kindly to an inflexible piece of cold metal sitting on my back teeth. Whether Soulmate appreciated it or not, forming a mutual respectful relationship with your horse was one way to get the best out of them when out on the racecourse. A lot of that relationship came from reading each other's minds, and right now, mine was giving off positive vibes. Holding the reins, I led the mare out into the yard.

Most of the other horses comprising first lot were already circling the yard awaiting their jockeys to be legged up. There was one more horse to be led from its stable before we all pulled out.

Soulmate's stable lad cupped his hands together, I raised a leg ready and he flipped me up, effortlessly, into the saddle. I circled Soulmate with the rest and the last one, Junket, an iron-grey monster of seventeen and a half hands high, joined us. A final girth check and we were ready to go.

First lot snaked out of the yard gates and set off in single file up the lane towards Mike's gallops, metal striking tarmac with a rhythmic beat from all the shod hooves. I slipped Soulmate in towards the back of the string away from the couple of colts in front until I'd had a chance to assess her responsiveness. But there was no sign of any mulishness or trying to take off sideways.

Instead, with her ears flicking back and forth listening as I kept up what I hoped was a soothing low whistle, the one I always used that my horses recognized and found calming – Dvořák's 'Largo' from the *New World Symphony*, but most people would probably know as the 'Hovis' advert – Soulmate was a model ride.

She did do a lot of head tossing, extending her neck to its fullest, but apart from that, I didn't find any undesirable traits at all. However, I reserved final judgement until we'd been on the gallops themselves.

By the time we'd reached them, Mike had already overtaken the string and was parked up in his usual spot about halfway along, binoculars slung around his neck in readiness to watch each horse more closely at its work. This was a vital part of his daily assess-ment in preparation for bringing each individual to its fittest, fully ready for the correct race. I knew that it was now second nature for Mike to judge a horse and have in mind a particular race. The pairing of horses to races was a skill he'd spent years honing and for which he had a superb flair.

It was just one of the reasons why Mike Grantley was a name well known in horse racing and one that commanded justified respect – to which his many wins, especially over jumps, testified. Prospective owners felt confident in looking to place their horses with Mike. They knew he was a first-class trainer and they trusted his judgement.

The first lot began peeling off and working up to half speed as they galloped to the end of the track and Soulmate eagerly followed. We turned at the far end and came back at a full-speed gallop. I was aware of the head lad's veiled warning and was alert for any display of headstrong awkwardness, but to my delight, I couldn't fault the mare at all. She gave me a beautifully smooth ride with no hiccups at all.

We pulled up at the end of the gallops, the air around us turning into white clouds as the gusts of horses' hot breath hit the cold air and, to me, the beautiful smell of horseflesh rose up from the sweating neck in front of me. I snuffed it up, very much I would think, like a confirmed glue sniffer might do. But this was no destructive, base-level addiction. In my case, it was the very reason I'd become a jockey – I loved horses. All horses, any horses, even the mean-tempered, vicious ones – it was never their fault, they weren't foaled bad; it was usually their upbringing that had led to them turning surly. And I always gave them the benefit of the doubt and sought to achieve some sort of calming influence.

I leaned forward over the steaming, sweat-lathered neck and withers in front of me and gently pulled Soulmate's ear. 'You're all right, girl. There's nothing wrong with you.' And I patted her wet neck, which gleamed in the weak rays of the winter sun.

Thoroughbred horses were born to race, it was hard-wired in them, but I never failed to show them I appreciated their efforts. Soulmate arched her neck and tossed her head. Horses knew when they'd done well, and like other animals, including humans, responded to praise. And they continued to give of their best. A little respect between horse and jockey went a whole lot further than most people would imagine.

Hearing the sound of an engine, I sat up in the saddle and turned and gave a thumbs-up to Mike as he drove back to the stables. He would be pleased with the piece of work Soulmate had just done.

And he was not alone; I was very pleased too. I couldn't wait to be in the saddle riding her at Huntingdon races. But that was tomorrow. Today, I was booked to ride at Doncaster.

I left Mike's yard at about eleven o'clock and toed it up north. I had two earlier rides booked before the big one, my three o'clock ride on Dark Vada, belonging to the famous Dame Isabella Pullbright. I'd managed to fit in going over to Barbara Maguire's a couple of times to ride work on Dark Vada and was confident that today's race should be a shoo-in – not that there was *ever* such a thing in horse racing. But her performance had impressed both Barbara and me. Whether her famous owner would also be there was an unknown. I don't think Barbara herself knew.

The first two races were on horses trained by a northern trainer who used my services fairly regularly and we were both well satisfied when I brought them both into the winners' enclosure in first place. But the next race was the one I really wanted to win. It was an honour that Dame Isabella had told Barbara I could have the ride. A lot depended on today's result. If we could pull off a win, there was every chance she would continue to use me as her jockey. It all added up to a win-win for Dame Isabella, Barbara and, of course, put much-needed numbers on my tally towards retaining the championship.

I trooped out with the rest of the jump jockeys, all dressed in their brightly coloured silks. I was wearing new colours for the first time – the colours chosen by the owner of Dark Vada. And they were certainly very striking – sugar pink with black chevrons topped off with a sugar-pink cap. Not only would the commentator have no trouble calling the mare's name, but he would be able to pick out Dame Isabella's colours even on a gloomy and overcast winter's day. If the lady herself was an equally flamboyant character, we were in for an interesting working relationship.

TWENTY-TWO

Dotted about in small groups, owners and trainers were standing chatting in the parade ring. A quick glance around showed me where I needed to be. Not only was the trainer,

Barbara Maguire, waiting, but she was deep in conversation with another woman. A tall, slender blonde who was dressed in a full-length black coat complete with knee-high black boots and topped off with – I could have put money on it – a tiny sugar-pink fur hat. It couldn't be anyone else but Dame Isabella Pullbright. She'd obviously found time, or made it, in her exacting schedule to be here and see for herself what sort of performance her mare put in.

I made my way across the grass towards them.

Dame Isabella turned her head and looked at me, at exactly the same moment as I, drinking in the undeniably delightful picture she made, was staring at her. The famous wide smile – eat your heart out, Julia Roberts – flashed across her face. Putting out a hand, she tapped Barbara's arm and nodded towards me. Then, unable to stop herself, she laughed out loud.

'Snap!'

Barbara and I both smiled back. There we stood, owner and jockey, both dressed alike as racegoers, getting in on the act, began enthusiastically clapping with amusement.

Dame Isabella bent forward, whispering in my ear. 'I'm not sure picking these colours was quite such a good idea . . .'

'Nonsense,' I replied, momentarily overwhelmed by her beauty and beguiling perfume at such close quarters. 'We make the perfect couple.'

There were immediate wolf whistles and guffaws from the crowd lining the rails who had caught what I'd said.

'He means himself and the mare, of course,' she said, raising her voice so they could hear her. 'See, she's wearing a pink brow band.' And Dame Isabella pointed to the mare's forehead that was adorned with a flashy bright pink band.

That only served to incite more whoops and laughter. It was the custom with some owners to incorporate their colours into brow bands for their horses when they were about to run in a race. Into these moments of merriment, whether we were ready for it or not, the bell rang and instructions, which had to be obeyed, were called out: 'Jockeys please mount.'

Sydney, Barbara's stable lad, walked Dark Vada from the circling track over the grass into the centre of the parade ring.

'Wow.' Dame Isabella's eyes widened in admiring appreciation.

'What a lot of hard work you've put in,' she said to him. 'The mare looks wonderful. I'm not surprised you won the "Best turned-out". Thank you.' She patted Dark Vada's glossy shoulder.

Sydney smiled with pleasure and I silently applauded the woman for taking time in the midst of all the excitement she must be feeling as a first-time owner to acknowledge the stable lad who looked after the horse at least six days a week. Without stable lads' hard work, racing wouldn't take place. Not only did they work hard, they were very poorly paid. One of the coveted perks was winning 'Best turned-out' which carried a cash prize. Sydney was going to remember this day.

Should I be able to ride a winning race, it would surely be the cherry on top for all concerned. The world of racing was like a family: each person supported the others.

Dame Isabella was paying out a great deal for the care and training of her horse. That money kept the trainer in a job and the stable lads in work, not to mention myself, plus if I could achieve a win, Dame Isabella would be recompensed, so would I, and Sydney would be in line for a hand-out. As for Barbara – well, Barbara would add another win to her impressive list in the successful trainer reputation stakes.

So, yes, all that was needed today was for me to win on Dark Vada. That would make a treble for me – not something that came around every day. But I was going to give it a damn good go.

Barbara stood smiling, pleased that her new owner was so obviously enjoying her brand-new racing experience. I was reminded of Mike's motto: 'Keep the owners happy.' And it was true – happy owners were owners that continued to want to engage with racing. It seemed that the racing bug had just bitten another willing victim.

'No instructions, Harry,' Barbara said as I got flipped up into the saddle. 'You've had a couple of gallops, you know what the mare's capable of. I don't doubt you'll find out a lot more about her during the race. But we would like a winner . . .'

'Do my best,' I said, touching my cap to Dame Isabella.

'Take care – of both of you,' Dame Isabella said.

I exchanged a quick glance with Barbara as Sydney urged the mare to walk on. We both knew it wasn't possible to go around a racecourse wrapped in cotton wool – races weren't won like that. However, any risks I took were calculated ones. But today, with the owner being high profile and the mare not having raced for her before, my risk-taking would have to be tempered by avoiding disasters and any subsequent fall-out should anything go wrong.

The chat and laughter followed us out to the start of the course.

'Nice, in't she?' Sydney said, looking up at me just before he released the lead rein.

'Dark Vada or Dame Isabella?' I asked, pulling his leg, and smiling as the blush rose up his young cheeks.

Then I was away, cantering down to the start.

I joined the other jockeys and horses and kept an eye on the starter and his yellow flag. The usual banter was flying about plus suggested placings that might or might not be right. I merely smiled at the comments, slipped in my gum-shield and turned Dark Vada around in a tight circle following the pack now heading forward towards the starter.

She was keen – and strong – and I had to hold her back in midfield. Her attitude was great but I wanted to know there was still some fuel in the tank when it was needed, probably two or three furlongs out from the winning post.

We met the first of the fences: Dark Vada made light of it and was away swiftly on the far side. As she continued to lift, effortlessly it seemed, over fence after fence, my spirits rose in tandem. We were still travelling smoothly in the centre of the field until four fences from home when I allowed her to begin to sneak up. By the approach to the third from home, we'd left behind six of the ten horses that had started off and we were lying fourth now with just two short-odds favourites in front who were chasing the front runner, Dustbowl. It was an apt name because for most of the race we had been following his dust – well, we would have been if the ground had been dry – but as with a lot of front runners, he'd shot his bolt by racing away to a massive ten lengths lead at the start. However, it was a pace that was impossibly fast and couldn't be maintained.

By the time we were approaching the second last, his speed had dropped as had his lead – it was now little over one length. The two horses in front of me were racing upsides now and preparing to challenge Dustbowl for the lead over the next fence. I urged Dark Vada to quicken and in seconds we were racing alongside the other two. Dustbowl, hanging like a barn door now, a sure sign of a tired horse, made a hash of jumping the final fence. He dragged his hind legs through the top, sending brushwood flying, and lost ground on the far side.

In contrast, I and the other two jockeys urged our horses on and the three of us flew the fence as one. Now I pressed the button and asked Dark Vada to show me what she could do. Working with hands and heels, she needed no whip, she annihilated the other two – taking off in an unbelievable burst of speed that ate up the muddy ground. We had now less than a furlong to run and already I knew we'd won. The mare was still drawing away, her speed precluding any chance the other two might have of catching us.

I bent over and risked a quick glance between my legs at the horses behind us. It was in the bag. Only Pegasus with his wings could take the race away from us and he certainly wasn't entered.

We fairly zipped over the finishing line, Dark Vada relishing every second of the running and sticking out her neck to make sure of victory. But she had no need to. We'd won by three lengths.

I was as delighted as I knew Dame Isabella and Barbara Maguire would be. This horse not only had the will to win, she was determined to win. I could see a very bright future for her. And, if her owner wanted me to be her regular jockey, a correspondingly happy future for me, too.

It was champagne all round in the owners' and trainers' bar. Barbara had given very firm instructions that, win or lose, I was to join them after the race.

'Ha, Harry . . .' Barbara seized me immediately. 'Now, you will have a flute, won't you?'

It would have been churlish to decline but, like on other occasions, I usually took a sip to cement good relations and simply played with the glass, maybe took another sip as I was about to leave. As a jockey, I spent a good percentage of my working hours behind the wheel getting from A to B and driving to different racecourses – no way could I afford to lose my licence.

'I can't tell you how thrilling I found that, watching you win the race.'

I nodded, smiling at Dark Vada's fizzing owner. 'I'm glad. You've got yourself a very good horse. She jumps like a stag *and* she stays. That burst of speed she produced in the last furlong . . . she's quite something.'

'Like her jockey. And talking of riding, how would you like to be her regular rider?'

Dame Isabella turned on the full wattage as she focussed her baby blues intently on mine. I could see why she was one of the leading film stars in England. She radiated a pull strong enough to control tides.

'I'd like that very much, thank you.'

'Well if, as you say, Dark Vada is a very good horse, it makes sense to make sure her jockey is very good as well. Don't you agree?'

'That's difficult to answer.'

'Really?' She put her head on one side and curved her lips ever so slightly.

'Hmm, if I disagree, I'd be wrong. On the other hand, if I agree . . . well, it seems like I'm blowing my own trumpet.'

'Harry, you *are* the champion jockey.'

Her smile spread now and I was treated to the famous full McCoy job – at such close quarters, it was devastating.

Barbara threw back her head and laughed out loud. 'Oh, dear, Harry. I think you've met your match.'

'I don't think, I'm certain I have. But thank you, Dame Isabella, I appreciate your trust. And I'm sure I've got the best of the bargain. With Dark Vada's qualities it would be very hard to be beaten in a chosen race. And I know Barbara can certainly pick the right races. She's like a female version of my business partner in crime, the trainer, Mike Grantley. He's the cream at picking races.'

'I'm not sure if you've just given me a compliment, Harry, but I'll take it as one.'

'And so you should, Barbara,' Dame Isabella said. 'I have complete confidence in both you and Harry. Now – more champagne, yes? It's a day for celebrating.'

'Not for me, thanks.' I made a show of taking a glug from my flute. 'Must go, I'm afraid.'

'Oh . . .' She did a seductive pout.

I replaced the glass on the table and took my leave.

Outside, the cold air was a wake-up after the warmth of the

bar. I made my way past the back of the stands heading towards my car. The delightful smells lingered in the air from the fast-food stalls and vans. Like a Bisto kid, I sniffed up the tantalizing, competing scents of hot dogs and onions, fish and chips, jacket potatoes and curry . . . I heard and felt my empty stomach rumble in appreciation. I'd be ready for a meal when I reached home tonight. Unlike the great Willie Carson, now retired, who'd effortlessly maintained his low weight – and had the quote, 'He performs magnificently at the dinner table', said about him – all the jockeys I knew, me included, suffered for their rides.

Turning from having a good lungful of fried onions, I caught sight of a large works vehicle. Pale blue, it had navy writing along the side proclaiming 'Dust Chasers', followed underneath by smaller letters: 'We always clean up.' I smiled at the pun. It had obviously ferried in a team of necessary cleaners for the race meeting.

But at the same time, I was reminded of Ginnie Cutler's words when I'd last seen her. Ginnie worked for a firm that specialized in supplying cleaners to the racing world. A twinge of conscience made itself felt. The poor woman had been in a bad state when I'd bumped into her at the Queen's Hospital. I'd heard nothing further from her. I really should have made contact, found out how she was – and if the granddaughter was still OK. And another phone call to the hospital was also in order to see if Keith had regained consciousness yet. The moment he did, I needed to get myself over there.

I carried on walking and was passing the outside toilets when I heard someone softly call out my name. I came to a halt, at a loss to see where the voice came from. Whoever it was whispered my name again followed by the words, 'To your left'.

Without turning my head, I looked sideways. Standing just inside the outer vestibule that led to the ladies' toilets was a small person dressed in a pale blue overall which had navy writing across the bib. I was too far away to read what it said, but I knew it had to be Ginnie. I gave a slight nod. Seeing she had my attention, she darted a glance nervously left and right.

Then, crooking a finger, Ginnie beckoned me – urgently.

TWENTY-THREE

Ginnie backed further out of sight inside the entrance to the ladies' toilets. Casually, I walked over and leaned against the outside wall. Fishing in my jacket's inside pocket, I brought out my wallet, mimed a juggling act of trying to hold on to it before 'accidentally' letting it slip down on to the tarmac, right outside the step at the entrance to the toilets.

Trying to do the near impossible of looking into the ladies' whilst avoiding looking like a pervert, I saw at a height of a foot or so above the cold grey floor tiles the hem of a blue overall. 'Quick, Ginnie, what's up?'

'Come inside,' she hissed.

'Uh-uh. No way. You'll get me locked up.'

'There's something I have to tell you.'

'Not ideal, talking here. I'll call round your place, tonight.'

'But—'

'Eight o'clock tonight, OK?'

'—I *need* to speak to you.'

Above my head I heard the irate voice of a female in a Yorkshire dialect.

'Aye, an' I *need to pee*, alreet?'

I hastily snatched up the remaining contents of my wallet that still lay strewn on the doorstep then backed out – still keeping my face averted and head down.

A lethal pair of six-inch white stilettos stomped by in a great hurry, narrowly missing clipping my left ear on their way to find a free toilet.

I made a quick exit and trotted the rest of the way to the jockeys' car park. What a field day the press would have had if I'd been caught. With, no doubt, headlines screaming: 'Champion jockey found on his knees looking up ladies' skirts.' Sweating buckets at the very thought, and firing up the Mazda, I heaved a deep sigh of relief at avoiding being accosted by security staff and drove swiftly away from the racecourse, heading south.

Whatever it was Ginnie was desperate to tell me would have to wait.

I toed it down the A1 and took myself home to Harlequin Cottage, where, locking the back door safely behind me, I ran a deep hot bath and climbed in.

I did some of my best thinking in the bath and right now I wanted to run through everything Ginnie had told me previously – plus swill off all the rancid, fear-laced sweat.

At half past seven, sweet smelling now – cat fed, me fed – I drove the car out of the five-barred gate and turned east towards Belvoir country.

Ginnie lived in a tiny cottage in the village of Redmile in the Vale of Belvoir. I drove down the narrow lane past the cottage: there was a light on in the living room but I drove on further to the next road junction. There were no other vehicles in sight. I drove part way back before parking and locking the car, then walked the rest of the way. If Ginnie were being kept under surveillance, I didn't want to risk her safety by advertising my visit.

I walked up the path and tapped discreetly on the front door. It was opened immediately – on the chain.

'Good girl,' I murmured as she closed it momentarily before allowing me a gap of a few inches to enter.

'Got to take precautions, Harry.'

'You certainly have.'

'I knew you'd be riding at Doncaster today.'

'If security had got their hands on me loitering by the ladies', it would have been the last ride for a bit.'

'Yeah, sorry to risk things for you.'

'Strikes me the boot's on the other foot – it's *you* who is taking risks. And they're on my behalf.'

'Yes, you're not wrong there, but listen.' She grabbed my arm, shook it. 'Listen to me, Harry. I have to warn you. That's why I had to catch you at the races.'

I stared at her. Her face was pinched with anxiety and she looked haunted. 'Warn me? What about?'

'This whole bloody mess . . .' She gulped. 'You have to stop investigating, Harry. Let it all go. If you don't, there's going to be more deaths.'

'Ginnie.' I reached for her as sobs shook her thin frame. She clung to me.

'Please, *please*, stop.'

'I can't, you know I can't.'

'You must! Oh, God, you're not listening, are you?' She wriggled free of my arms. 'Do you understand what's at stake?' Then she shook her head wildly. 'No, you don't, do you? I can see you don't. What does it take to convince you?'

'Calm down, girl.' I guided her to a chair, sat her down. 'Now, tell me what's happened.'

'What's happened is two heavies on my doorstep. And they didn't come in for a cup of tea . . .' She caught back a sob. 'Bastards, they were . . . threatened our little Sophie.'

I stared at her, speechless, her fear translating itself to me, curdling my guts.

'They said it wouldn't do any good to threaten *you*. Said you were a tough swine and it wouldn't have any effect. But they also said you'd got a weakness – protecting other people. An' they're right, aren't they?'

I nodded grimly. 'Yes.'

All the cases I'd been involved in had been initiated on behalf of other people's safety. It was indeed my Achilles' heel. But now, it seemed, the opposition had cottoned on to the fact and were using it to manipulate me over the all too familiar barrel.

Except this went to new depths – I'd never been called upon to defend a child. And not only an unknown child I'd never seen, but the four-year-old daughter of the man who had once saved my life and was even now in hospital, fighting for his own life.

However, I had to calm the distressed woman in front of me. It wouldn't do for her to see the effect her words had had on me. No wonder she had been desperate to speak to me at the races.

'It's just a threat, Ginnie,' I said, playing it down on purpose. 'They're bluffing.'

'Oh yeah?' she said scathingly. 'Like it's a bluff Lenny Backhouse's body was fished out of the Smite River?'

'But he was part of an organized drug-dealing syndicate. If you get involved in that sort of stinking business, well, you accept whatever is coming to you. Like the strong chance of getting bumped off.'

'Maybe, but how do you deal with the same bastards who topped Lenny when they come calling . . . actually coming right into your home . . . threatening little Sophie?'

'Bluff, Ginnie, that's all it is, just a big bluff.' I didn't believe my own words. And I could see she didn't either.

Pushing back her chair, she rose to her feet, drew herself up ramrod straight and looked me in the eye. 'Is that so? You *really* believe that, Harry? Well, I don't call this a big bluff, I call it bloody scary. An' it's bloody painful.'

She pushed up her left sleeve. Then, turning her arm over, she exposed the inner skin above her elbow joint.

I took a sharp intake of breath between my teeth. An ugly red circle complete with partially healing blister told the tale of a cigarette being stubbed out on tender flesh.

Ginnie stuck out her chin defiantly and eyeballed me. 'Burns heal quicker if they're not covered up, don't they?'

It was like watching a rabbit baring its teeth and challenging a fox.

It completely did me in. 'Those goons did that to you?' I managed to whisper.

'Yes, said it would prove they meant what they said.'

'My God, I'm so sorry—'

'An' that's not all. They told me that if I didn't pass on their message to back off from your drugs investigation, Harry, they'll do the same, and much worse, to Sophie. So, promise me you're going to call a halt, stop digging around. Let it drop. Promise me, go on . . . *promise!*'

TWENTY-FOUR

'Here, Ginnie, drink this.' I'd found an opened bottle of whisky in the sideboard. I held out a half-filled tumbler to her as she sat pale and shivering on the settee. With teeth that chattered against the glass, she obediently took several sips. Relieved, I watched the colour slowly return to her face. 'Feel better?'

'Better, yes. Thanks, Harry,' she said, nodding. 'It was like . . . like it was happening all over again, y'know? All the fear, the pain . . . I could feel it as though it really was the first time. I was terrified. Weird.'

I reached over for the bottle and poured a top-up of whisky into her glass.

'I know exactly what you mean. I've been there myself. The medics have a name for it. The modern name is post-traumatic stress, but years ago it wasn't called that. Basically, the nervous system replays the bad stuff and massively reacts to the memory – as though it is *actually* happening again. And it's bloody awful.'

She nodded. 'You're not wrong.' She shuddered. 'Promise me, Harry. Promise you'll stop investigating. I couldn't live with myself if Sophie came to harm.'

'Hush now, Ginnie. We aren't going to let any harm come to the child. Tell me where she is right now. Is she here, in the cottage?'

'Oh, no. I wasn't going to take any chances of those gorillas coming back here and having a go at her. I didn't know if I'd manage to get hold of you at the races. An' I was all but tearing my hair out in chunks, knowing those bastards meant every word they said.'

'So? Where is she?'

'The only other place I could think of.'

'Tell me, Ginnie. We don't have time to waste.'

She raised a frightened gaze up at me. 'You think she's not safe, don't you?'

'I'm not going to tell you any fairy stories. The child needs to be in a place of safety. Is she, Ginnie?'

'She's with my daughter, Rosy. They're both at Dottie's.'

Keith's mother. I nodded. 'Certainly safer than here, but it's not safe enough.'

Ginnie bunched her knuckles and crammed them against her mouth, her eyes imploring me to come up with an answer.

'I'll get over there straight away. Did Rosy take spare clothing, toiletries, that sort of thing with her?'

'Oh yes, she packed a suitcase and a bag of toys – and her favourite teddy bear – for Sophie.'

'Sorted then. Now, I just need to get myself over to Dottie's and speak to her and Rosy. See if they agree with what I'm going to suggest.'

She nodded silently. I reached for her hand and gave it a reassuring squeeze. 'Trust me, Ginnie. I'll get back to you as soon as I've got a result. OK?'

Again, eyes wide with fear, she simply nodded her agreement.

I checked the lane in both directions as I left her cottage. But there was no one about. I drove over to the A52, turned left and headed for the village of Aslockton. It wasn't far away – certainly not far enough to deter the bastards who had burnt Ginnie. The barrel I found myself over had suddenly expanded in size. There was a child to be saved now, and that added a whole new dimension.

Although Sophie was unknown to me personally, she was Keith Whellan's daughter. The man I owed an unpayable debt to. Keith, who had taken a bullet – most likely meant for me – and ended up in hospital. The outcome of which was still as yet unknown. And it also meant there was no way I could duck out. I had to do my best to try and safeguard the little girl, whatever the cost to myself.

I'd vowed never to get involved in any more unsavoury crimes; however, here I was up to my eyebrows in the evil-smelling sewage – yet again! And nothing I could do about it.

I drove over the railway crossing in the centre of the village and on down Main Street. It was impossible to tell if there was anyone keeping tabs on Dottie. Cars lined the whole of the street. I dropped to second gear and crawled past Dottie's terraced cottage then on past the village church and found a vacant spot. It was far enough away from her home to deflect suspicion. But I had no intention of knocking on her front door where it fronted straight on to the pavement.

There was a passageway running between her cottage and the one next door, and I checked the street was empty in both directions before sliding unobtrusively along the dark passage round to Dottie's back door.

I tapped discreetly on the inset glass panel. Dottie's frightened face appeared on the other side of the glass followed by the door being opened a scant few inches to allow me access.

She grabbed my arm and pulled me inside, closing the door and running a thick bolt across into its socket. It was strong enough to keep a vault secure.

She expelled a deep breath and leaned back against the closed door. 'Am I relieved to see you, Mr Radcliffe—'

'Harry, please, Dottie.'

'I feel a lot safer now you're here.'

She went across to the door fronting the stairs, opened it and then bellowed, 'Rosy, it's OK. You can bring Sophie downstairs. It's Mr Rad . . . It's Harry.'

There was the sound of footsteps running along the landing and seconds later a young woman, blonde hair in an exaggerated pile on the top of her head, came into the kitchen closely followed by a little girl, also blonde, but whose hair was contained in a pair of perky plaits complete with a pair of scarlet bows.

'Say hello to Mr Radcliffe, Sophie.' The child was given an encouraging push forward as she instinctively clutched her mother's jeans.

'Hello, Sophie.' I held out my hand to the child. 'I'm a friend of your daddy.'

'Daddy?' She looked earnestly up at me. 'Where's my Daddy? I *want* Daddy.'

I turned to Rosy and grimaced slightly. 'Sorry . . . sorry.'

'Oh, don't worry about it. She misses him, all the time going on about when is he coming to see her.'

I felt in my jacket pocket and then hunkered down. 'I'm sorry, Sophie, I can't bring your daddy. But do you want a sweetie?' I held out a new, unopened roll of Polo mints. I was never without a pack – using them as treats for the horses who, oddly, adored them. Her big eyes fastened their intent gaze on mine.

'I *want* Daddy.'

'I'm sure you do, but he can't come right now, sweetheart.'

The blue eyes slowly filled with tears that overflowed and trickled down her cheeks. It was made all the more poignant because the tot didn't make a sound, simply stood in front of me, her grief expressed silently on her face. It damn near moved me to tears, too.

I held out my arms. Sophie collapsed against me, clutching my jacket and burying her face in the thick material. Above her head, I exchanged looks with the two women. Both of them were struggling to hold back emotion.

'They're optimistic, Harry. They told me when I rang the Queen's earlier today . . .' Dottie choked on her words.

I nodded. 'Pleased to hear that. You'll let me know if you hear when he's allowed visitors, won't you?'

'Oh, depend on it, Harry. But now . . .' She nodded down to where Sophie, face buried in my jacket, was still clinging tightly to me.

'I've just come from Ginnie's.'

Dottie lowered her voice to a whisper. 'She showed you what they did to her?'

'Yes. I'm appalled. That's why I've come to see you, get your approval and consent.' I had their attention now.

Rosy pulled a finger from her mouth. 'Go on then.' She reinserted the fingernail but not before I'd noticed it was bitten down to the quick. It gave a lie to her seeming lack of maternal concern regarding Sophie and the situation.

I smiled reassuringly at her. 'I suggest you and Sophie would be far safer up in Yorkshire.'

Rosy met my inquiring look and gave an exaggerated shrug of her shoulders. 'Whatever.'

Dottie and I exchanged exasperated glances. 'We've no money, Harry . . .' she said.

'Don't worry about it. That's the least of our problems.'

'And the first problem is?'

'Do you hold the keys to Keith's rented cottage?'

'Yes.'

'What about the name of the owner? He's the farmer that rents out the cottage to Keith.'

She nodded. 'Yes, Mr Percell. He's looking after Tugboat, y'know, Keith's dog?'

'Oh, yes, I certainly do know old Tugboat. Without his help, I wouldn't be standing here now.' Because of Keith and Tugboat's efforts, I was still this side of the veil. He was an enormous Newfoundland, big as a bear and just as strong.

I took my mobile from my pocket. 'If you could just give me Mr Percell's number, I'll get hold of him.'

A couple of minutes later, he fell in with my suggestion. 'Rent's paid, nothing to stop his family coming up. Sorry he copped it from that trigger-happy bugger. Hope he's making good progress. Tell you what, because of the weather, I'll get one of my men to drive over, light the fire, stick the fridge back on, put in a couple of pints, OK?'

'Very much so. Thank you, we all appreciate it.'

'Shall I send Tugboat over as well?'

I thought about the little girl – still glued to my chest. 'I think that might be a really good idea. His daughter will be the dog's willing slave, I'm sure. Just what she needs, I'd say.'

I ended the call and thought about what he'd said. It was an excellent idea to have the huge dog at the cottage. As a reliable guard, he couldn't be bettered.

'All sorted,' I informed Dottie and Rosy. 'If you agree, Rosy, I'll drive you and Sophie up to Yorkshire. You should be safe there at the cottage. Is that all right?' Both women nodded. 'Could you get a suitcase packed straight away? Take as much as you like. Don't forget, you'll need food as well as warm clothes.'

Then, very gently, I peeled Sophie away from me. 'Now then, Sophie. I'm taking you and your mummy for a ride in my car. You'd like that, wouldn't you? You're staying in your daddy's house. It will be like a holiday.'

Hesitantly, she nodded.

'And you must take your teddy bear with you. We can't go on holiday without him, can we?'

This time she shook her head vigorously.

'And when we get to where you're staying, guess who'll be there as well?'

'Daddy?'

I cursed myself for asking such a stupid question. 'Not yet, no. But Tugboat will be there to play with you. You love Tugboat, don't you?'

This time there was no hesitation. 'Yes. He's my doggie.' Her face was transformed now by a radiant smile. 'I love him, lots and lots,' she said happily.

I pushed the packet of sweets into her hand. 'And you can take these to eat on the way.'

'T'ank you.' She reached up and kissed my cheek. 'I love you, too.'

There wouldn't have been a dry eye in the house had we been on stage.

TWENTY-FIVE

'd exceeded the speed limit by a long way on the journey up to Yorkshire. Now, on my way back, I maintained a more lawful one. Partly because the fuel gauge was showing ominously low, but also due to the cross-country diversions I'd taken to throw off any possible followers. Another incentive was that at this time of night, the roads were icy and deadly.

Arriving at Harlequin Cottage, I scrunched over the gravel and pulled up near the kitchen door. The curtain at the tiny side window twitched and an inquisitive furry head thrust itself round. I just had time to brace myself after I entered the kitchen before eight kilos of ginger tom landed with a thud on my shoulder. 'Y'know what, you're putting on weight, Leo. If you get much bigger I'll be able to put a saddle on you.'

Leo didn't care. He was impervious to low remarks about his expanding girth. He rubbed his bullet-hard head against my chin and declaimed that it was time to eat in a bass bellow that rattled my eardrum.

'Soon, old son, soon,' I assured him, closing the outside door and locking it. It wasn't just Ginnie who needed to be extra cautious. 'Something much more urgent to attend to first.'

Going into the lounge, I picked up the landline receiver and keyed in Ginnie's number. It had crossed my mind on arriving at the cottage in Yorkshire that the poor woman would be in a state of fear and agitation until I contacted her. In fact, I'd begun to dig in my pocket for the mobile to let her know we'd arrived safely when I realized that with the sophisticated tracking systems these days any call made on the mobile would pinpoint my location. It was entirely the opposite of what I wanted to achieve. Only while Sophie's address was kept secret was the child safe, so I'd pushed the phone back inside my pocket and decided it would have to wait until I was back at home.

But now, a landline was so much safer. Ginnie could be informed of her daughter and granddaughter's whereabouts in complete safety and she could down a whisky and relax.

She answered on the second ring. 'Who is it?' Her voice came out in a mouse-like squeak.

'You OK, Ginnie?'

'Oh, oh thank goodness you've rung, Harry. Been out of my mind with worry.'

'Well, your worries are over. I'm not saying too much, but the fledgling is now in a safe nest.'

There was silence for a second or two, then I heard Ginnie break down in a spasm of tears of relief.

'Pour a stiff one, Ginnie. If you need me, don't hesitate to call, OK?'

'Yes,' she sobbed, barely able to get the words out. 'Thanks, Harry.'

'None needed. Bye now.' I put the receiver down and checked my watch: 2.17 a.m. No wonder Leo was delivering a strident diatribe about dilatory owners who left their feline partners unfed.

'OK, mate. Come on . . .' I went into the kitchen and quickly filled the cat's dish while Leo stood on his back legs and batted at my trouser leg with his front paw. He was on the food in a flash the instant I placed it on the quarries. A blessed silence ensued.

I, meantime, made a scalding mug of strong tea and wearily climbed the stairs and drank it in bed. All the pain from my bruises and stiffness from the racing fall I'd taken had come back with full force now my attention wasn't fixed elsewhere. It seemed an age since I'd taken three painkillers at the start of the day – no, yesterday, I corrected my thought – and those had worn off a very long time ago. The discomfort had me reaching for some painkillers I kept handy in my bedside cabinet. Tossing three down with the remains of the tea, I slid thankfully under the bedcovers. It had been a bloody long day.

Then a memory surfaced. Despite the pain in my battered body, a smile stretched my lips just as I was about to crash out. No wonder Leo was getting fat. The jammy sod – I had been well and truly cat-conned. Before I'd set off for Ginnie's cottage, I'd fixed us both a delicious meal.

He'd had double rations.

*   *   *

At six a.m. I groaned my way out of bed. It was freezing, the windowpane delicately lacy-patterned when I dragged back the curtains. Outside, Leo, keeping low to the ground, was just as delicately padding across the stiff white lawn. The blackbird he was stalking was busy tossing over crisp dead leaves beneath the holly tree. Above, in the top of the laburnum, another blackbird spotted the cat and rattled off a sharp warning. Both birds lifted to the blue sky and Leo was left grounded and lashing a ginger tail in frustration. Had his hunt been successful, I'd no doubt that despite putting away double rations last night he'd have indulged himself in yet another one.

I wobbled downstairs and sent off an email to Mike assuring him that, although I was late, I would be with him shortly. He pinged one back immediately: *'Hope so, U're riding Soulmate in the 1.30 @ Huntingdon . . .'*

'Haven't forgotten. Thanks,' I sent back. I didn't bother to remind him that, prior to that race, I was also booked to ride Matrix for another trainer at one o'clock.

Then I brewed a mug of tea and fixed a slice of Marmite toast which I ate standing up in the kitchen. It would be a grave mistake in my present fragile state to take myself through to the lounge and have breakfast in comfort cast on the couch. There'd be a really serious danger of dropping off to sleep.

At about nine o'clock, I was seated on a chair in Mike's kitchen gratefully accepting a honey-sweetened mug of black coffee from Pen. I'd opted to give Soulmate a good grooming prior to her appearance at Huntingdon Racecourse. It cemented good relations between us – a Polo mint worked wonders, I found – and had the added advantage of loosening my tight muscles and thoroughly warming me up. Both things were needed before setting off to ride later. It certainly wasn't what a champion jockey was expected to do, however right now it suited me.

Pen had already fuelled me up with a generous helping of scrambled egg – no toast – and I ended the meal with another three painkillers. Hopefully they would see me through most of the day or at least until after my last race. The return drive home scarcely mattered once the business had been done. Pen had been positively twitching between cooker and table before, seeing I'd finished eating, she plonked her heavily pregnant body down on a kitchen chair.

'Now, tell us about what happened at Doncaster yesterday,' she demanded. 'You were seen, you know, hanging about – no, positively *loitering* – outside the ladies' toilets. So, come on, give.'

'Good God,' I said, aghast. 'Who told you that?'

'Don't look so surprised, Harry. You can't deny it, can you?'

'Well, no . . . But there was a very good – and completely innocent – reason.'

'Don't do it to the poor sod, Pen.' Mike remonstrated gently. 'You've really got him going.' Indeed she had.

She grinned. 'Oh, all right. I had a phone call earlier while you were out in the stable. It was Ginnie Cutler.'

My head jerked up. 'She OK?'

'Don't worry, she's fine, and she wanted me to pass on her grateful thanks for going the extra mile last night. So? Tell us what you've been up to. I did try to pump Ginnie, but she wouldn't say.'

'Good for her. I'm very glad to hear that.' I filled them in on developments.

'And is Rosy staying in Keith's cottage, then?' Mike asked.

'Yes, for the foreseeable, anyway.'

'What happens if Keith regains consciousness and the hospital discharges him? He'll want to go back up there, won't he?'

'At that point, we'll have to think again. But right now it seems the safest place. Tugboat's with them and the farmer's keeping an eye out.'

'And you drove them all that way – and then came back yourself, last night?' Pen said, wide-eyed. 'What time did you get home?'

'Two seventeen a.m.'

Her eyes opened even wider. 'Wow, that's very specific.'

'Hmm,' I agreed, and proceeded to drop Leo in it about giving me a guilt trip for his own ends.

'Love it.' Pen giggled. 'You know what you are, Harry, don't you?'

'What?'

'Just a big softie. And I love you.' She heaved herself up from the chair and flung her arms around me, giving me a hug. 'Thank you from me, too.'

'Give over, woman,' Mike growled. 'The bloke's got to concentrate on his racing.'

She laughingly released me. 'Just because you're jealous . . .'

I stood up quickly, drained my coffee and set the mug down on the draining board. 'High time I was off.' Mike and I were great mates and I aimed to keep things like that. 'See you at the course, Mike.'

It took me about a couple of hours' driving cross-country to reach Huntingdon Racecourse where I parked up in the jockeys' car park. Not only was I down to ride Soulmate in the one thirty, I was also booked by an Oxfordshire trainer to ride his horse first at one o'clock.

For once, I was relieved that I only had the two races. I was feeling far from fit, what with the after-effects of my fall and the miserable amount of sleep I'd managed last night. Tonight, thankfully, I had nothing planned other than a very early night.

With the appropriate silks on – brown with bright orange stripes for this owner – I walked out of the weighing room into the parade ring and was hailed by the Oxfordshire trainer. He was standing beside the horse while the stable lad clung on to the lead rein as Matrix tossed his head vigorously up and down, clearly demonstrating his pent-up energy and willingness to get out there on to the racecourse. He looked well. My hopes for a possible win rose as I chatted to his excited owner and the trainer.

And those hopes were upheld as I was given a superb ride on the eager horse and from mid-field position, which I held for all but the last two furlongs; when I urged him, he delighted in surging forward for the line and ended winning by a length and a half.

On the back of the win, I went into the weighing room wearing the brown and orange silks and returned out through the weighing room some fifteen minutes later wearing new colours, this time of navy and pale blue, the ones chosen by Soulmate's owner. Mike was waiting for me in the parade ring together with the owner. He introduced me to Mr Elliott.

I touched my cap in response. 'Good afternoon, sir.'

'Well done for winning. I watched your last race.'

'Thank you.'

'I trust the winning streak will continue.'

'Indeed, so do I.' We smiled at each other while Mike stood back, beaming broadly. His owner was a happy man right now and, in accordance with his racing mantra, so was Mike. Except that, when Mr Elliott turned his head to swing a glance around at the other jockeys who were all now waiting for the order to mount, Mike's beam changed in an instant. He gave me a penetrating look before immediately looking at Soulmate. Something was bugging him. I looked at the horse and noticed what Mike was silently trying to convey to me, and of which the owner was thankfully unaware.

It could of course simply be that Soulmate was extremely laidback and feeling calm. Or it could spell trouble. Right now, I didn't know which. The stable lad was merely resting a hand on the lead rein. It was in sharp contrast to the struggle the previous lad had had holding on to Matrix. There was no tossing head, no skittishly swinging hind quarters, and certainly no sign of sweating up.

Soulmate in comparison appeared half-asleep. I wouldn't know until I was in the saddle, but I felt, probably like Mike, a disconcerting flicker of apprehension.

'Jockeys please mount,' was called, and I pushed away the negative feeling and accepted a leg up into the saddle. Soulmate was rated third – after the joint favourites. The horse had performed very well since coming into Mike's stables, but today was her first time on the racecourse.

And just how well she could do was very much an unknown. I took her out on to the track and gave her a good squeeze. Her response allayed my forebodings. She had raced before and knew what was expected from her. She cantered off down to the start where the other horses were grouped.

I knew Mike would most likely be in the owners' and trainers' bar watching the race and he also must be feeling a measure of reassurance from the way Soulmate had responded. Meantime, along with the other jockeys, I kept Soulmate on the move, circling around so she didn't get cold while we awaited the starter's instructions.

There were thirteen horses altogether and it took some little time for him to be satisfied as to the line-up. But eventually he was ready to drop the yellow flag and we swept up the course in a colourful wave.

Predictably, after the first couple of furlongs, we were all following the front runner who was going away like a train, but who we knew would be unable to sustain the pace to be in with a chance in the last couple of furlongs heading for the finishing line.

I urged Soulmate into the middle of the pack and was content then to let her run with the others and take each fence collectedly and safely. My initial misgivings had disappeared by the time we were over halfway and were coming down the back stretch. While not extending herself, she had kept up with the rest and I hoped she had conserved some energy for the last part of the course.

However, approaching the fourth-last, I felt her slacken speed and she not so much jumped it but fell over the fence, brushwood flying as she scrambled her way through before she staggered on. Far from being able to begin to urge her on for home, I could feel her continuing to weaken beneath me. I could feel she was going nowhere. I took the only option open to me.

I pulled up.

It wasn't the first time I'd ended a race walking the horse back to the stable, but today it was the first time I'd actually anticipated this could happen. And I was extremely concerned. I just hoped to God they wouldn't call us into the doping box for testing.

TWENTY-SIX

Mr Elliott was very magnanimous. 'You can't expect to win every race. It's Soulmate's first race for Mr Grantley. There's nothing to be sorry about, Mr Radcliffe . . . Harry.' And he smiled at us both. 'I'm sure she'll be fine next time out.'

'I certainly hope so,' Mike said grimly.

I couldn't meet his eyes. We both knew there was something wrong with the horse, probably had the same idea as to what it was, but neither of us were prepared to say.

Somehow, God knows how, the horse had been nobbled.

The authorities hadn't called us in for a dope test. Thank goodness they hadn't. I was as sure as I could be that they would have discovered some evidence.

I drove myself over to Leicestershire and arrived back at the stables before Mike.

Pen took one look at my face as she opened the back door and gave me a sympathetic smile. 'No winners, then? Still, you can't expect to win every race.'

'Oh no, not you too, Pen. That's exactly what Soulmate's owner said.'

'There you are then. If *he's* not having a go at you, why the long face? Stop having a go at yourself.' She proceeded to make us a mug of tea each.

If she hadn't been so far gone in her pregnancy, I might have been tempted to unload my worry on to her. But she was and I didn't. I'd leave that up to Mike. If he wanted Pen to know, he'd tell her. So I stayed silent and wrapped myself around the very welcome hot tea. Something was cooking in the Aga and I must have betrayed my hunger as I sniffed the very tempting smell because before I'd even drained the tea Pen was offering to feed me.

'Now, come on, Harry. There's plenty for three. I don't expect you've had much at all to eat today. Please stay and have some food with Mike and me. It's just a simple chicken stew. I'll excuse you not eating the dumplings. What do you say?'

'I really ought to get home after I've had a word with Mike when he gets back. He'll be here soon. Plus there's Leo to see to . . .'

'What? Don't tell me you're going to feed that furry barrel any more today. I'm sure he wangled a breakfast out of you before you left this morning. He had more than enough, you were telling me over the phone last night.'

At her words, a smile found its way to the surface and I smiled for the first time since finishing the last race. 'OK. I guess I haven't got an excuse to rush back.' I shook my head. 'That cat's got enough fat on him to last a month.'

At that point we heard Mike's car circling round outside before pulling up and a couple of minutes later he came striding in.

He gave Pen a quick hug and a kiss. 'You all right, sweetheart?'

She nodded. 'I'm fine.'

'Good, good.' Then he turned to me. 'Well, what do *you* think about Soulmate?'

He accepted a steaming mug from Pen and flung himself down on a kitchen chair.

'I think we did very well not to be called in at Huntingdon.'

He pursed his lips, nodded and made inroads on his drink. 'And?'

I shot a quick glance in Pen's direction.

'Oh, don't worry about Pen knowing, we have no secrets.'

'Well, the mare obviously had to be pulled up and walked back. I must admit, I was pleased when she decided to water the course on the way back. That could have drained off some of whatever might have been in her system, I would think. And they'd have been waiting a good while in the stable until she passed water again for checking.'

He nodded. 'So, you're thinking along the same lines as I am, then?'

I screwed up my lips ruefully. 'I think we're both considering she must have been got at, somehow . . . although how she got nobbled . . .' I shook my head.

Pen was standing beside Mike and her mouth dropped open. 'Are you saying Soulmate was doped, Harry?'

Mike and I looked at each other and nodded simultaneously.

'I'm very much afraid so.' Mike finished his tea in one more gulp. 'I'll go and ring the vet. Get the mare thoroughly checked over. Get her scoped, as well. See what he says.'

'Did Rantby get back regarding his stock at the surgery?'

'Hmm, couldn't find anything missing.'

'Doesn't make sense,' I said, frowning and shaking my head. 'If Paul Oats didn't get the drug from the surgery, where the hell *did* he get it?'

Mike shook his head too. 'Can't help you, but I have to ring Rantby, get him over.'

But he was out of luck. It seemed the vet was out on an emergency call, so Mike had to leave a message.

'Sod's law,' he growled.

'Never mind.' Pen reached up and kissed his cheek. 'Now, how about getting your oats?' She bent over the Aga.

'Eh?' His eyebrows shot up.

She started to grin wickedly. 'And Harry's joining in as well.'

'I am?'

'Oh yes.' Her grin widened. She lifted a wooden spoon and tapped it on the side of the cast-iron casserole dish she'd lifted out of the oven. Then, as she removed the lid, the kitchen filled with a beautiful aroma of herbs and chicken and we both grinned back.

'*Now* you're talking sense.' Mike shoved back his chair and went to wash his hands at the sink.

The three of us sat down to a much appreciated, tasty and comforting meal – one serving predictably, regretfully missing out on a helping of herb-filled dumplings.

I'd waited until we'd all finished eating – the minuscule leftovers being scraped into Sunny, Pen's yellow Labrador bitch's bowl, and instantly demolished – before I asked the question. It wasn't something I wanted to raise knowing that it was a potential bomb. But it had to be asked. Mike's head lad would have taken charge of Soulmate when the horse arrived back at the stables. Mike would have initially entrusted him with the care of the horse and intended going round to the stables later as usual.

I accepted a welcome hot coffee from Pen and took a gulp. Then I pulled the plug on the grenade.

'Thanks for a great meal; I really enjoyed it. But I'm sorry I've got to throw a curve ball at you both.' I had their attention.

Mike sat up straight in his chair. 'Throw it then, Harry.'

'We think that Soulmate was got at, yes?' They nodded. 'But have you thought that instead of the target being Tal Hunter's stables, it's actually Mike's stable that's the target?' This time they gaped. 'I'm really sorry, but I've looked at this every which way and it does seem like it's your stables in the firing line.'

Mike was the first to regain his composure. 'So,' he said, and took a deep breath, 'are you saying that the nobbling probably took place, like Tal Hunter's, in the horsebox?'

'Yes.'

He digested this for a moment. 'That answers the question of why you rang me up late at night to ask about the box. You were expecting this to happen, weren't you?'

'I wasn't expecting it. But, yes, I did think it was a possibility. Was the other horse a bay with similar colouring to Soulmate?'

'It *was.*'

We were all silent, pondering on the consequences.

'Who was the trainer who owned the box? And, even more important, who was the lad with it?' I asked.

'I don't think for a second the trainer was aware of anything underhand. As for our stable lad, I'll grill him. Find out if *he* knows anything about it. There must have been a point when the box was stopped before it got to the course.'

'If it's following a plan, like last time, I'd say that was a certainty. However, I *need* to make tracks. Thanks again for a great meal, Pen. I'd love to stay, but—'

'You've got to see a man about a dog, I know.'

'Something like that,' I agreed.

In actual fact, I was going to see a woman about a horse. But for now I was keeping quiet about that.

I opened my car door and turned on the engine but I only drove a couple of miles down the dark lane before pulling over on the grass verge. Opening the dash, I felt around for the plastic container I'd taken from my jacket pocket before going in to see Pen. At some point I'd tell both of them, but for now, I was keeping this information close to my chest. It had long been a habit of mine to carry an empty container of some description, depending on where I was heading for.

It was a habit I'd adopted since working on my first case. On that occasion I'd found a partially smoked cigarette and had to secrete it in my handkerchief. The cigarette proved very necessary evidence. Now, I was in front of the game and always had either a plastic zip-lock bag or, in this present case, a tiny plastic tube with stopper.

However, I was limited in what I could secretly conceal on my person, especially when I was racing. Fortunately, the white breeches did contain a pocket, albeit not a very big one. I'd chosen the present tube because of its small dimensions. It was actually a clean eye-dropper. One used by vets for feline patients. I placed it into my jacket pocket, engaged gear and drove on down the lane.

Leo had had an eye infection a couple of weeks ago and I'd

had to act as his nurse between visits to his veterinary surgeon. She was yet another female who was besotted by him. How did he do it? I was on my way to call on her now. Eliza Grey was her name and she was an efficient, caring woman.

It was doubtful she would still be working in the evening surgery; it was getting late. But she was very interested in Leo and, by association, also with me. It was Leo's exploits in saving my life on more than one occasion that had enamoured her to us both. I suppose the fact that I was famous as champion jockey also helped, but I'd found her to be nothing other than extremely helpful in any medical situation. Leo, however, had moved things along and was on up-close-and-very-personal terms, allowing her to examine every inch of his furry person, the jammy sod.

I reached for the thin tube, drew it out. It had started out empty this morning but now it was nearly full of horse urine – to be exact, it contained Soulmate's urine. I always liked to be doubly sure of my facts and checked everything I was told before relying on the information. Rantby, I didn't doubt, would do a first-class job when he saw Soulmate. But caution had become my middle name and the one person I trusted 110 per cent was myself. This was because I checked, double-checked and, in some cases, checked a third time if I thought it was needed.

In today's situation, I needed the experience of a second professional. Only when I was totally convinced could I stand firm against whatever was thrown at me.

And now with the dirt being aimed at Mike's stable, I couldn't afford the slightest mistake. No use going to the police with half-baked tales. Unless there was concrete evidence of wrongdoing, they wouldn't take any action. Then I thought again about poor Ginnie Cutler and her blistered arm. And I felt the anger rising again inside me. Yes, that was proof somebody had intended to cause her pain, but I knew she would never follow it up through the official channels: Ginnie's motivation was not revenge for herself, but to ensure safety for her granddaughter, little Sophie.

So, until I could produce facts, backed up by tangible evidence that the police would act on, it was once again down to me. What was it Mike had said? There were at least six people depending on me. Now I could also add two more to that list – Pen and Mike himself.

The journey to Miss Grey's didn't take long and I pulled up outside the entrance to the surgery at Cropwell. The lights were on but there were no other vehicles parked up. I locked the Mazda, went up to the door and pressed the bell. Eliza, tall, slender and dressed in white scrubs, opened the door. When she saw who it was, a wide smile welcomed me.

'Come along in, Harry.' She bent slightly, looking to either side of me. 'Where's the lovely boy, then?'

'Sorry, Eliza, I've debarred you the pleasure of the greedy sod.'

Her dark eyes widened. 'Are we talking about dear Leo, your beloved sidekick?'

'Oh, yes, we sure are. But tonight I've got another problem for you.'

'Come in.' She stood aside. 'Let's see if I can solve it for you. But of course, I'm not promising anything – at this stage.'

'Quite right. In this case, I'm absolutely sure it will be best to wait until I tell you what it is.'

She laughed. 'Now I'm intrigued.'

I walked into the entrance hall and turned left into the examination room. I was getting to be on as familiar and frequent terms with Leo's medical venue as I was with my own in the Queen's Hospital in Nottingham – unfortunately.

Eliza followed me in, closed the door and leaned back against it. 'I can't wait for this.'

I grinned, dug into my jacket pocket and pulled out the thin plastic tube. 'I want you to analyse the contents of this for me, please.'

'What is it?'

'Guess?'

She shook her head. 'I wouldn't dare. Come on, just tell me.'

I placed it on her outstretched palm. 'It's horse urine.'

TWENTY-SEVEN

'Horse urine?' Eliza's eyes widened to their fullest. 'You slay me, Harry. I *never* know what you're going to come up with next.'

'Could you do it for me?'

'Firstly, why do you need to find out?'

'Double-checking, Eliza.'

'Hmm, I take it another vet is also doing some checking.'

'You take it right.'

She pursed her lips. 'Not sure I should be getting into this. I mean, I can't possibly—'

'I'm not asking you to do down another vet's work or findings.'

'And I wouldn't.'

'No, I respect that. But I do need my own independent vet to tell me what the urine contains. Please?'

'Neither would I want you to go running around begging.' Her lips curved a little.

'So you'll do it?'

'If you could supply me with the name of the substance I might possibly identify . . . yes.'

'I've an idea, but that's all. If you want something more concrete, I'd have to dig a bit more.'

She looked pointedly at her watch. 'Look, you go and get your spade and dig. I'll make a start. I take it that I'm looking for a drug that affects a horse's performance, right?'

'Yes,' I said humbly. 'And thanks, Eliza.'

'One thing, can I know this horse's name?'

'Safer if you don't.'

She shook her head. 'You're not on my wavelength. I *must* be sure it isn't one of the horses I treat.'

'OK. It's a mare actually, called Soulmate.'

'That's fine then.' She relaxed. 'It's not one of Lady Branshawe's.'

'Why do you need to be sure?'

'Because I've only recently been given the sole responsibility for her string – it's lucrative, Harry. And I wouldn't want to lose her patronage. It counts with other owners when they know she trusts me with her horses.'

I saw exactly how she was placed. 'I'm in your debt, thank you.' But the mention of Lady Branshawe's name reminded me I had an invite to attend a party at Hempton Hall. And I still hadn't decided who to invite as my partner. Yet another of the loose ends I needed to tie up.

'I'll send you an email with the name, or names, of the drugs as soon as I find out. Could be later tonight. And thanks again. Bye.'

Unlocking the Mazda, I slid in, closed the door against the chill evening air and thought about my next move. I needed to speak to Gary Butt. He knew more than he'd told me at our initial meeting. But did he know any specific names?

It was well past happy hour, but I thought it was a fair bet that Gary would be down the pub putting in some darts practice. The only question – which pub?

Logic said it would be close to Mike's stables. I knew the most popular one was the Three Horseshoes at Waltham-on-the-Wolds. It was most certainly worth a try. Many of the stable lads from several stables close by gravitated to the Horseshoes: it was very popular and undoubtedly would be heaving with bodies. It should be fairly easy for me to remain unrecognized, in the crush and racket. Well, I hoped so. Gary had certainly been in there before, because I'd seen him the night Mike's sister and his niece had suddenly turned up from Italy. What a night that had been. I'd also been in the thick of another case at the time. Thinking about it, I was fairly confident it would be a good bet.

I nosed the Mazda back down the dark narrow lanes into Leicestershire and, just before reaching Waltham, the bright lights of the pub came into view. As I'd anticipated, the car park was jammed with cars. I'd take a punt on Gary being somewhere inside among the crowd.

Now, as I pushed my way in through the heavy doors, the heat and noise flooded out and over me in a great wave: The Rolling Stones were certainly giving their all. Unless there was a darts match going on somewhere else, it was a pretty good bet that I'd picked the right pub to start with and I'd find young Gary in here.

I inched my way in, taking advantage of an alcove. No way was I going to battle my way to the bar and have everybody clocking my progress. There was an empty pint glass resting on a lip of the wide window ledge and I quickly reached for it, bringing the glass up in front of my cheek. There was still half an inch of beer in the bottom and the sides were smeared with froth. As a disguise that didn't seem out of place, it was perfect. It would certainly deflect any casual glance from identification, although I knew it wouldn't be for long.

Leaning back against the wall to reduce my height, I quickly surveyed the boisterous, well-oiled throng. The lads tended to stay in their stable groups and I recognized some of Mike's staff about halfway down from the bar on the right. Sure enough, Gary was one of them. At least I hadn't wasted my time going to the wrong pub. But how to extricate him in order to have a few quiet words could be a problem.

My time now was entirely my own, no calls from anyone else needing me. I could afford to wait. With the amount of beer being thrown down throats, I knew it was a fair bet there'd be a good footfall heading in and out of the gents.

Taking my time, I eased my way towards the toilet door. Fortunately, it was this side of the room and I continued making progress, unobtrusively keeping close to the wall, until I was within three feet of the toilet. Then I stopped, leaned back on the wall, angled my face towards the hinge side of the door so that for a good deal of the time, with the amount of action the toilet was seeing, nobody would be able to see my face, and partially disappeared behind the beer glass again. And it worked like a charm. I could have been the invisible man. And the beauty of it was, I didn't have long to wait.

Peering through the side of the smeared glass, I spotted Gary trying to make swift headway through the unyielding throng. He all but burst into view and flung open the door in my face. Equally quickly, I lurched inside after him and the door closed behind us.

I shot a swift glance across to the two cubicles and noted there were no shoes showing beneath the doors. Then I seized Gary's shoulder as he was preparing to unzip in front of the line of urinals and dragged him into the first cubicle.

'What the bloody . . .?'

'Shut up. I'm in the next one.' And I followed up the words by the action.

Only just in time. The outer door to the bar sprang open and two or three chaps came barging through, all headed straight for the urinal basins. I'd arranged my shoes so that the toecaps were pointing towards the cubicle door and just hoped Gary had the foresight to have done the same. Then I waited whilst the men finished relieving themselves and exited on a chorus of bawdy laughter. Silence followed.

Then, above my head a voice softly whispered, 'Harry?'

I looked up to where Gary was precariously hanging over the dividing section.

'I'll make it quick. Did you find out any more about the post-mortem on Lenny Backhouse? Like, the name of the drug they'd used to knock him out?'

He played for time. 'Why do you want to know?'

'I *need* to know. A child's life may be at stake here.'

He swallowed hard. 'That bad?'

'Yes, *that* bad, Gary.'

'Yeah, well, don't suppose *you're* going to let on where you hear it.'

'Damn right. Now come on, be quick before a football team walks in.'

He made his mind up. 'Detomidine, that's what they found in his body. That and traces of cocaine.'

'Thanks, thanks very much.'

I reached into my wallet and drew out a twenty-pound note. 'Get yourself a drink. You've earned one.'

'Oh, great, yes, thanks, Harry.'

'And stay in here for another couple of minutes. I'm going to try and get out without being noticed.'

'Sure.' He nodded, allowed his boot toes to slide down the side of the cubicle, and he disappeared out of sight.

I opened the door to my own cubicle and returned to the bar and the ear-punishing beat of 'I Can't Get No Satisfaction' from The Stones.

Running one hand slowly through my hair, I managed to successfully shield most of my face as I kept close to the wall and slid out through the front door. I exited the Horseshoes with relief and drove off quickly.

I waited until I reached home before trying to contact Eliza. I was very mindful of the need to protect her from becoming involved in any way. Drugs were a nasty, dirty business. So I rang her from my landline. But I was out of luck. Despite being exhorted to leave a message on the answering service, I simply replaced the receiver, swore a couple of times, and then made a scalding mug of tea. Flinging myself down on to the settee in the lounge, I considered what Gary had told me. Detomidine, if indeed it was used for slowing down horses, would no doubt poleaxe a man.

And if Detomidine had definitely been found in the post-mortem on Lenny Backhouse, the poor sap wouldn't have stood a chance: they'd certainly made sure his particular link in the chain had broken and would stay broken. On top of the drug, he'd been felled by a heavy blow to the head, pitched over into the waters of the Smite and left to drown. I dare say they – whoever *they* were – had been absolutely sure he'd died; a most definite closing of his mouth. But the names of the murderers were unknown.

Gary hadn't volunteered any further information but somehow I didn't think he knew their names. Which then threw up a snippet of conversation in my mind that one person *did* know. And they'd been too frightened to tell me. Ginnie Cutler, the night I'd driven her home from the Queen's Hospital, had been scared witless and refused to divulge the identity of the two men that she'd seen and heard talking in the cloakroom.

However, after the burning of her arm and the following threats to herself and Sophie, I thought it most unlikely that she'd come clean and divulge the names. And I didn't blame her.

I glanced at the clock. It was getting late. The lack of sleep recently seemed to have caught up with me – that or I was getting old. I was having a job to keep my eyes open and the yawns were getting more frequent and cavernous.

I hauled myself up, took the empty mug back to the kitchen – no sign of Leo, with his luck he'd no doubt got queens queueing up for his favours – and took myself off to my empty bed.

I clocked up a solid eight hours and, much restored, padded

downstairs. Even as I approached the kitchen door I could hear some seriously loud snores. Sure enough, when I entered the kitchen I could see a large heap of ginger fur curled up in the cat basket on top of the worktop. I smiled and stood for a moment marvelling at the amount of noise one sleeping cat could produce.

Then into this delightful tableau, the telephone rang.

Leo shot up, ears flattened back against attack and a look of sheer aggression in his green eyes. I hastened over, lifted the telephone receiver and stilled the shrill noise. 'Sorry, old man, but you don't like it when your bed's down on the floor.'

'I *beg* your pardon,' said a disembodied voice from the receiver. It was Eliza.

'You've just woken Leo up. He's been out on the tiles and by the look of him he's had a rough night.'

She gave a delightful giggle. 'Do give him my very best, won't you, and apologize for my insensitiveness.'

'Oh, the way he is with females, I'm sure he's forgiven you already.'

I glanced at the basket; once more it resembled a recumbent furry heap.

'I have something to tell you, Harry. I've spent a lot of my valuable sleep time on the job—'

'Just like Leo.'

Another giggle. 'And I've discovered there is no Ketamine and no Etorphine present in your sample.'

'Er, not *my* sample,' I said gently.

'If you'd like me to check on that . . .'

'No, no,' I said hastily, 'but carry on, please.'

'OK.' Her voice became brisk and professional. 'What I have found present is Detomidine. A minute trace. So minute, I don't think it would be called "conclusive".'

'Right.'

I thought about her choice of word – 'would', not 'could'.

Eliza was in front of me on this.

TWENTY-EIGHT

I owed this woman. Not simply for doing the analysis, but for all the compassionate care she'd shown for Leo.

'Would you like to come with me to Lady Branshawe's party? It's on the seventeenth of October.' I'd blurted the words out before I'd realized.

'It's the seventeenth today, Harry.'

The days had slipped past without me being aware. And there was also the slight hiccup of just which of the four women I knew well enough to ask was the right one to take – minefields were easier to traverse. However, I'd shot my bolt now, of course. I'd felt that I owed Eliza for doing me a really big favour – and I did. Not many vets would have put themselves out to do the job, and so swiftly.

'Yes,' I said, trying to regain a foothold plus save face, 'it is short notice, I must admit.'

'The others turned you down, did they?'

I could tell from her voice she was smiling at my discomfort. 'No, I haven't asked them.'

The smile turned into an audible laugh and, after a few moments, I began laughing too. 'Well, what do you say?'

'I'm going to give you the benefit of the doubt that they all turned you down. And forgive you for a last-ditch offer and say, yes, I'd love to.'

'Oh, that's great.' And I realized that I did mean it. Somehow it was just what I needed. I liked her and she had a delightful sense of humour that resonated with my own. It would remove the case from my immediate focus and I'd be able to relax. Very often on a case, I'd be so submerged in details and impressions, so uptight, that it defeated the objective of allowing the superior intuition of the subconscious to come through with a possible solution. I definitely needed to relax.

'We have to be there for eight o'clock, at Hempton Hall. Shall we say I'll pick you up at the surgery, at seven thirty?'

I didn't want to embarrass her by asking for her private address – that would probably be a bridge too far.

'Yes, that would be lovely, thanks.'

'No, *thank you.* I'm definitely in your debt.'

The smile was back in her voice. 'Bye, Harry.'

I put the receiver down and there was a corresponding smile now on my face. It was nice to have something enjoyable to look forward to. Best of all, I didn't see it developing into something heavy. There was no space in my life at the moment to think about starting a possible love affair. And I was equally sure that neither did Eliza. We seemed to be two of a kind – both dedicated to our careers. But we both needed an evening off.

Meanwhile, there was work to be done. I had three rides for Mike at Leicester, our local course. They were all early afternoon ones, fortunately. Mike had been well ahead of me. He'd put the declarations in two days previously. He'd kept track of the passage of days and was also well aware of Lady Branshawe's party scheduled for this evening – as I found out when I arrived at the stables. I wasn't surprised. He was always on the ball.

'So, who are you taking tonight, then?' Mike transferred a mug of black coffee from Pen's outstretched hand and pushed it across the kitchen table to me. 'Which poor woman has drawn the short straw?'

Pen giggled. 'Mind your own, Mike.'

'A lady who has done me a very big favour.'

'Uh-oh, and that's *before* you take her to a party.' He gave a snort of laughter. 'I call that good going. You must have given her a load of soft soap.'

'Oh shut up, Mike.' I took a slurp of the coffee. 'Anyway, I'll drive myself to Leicester today. I need to get back. There's something I have to do before I get my best gear on.'

'You've got that look in your eye again. I know what that means. Are you going to tell us where you're going?'

'No. I'm not, Mike. I told you, I'm going it alone this time.'

'But you will shout if you need his help, won't you, Harry?'

'Cross my heart, Pen, I will.'

Mike and I exchanged glances.

'Write it down, OK?'

I pursed my lips. 'Under Leo's bowl, do you?'

'Yep.'

We all parted company later in the morning – Mike in his own car, me in mine, both to Leicester Racecourse – and we left Pen in peace in the kitchen.

It was a productive afternoon. I won the first race, lost the next and came second in my last race. After which I showered, changed and was driving back to Nottinghamshire by just after three o'clock. I could have had a couple more rides. I only had to accept the offers and book them ahead of the meeting – and I *was* mindful of my winnings total – but there were only so many hours to do stuff.

However, I was also very aware that there was a developing urgency about the situation. Nothing concrete about it, simply an instinctive feeling that everything was beginning to speed up. I could sense it; I'd been here before while investigating other cases and, like the prickle at the back of my neck, I ignored it at my own risk.

I drove back to Harlequin Cottage, but all the way home I was mulling over what Patty had said just before he'd left – plus what Mike had said earlier today. It had been a throwaway remark, said without any thought behind it. But putting them together, I'd found they gave me a totally different and exciting angle on things. The beauty of it was it also tied in exactly with my earlier plans for this afternoon.

Reaching home, I changed again, this time into jeans, sweater and trainers. I needed to blend in where I was going. Reaching for Leo's bowl, I wrote 'Tal's place' on a sticky label and stuck it underneath. I'd promised – and I *always* kept my promises. On the landline, I dialled Tal's number and had a quick word with her.

'He's out somewhere right now, I think. Well, certainly as in not working, but if you hold on, I'll slip round the back of the lads' hostel, see if I can get a quick peep in his window.'

'Only if it's safe . . . Tal . . . Tal?'

She'd gone. I hung on as requested.

A few minutes later her voice came on the line. 'Harry, you still there?'

'Sure am.'

'It's fine. Nobody is at home, so come over.'

'Coming, as we speak.'

I replaced the receiver then shrugged on a jacket and also added a flat cap with a decent peak.

The Mazda made nonsense of the mileage and I parked up about a quarter of a mile away from the entrance to Tal's stables. Locking the car, I tugged the peak of the cap down over my eyebrows as far as it would go and, hunching my shoulders, walked down the lane and slipped in through the back way. I knew the layout of the stables and made a discreet visit to the deserted tack room.

The door wasn't locked, simply on the latch. A quick glance each way ensured there was no one around so I slipped inside and closed the door. Avoiding the lines of bridles hanging down from overhead hooks, I worked my way down the long benches containing all the daily equipment needed for cleaning horses and their tack: rubbers, curry combs, body brushes, cleaning sponges by the dozen. And what I'd come to find – boxes of saddle soap. I checked them all out.

And I didn't find a thing.

I forced down the feeling of disappointment. It had certainly been worth a try, but to have found what I was looking for would, probably, have been a bit too easy. It would also have eliminated the need to do a search of Paul Oats' room. But on the plus side, if I had found it in the tack room, it wouldn't have the same damning significance – any one of the staff could have put it there. And, of course, there was always the chance that I was allowing my imagination to run wild.

I took a glance both ways before leaving the tack room. There was no one in the yard. Tal must have been watching out for me though, because she beckoned from the corner of the hostel.

'Come round the back. I've already been inside and left the window unlatched. Easier to get in that way, less likely to be seen.'

'That's my girl.'

I followed Tal along the length of brickwork and round the right-hand corner. At waist height there was a short run of windows, all tightly shut – except for the last one. It was only open about half an inch, but it was enough to know that it wasn't fastened inside. We came to a halt.

'Go on, then,' she whispered, 'get it open and climb in.'

I nodded and, taking out my wallet, I removed a strong plastic debit card. Slipping it between the window frame and the window itself, I gently eased it open sufficiently to hook my fingers in and pull the window wide open. I took a quick look inside. The room was empty. I released a breath I didn't know I was holding and heaved myself over the sill.

The room was as basic as I'd expected. Stable staff didn't warrant luxury, but Oats' room was practically bare. It crossed my mind that perhaps this was the way he always lived, little to pack, being able to cut and run at very short notice. This search wasn't going to take long at all.

On the back of the door were four hooks – presumably in lieu of a wardrobe.

The bed was, of course, the main piece of furniture. But it didn't sport a headboard and the framework was a solid wooden one – nowhere to hide anything there. I reached over, took off the one pillow and shook it, patted it all over and placed it to one side on the one wooden chair in the room. Then I heaved up the mattress and examined it on both sides and also underneath the two flat mattress handgrips that were fixed to the sides. There were no signs of it having been slit open, no edges re-stitched. And the mattress itself sat on top of laths of wood attached to the base and four legs, far too thin to hide anything inside them.

I passed my hand underneath and ran my fingers the whole length of each lath. There was nothing attached to them on the underside. Another blank.

I moved to the rickety chest of drawers in the corner, eased it away from the wall into the middle of the room and began a careful systematic search, checking all the contents and the sides and bottoms of each drawer. It proved entirely innocent of concealing anything. I was running out of ideas and places to look.

Tal, meantime, was continually dancing between the window and the door leading out of the room and back into the main reception, kitchen and bathroom areas. 'Do be quick, Harry,' she begged.

I picked up on her anxiety. Neither of us wanted to be caught in here. It was gross violation of private space. To give myself time to think of where else I could search, I reassembled the bed and smoothed down the cotton spread on top. If Oats were to come back now, he wouldn't notice anything amiss and we could make a swift exit through the window.

But he hadn't returned, not yet, and I was desperate to find some evidence that would tie him in with the drugs scam. I scanned the walls – no pictures but a small mirror was screwed to the wall above the gap where the chest had been. I pressed my face up against the cold plaster. There was a good quarter of an inch gap at the bottom edge. And the wood was a substantial thickness – glass was heavy.

It was a possibility. I knew if I could release the screws and lift the mirror down, it might prove a hiding place. But I'd no tools with me, on purpose. Carrying tools like chisels and screwdrivers could constitute housebreaking implements and compromising evidence.

The screw heads were the old-style straight-cut ones. It represented half a chance. Had the screw heads been the more modern Posidrive variety – no chance. But either way, I had no tools.

'Any ideas, Tal, on how I can unscrew the mirror? Do you keep any tools in the hostel at all?'

She shook her head. 'Nothing, I'm afraid. Except, I suppose there will be cutlery in the sink unit drawer.'

I grimaced. 'The blades will probably be too thick . . . need something with a narrow edge.'

'Well,' she said, rummaging in her pocket, 'there is this, not a blade as such but it is thin, if it's of any use.' And she held out a nail file. Not a flimsy one but sturdy with a short, solid handle.

'Tal, you're a star . . .'

I took it from her and began loosening the two bottom screws holding the mirror. It wasn't as good as a real screwdriver, but it answered the purpose. One after the other the screws loosened in their threads until I was able to use my fingertips to unscrew them, enough to lift the mirror away from the wall sufficiently to see behind it.

I swore with frustration. There was nothing whatsoever behind the mirror. I quickly replaced it and gave the screws a few turns, enough to fox anybody that it was still firmly attached to the wall.

'I think we have to call it off, Harry. He could be back at any time.'

I was about to agree with her, was holding my hand out to return the nail file, but then I stopped. On the floor next to the skirting board was a light dusting of plaster from where I'd been unscrewing the mirror. But not only was there some plaster dust, there was also a smidgeon of fine sawdust. Not much, and certainly not enough to have attracted my attention on its own, but with my attention focussed downwards, there was enough to cause my pulse rate to quicken.

'Wait a bit . . .' I kept hold of the nail file and went down on my knees near the wall.

Tal leaned over me. 'What have you found?'

'Wait.' I inserted the tip of the nail file between the wall and the skirting board. Gently, oh so gently, I prised the wood away from the plaster. It had been recently cut about six inches along from the natural joint. Unless you were looking for it specifically, you would never notice. With extra care I continued to widen the gap until I could insert the tips of my fingers in and then I pulled. The small length of board came away easily in my hand.

Behind me I heard Tal give a gasp of surprise. Instead of the plaster being about half an inch proud of the floorboards, as it should have been, it had been carefully chiselled out to leave a good two-inch gap. It was a very neat job, I gave Oats that. Pressing my fingers into the tight space, I withdrew a small cake of saddle soap.

Getting to my feet, I placed it on the palm of my hand and showed it to Tal.

'Soap?' she queried, frowning. 'A cake of saddle soap? So?'

I turned it over. The reverse side had been scooped out to form a hollow and tucked snugly inside was a slim plastic tube. And it had a label stuck on the side. The label had one word scrawled on it. I looked at Tal – she looked back at me.

I read out the name written on the label. 'Detomidine.'

TWENTY-NINE

I was still smiling as I helped Tal back through the window and, bent double to avoid detection, we scurried back to the main house. She immediately made some strong coffee.

'Your nerves may be able to stand all this twanging, Harry, but mine can't.'

'What makes you think mine can?'

'Get away with you. You love the game. Maybe not as much as winning races, but you do.'

Her words gave me a jolt. It had been said before – and by a very worthy person, Pen – but being seconded by Tal, equally worthy, made me give the idea credence.

'Here's your coffee . . . strong and black. Oh, did you fancy a whisky, maybe?'

'No, no, Tal. Coffee is just what I need. I've some mileage to cover later.'

'So, is the Detomidine what you were looking for?'

'Hmm . . .' I said, nodding. 'But *expecting* to find it would be more accurate.'

'A horse sedative, then?'

I nodded again.

'But you've left it there, behind the chest of drawers.'

'We don't want Oats to realize we've found it, Tal.'

'Will he use it again, or am I being really naive?'

I spread my hands. 'Your guess, et cetera. But one thing I do know is I'm afraid you have to get back now, to the hostel, to his room, before he gets back.'

'*Whaaat?*'

'Hmm, sorry, but you have more credibility to do this than I do.'

'And just what am I going in there for?'

I smiled at her, trying to defuse her indignation. 'There's a window that needs closing, securing against burglars, on the inside.'

*   *   *

It was twenty past seven when, suited, booted and eager to see Eliza, I arrived at the veterinary surgery. She opened the door still dressed in her working scrubs.

'You're early.'

'True, but I've brought you something. However, I wouldn't call it a present.' I held out an eye-dropper. I'd extracted a tiny amount from Oats' tube.

'Not horse urine again?'

'Oh, no, not this time. This time, if I'm not mistaken, it's pure Detomidine. Of course, I don't have the expertise to determine it for certain. But I'm sure you do.'

I dropped the tube into her hand. Her fingers closed around it.

'Tomorrow, yes? Tonight we take a night off.'

'I can't fault you,' I said.

And ten minutes later, with Eliza now more appropriately dressed in an ankle length midnight-blue dress with matching wrap, and shod in five-inch high heels, we were on our way to Hempton Hall.

'You know the way?'

'I do.'

'It's tricky to find, isn't it? I got lost when I came to be "assessed" by Her Ladyship.'

'Assessed?'

'Well, it wasn't exactly a job interview, because she'd already asked me if I would like to become her equine vet.'

'And you said you would.'

She grinned. 'I did indeed. The prestige is brilliant. It virtually says, "You can trust this woman with your animals." And, of course, then I have to live up to it.'

'Which I'm sure you already do.'

'Thank you.' She smiled prettily. 'My work is the most important thing in my life. I'll admit it because it's true. And your work, Harry, it's important to you, isn't it?'

'Oh yes, like yourself, it's something I need, that I eat, breathe and sleep.'

'Two of a kind.' She smiled at me. 'So, we both understand each other.'

And I certainly understood what she *wasn't* saying: tonight is just a dalliance, it means nothing. But then, it was what I'd anticipated. However, it cleared out any dross of misunder-standing and we could enjoy ourselves all the better knowing nothing further was likely to develop.

Arriving at Hempton Hall, we climbed the grand sweep of steps between the two grooved pillars leading to the impressive heavy oak door. Reaching up for the circular iron ring, I gave it a tug. We could hear it give a loud peel that wouldn't have disgraced the local church bell. The butler, in full fig for the occasion, took Eliza's wrap before showing us through into the main reception room and Lady Willamina Branshawe swooped down on us, her face one big smile – and it was a smile of genuine pleasure that we'd decided to come. She might hold a title and an exalted position in society but it didn't stop her behaving naturally and letting her delight show. She motioned to a passing waiter and we were supplied with flutes of champagne.

'I didn't know you knew each other,' she said. 'Has Eliza told you I've recently appointed her as my equine vet?'

'Yes, she has mentioned it.'

'Of course, with your backgrounds you are bound to be acquaintances.' Lady Willamina beamed at us. 'Now, do let me introduce you to a famous lady, also a rider, although not in racing.'

She did a quick glance around and located the right person. We were ushered across the crowded room and brought to a halt at the side of a woman in a very short, scarlet dress who was enjoying the attentions of a ring of admirers.

'May I introduce Miss Eliza Grey and Mr Harry Radcliffe,' she said. 'And this is Dame Isabella Pullbright, the famous actress.'

'Lovely to meet you,' said Eliza.

I looked at Isabella and smiled. 'Actually, we have met before, Lady Willamina. I must say you look very striking, Dame Isabella.'

'Well, thank you, Harry,' she said, laughing. 'I have to say, Lady Willamina, you do know the nicest people to invite to your parties.'

'One tries. But it is always gratifying to hear. Now, please do excuse me . . .'

Across the room, the butler was ushering in two more guests. I wondered just how many more would arrive – it was getting crowded. Eliza began talking to Isabella about the new film and was questioning her about the riding sequences. I listened with half an ear and let my gaze drift over the other partygoers. I knew quite a few of them – it wasn't the first time I'd been to a party here – and there were a few raised glasses and acknowledging nods in my direction.

I noticed the trainer, Jim Crack, sitting by himself at one of the smaller tables in an alcove over by the enormous four-foot inglenook fireplace in which logs were blazing beautifully. Excusing myself from the ladies, I walked over and sat beside him.

'How're things, Harry?'

I nodded. 'Good, thanks, and yourself?'

I'd heard that his divorce had finally come through: Joanne, his wife, had been amusing herself with their accountant. Jim played with a straight bat and was not the forgiving kind. He expected and deserved loyalty from her but, unfortunately, Joanne had had other ideas. It was a shame; he was a great guy, but life isn't fair, never has been.

'Which of your girlfriends have you brought with you tonight? More importantly, where is she?'

His words made me feel like a Casanova. Was that how other people saw me? God, I hoped not. There has only ever been one woman for me. But in the circumstances, although I could have protested, I didn't want to rub salt in. 'Not a girlfriend, Jim. Eliza is Leo's vet, actually.'

'That's the most unlikely excuse I've ever heard.'

I was relieved to see a smile play across his mouth.

'It isn't an excuse.'

'I'm supposed to swallow that?' he said.

'Yes, because it's true. She's a damn good vet, too.'

'Hmm . . .' Pondering for a moment, he became serious. 'Look, Harry, she doesn't do horses, I suppose?'

It was a fair question. Most vets tend to specialize in either small or large animal husbandry. 'I can only tell you what I've found to be true. She's been marvellous with Leo. And, do you know, he absolutely adores her.'

'Thought he was a one-woman cat.'

I grinned. 'Annabel.'

His eyebrows rose. 'Who else?'

I nodded. '*But*, Eliza is also Lady Branshawe's equine vet.'

'By gum, are you serious?'

'Of course.'

'Now *that* is interesting.'

'You in need of a horse vet, then?'

He tapped the side of his nose. 'I might be, Harry.'

I didn't press him as to the reason. Instead, I looked across the big room to where the two women were still chatting together. 'Look, let me introduce you, how's that?'

'Makes my effort in coming tonight worth it, I'd say. Well, it has potential.'

I suddenly realized it *had* taken effort. He would know that a good percentage of the people here at the party would be aware of his marriage break-up and I could see it might prove humiliating that Joanne had buggered off and left him.

Another thought crossed my mind. It was most likely that a new vet wasn't the only professional help Jim needed to find.

'Keep moving forward, Jim. If life's not too sweet at the moment, things are bound to get better. Nothing stays still – nature's law.'

This time he gave me a proper smile. 'Go and fetch your tame vet.'

So I did.

As I'd thought he would be, Jim was bowled over to be the meat in the sandwich between two beautiful women when they sat down, one on either side.

'You're a jammy beggar . . .' Jim shook his head reprovingly at me. 'Not content with one woman, you've got two.'

I reached over to catch the waiter as he passed with another full tray of flutes and relieved him of four. However, at that moment, the three-piece band struck up and conversation halted whilst we sipped and watched the talented musicians playing. It proved to be simply the introduction and within ten minutes they were bowing and smiling at the applause. Then waitresses moved along beside the cold buffet removing cloths and cling film and Lady Branshawe was exhorting everyone to enjoy the food.

We gave it two or three minutes and then we tacked on to the line of guests and applied ourselves to choosing some of the delicious food laid out before us. With well-filled plates – very spaced out in my case – we made our way back to the tiny table and munched away.

The last time I'd been here, it had been me and Jim, Georgia

– a girlfriend whom I'd taken with me on a trip to Switzerland – and Tally. As trainers, Tal and Jim were friends. And, of course, that was why Jim was on his own this evening. Tally had, very wisely, gone to ground. Until this doping was sorted out, the shadow of it would continue to hang over her.

'This is all so new to me.' Isabella treated us to her famous megawatt smile. 'I never realized that horse racing could be so much fun.'

'Hmm . . . I hear you've been bitten by the racing bug. You've bought a mare, yes?'

'That's right. Barbara Maguire's my trainer. I thought it would be a good idea to use a lady trainer, you know, a woman's take on things.'

'You see, Harry.' Jim shook his head sadly. 'She doesn't rate us men very much.'

'Oh, but that's not true,' Isabella protested. 'It's just there wouldn't be any possible misunderstandings.'

'You mean, a man would just see a beautiful woman, rather than an owner?'

'Since you put it so bluntly, Jim, yes. But beauty is in the eye of the beholder. All women are beautiful in some men's eyes.'

Jim smiled at her, then turned his gaze on Eliza. 'Indeed, they are.'

I was beginning to feel like a spare part, but I was pleased they all seemed to be hitting it off so well. Finishing my food, I excused myself and headed off across the room and through the door that opened on to the internal hall. I knew this led to the cloakroom.

I'd been here before at a party straight after arriving back from Switzerland. On that evening, there had been a magnificent pianist playing for Lady Branshawe: Jackson Fellows. His rendition of Beethoven's 'Für Elise' had been an absolute joy to hear. I'd run into him afterwards, accidentally on purpose, here in this opulent cloakroom, decorated from floor to ceiling in beautiful glowing amber wall tiles.

It had proved a fruitful meeting for us both. But tonight there was no one with whom I needed to strike up a conversation – well, not that I was aware of, and yet, as I came out and closed one of the three toilet doors behind me, I experienced the telling prickle at the back of my neck. Why? I didn't know why. And it was disconcerting.

On the wall opposite the three toilets there was a vanity unit, also in amber, that had some hand basins set into it. Leaning over one of the hand basins, I turned on the tap, ran the hot water and placed my hands in before peering at my reflection in the wall mirror. Strange as it seems, I knew the additional element of water would aid whatever it was my subconscious wanted me to know. It had helped me out on numerous occasions in the past when I'd been on a case. Too numerous to discount, if I was honest.

It didn't let me down now, either. On its own, the idea was tenuous. Had it not been for that tell-tale prickle I might have ignored the flimsy thought that had just clicked into my mind. But experience had shown me that, however bizarre the thought, it should never be dismissed.

I plunged my hands back deeper in the hot water and considered it. There were two options available to check this out: ask Lady Branshawe, or ask Ginnie Cutler. I was sure Lady Willamina would answer my question immediately, and without questioning me about it. As to Ginnie . . . well, if I presented the question to her, already knowing the answer, she might probably find the courage to tell me. Because backing it up was essential. And although Lady Willamina *could* tell me, it was Ginnie who held the key to giving me the right answer.

THIRTY

We left the party at a respectable hour, Eliza stating very firmly she needed her beauty sleep and tomorrow she was facing a long day of work. I reassured her she had no need to worry on the beauty front, but she was adamant: leave at eleven thirty, home to bed by midnight. Well, you couldn't argue with a lady.

I dutifully dropped her at the surgery where she'd left her car and motored on home alone. Coming off the well-lit A52, I took a left and carried on down the ink-black country lanes – both headlights now on full beam – and eventually swung in at my open five-barred gate. Gravel spat as I slammed on the brakes.

Parked up in my usual spot was a car I recognized – an old, red Ford. Dowsing my lights, I got out and locked my vehicle. There was a woman sitting in the Ford's driving seat. At my approach, she opened the door and climbed out, peering at me in the darkness.

'Harry? It is Harry, isn't it?'

'Yes, it's me, Mrs Whellan.'

'Can I speak to you? Is it OK, or are you tied up?' The anxiety in her voice was coming across strongly.

I lifted up both hands in front of her. 'No handcuffs.'

Her shoulders dropped at my horseplay, which was exactly what I'd hoped for. 'Come on in. I'll mash us some tea, eh?'

'Oh, yes, please. I've been sitting in that old car of mine for the last three hours. I'm perished.' As if to emphasize the fact, she rubbed her hands together vigorously.

But she didn't need to. I could see the poor woman was shivering. 'It's not often I'm out in the evenings, Dottie, but you would have to pick tonight.'

'No, not me. The hospital rang earlier and told me I could visit tonight. So, of course, that's what I did, drove over to the Queen's and saw my Keith.'

'You did?' I spun round from the Rayburn where I'd been putting the kettle on the hot plate. 'That's fantastic news. Is he conscious, then?'

'Yes. Seems he came round late this afternoon. I promised you that I'd let you know as soon as I heard, but I didn't want to risk using the mobile. Not very safe, are they?'

'No. They're dodgy things. All right for general use but if you need something kept secret, it's best to give them a miss.'

She nodded emphatically. 'Exactly what I thought. Anyway, the good news is Keith's awake now.'

'It's the best news, Dottie, it truly is. Does it mean that I might be able to get in to see him, do you think?'

'Can't rightly say, Harry. When I left, I told the hospital staff – and the policeman on duty – that he was to be kept safe. Don't want that gunman getting in his room, maybe having another go at him.'

'God forbid.' I handed her a steaming mug of tea. 'Would you care for a dash of whisky in it?'

'I would that.'

I poured a generous splash into both our mugs. 'So, did Keith actually speak to you, then?'

'Oh, he were a bit muddled, y'know . . . didn't make a deal of sense really. But at least he's alive, on the mend.'

I nodded. With my own experience of being concussed and out of it, I knew that I'd rambled a lot of nonsense when I was coming round. 'It will take him a while, but I'm sure he'll get there. At least it seems he's coming out of the unconsciousness.'

And I also knew that that was an extremely dangerous time as well. If the gunman who had shot him got wind that he was on the way back to recovery, they'd be likely to have another go at finishing him off before he could say anything. If indeed Keith did know anything – and especially if he'd seen who it was that had taken the shot at him. 'What time did you visit tonight?'

'Oh, about seven o'clock, I suppose. I didn't stay long, didn't want to tire him, you know. But then visiting hours are up at eight o'clock anyway.'

I nodded. I was only too aware of the timetable in the hospital – I'd been in there, mostly horizontal, too many times. 'Is it still just family? Or, do you think they'll let me in to see him?'

She shook her head. 'Not sure. But you could ring them, find out.'

'I will, but not tonight. I'll ring first thing in the morning. You said you told the policeman as well as the hospital staff to keep him safe.'

She set down her empty mug with a bang. 'Oh, I did.'

'So, was the policeman outside Keith's bedroom door?'

'Yes. He'd got a chair to sit on, well, I suppose, he would have. I mean, Keith's been in now several days.'

'Hmm, however, it would be rota staff, I suppose.'

We were both silent, thinking about Keith's lone ongoing battle to regain full consciousness.

'Well, I'm off now. I've told you like I promised. But it was the safest way to do it.'

'Oh, yes. And thank you, Dottie. I appreciate your coming over. I'm just so sorry it was the one night I was out.'

'Don't give it another thought. I mean, you went haring straight off up to Yorkshire with my granddaughter. I mean, *you* didn't even consider *not* going. We've all just got to pull together is how I see it. And I know my Keith will be very grateful when he knows about it.'

'No need for thanks.' I shook my head and escorted her to the door. 'I can never repay *him*. Take care on the way back. These lanes are a bit dodgy in the dark.'

'I'll be fine.' She slid into the driving seat and fastened her seat belt. 'I've got nice and warmed up now. I'll be home in a few minutes.'

I went back indoors, made a fresh drink and tried to plan out the next day. I'd got four rides. However, it would all hinge on what the hospital said when I rang them. Far too late tonight, of course. Anyway, it would give Keith at least another twelve hours to make progress.

If I was allowed to see him tomorrow, maybe he would be sufficiently improved and his memory intact to speak coherently. Until I had done, found out if he actually saw who the gunman was, it was still a matter of chasing up other people and continuing to dig.

Slumped on the sofa, shoes off, feet up, deep in thought of where and what I'd be doing the next day, I obviously hadn't heard any sounds of entry and I'd assumed I was the only one inside Harlequin Cottage. Until the door opened very slowly and a lithe ginger body emitting a bellow of welcome squeezed itself through the crack. I looked up at the very last second and saw a big furry cat launch itself at me.

Leo, all eight kilos of him, landed squarely on my solar plexus, knocking all the breath from me. He placed both front paws on my chest and clouted my chin with his head. His tiger-loud purr told me just how glad he was to see me home. When I'd got my breath back I told him a home truth I thought he should hear.

'You know your trouble, mate, don't you?' He squeezed his emerald eyes tightly and used me as a piano, pounding his pads – and claws – into my chest. 'You are anti-social. Why didn't you come in when Dottie was here? She could have done with a lapful of cat to stroke – good for stress. And God knows, she's stressed all right.' But it was water off a duck – he took no notice. 'Well, it's very flattering, knowing I'm your favourite person, but you're not getting any more food.'

He conceded, gave up cajoling and let his paws slide slowly down the front of my jumper before collapsing gently in a warm, furry heap on my lap. He made a very efficient, soothing hot-water bottle, I'll give him that. Within seconds, his purrs had given way to bass snores. Leo had fallen asleep, but even so, he was still working hard at stress-busting.

I yawned mightily. And realized I was damn tired too. It was way past my bedtime. But it seemed churlish, if not down-right rude, to push him off on to the floor, so I stayed where I was.

And that's exactly where I found both of us at six o'clock the next morning. Stiff as a brick with a bloody painful crick in my neck, I forced my eyelids open. Leo, the jammy sod, was still curled up in exactly the same comfortable position.

Feeling me move, however, he stirred himself, opened an impos-sibly pink mouth and all but swallowed himself in a massive yawn. While I watched, he did his version of yoga, stretching to the limit front and back before leaping down to the carpet. Then he high-tailed – and his tail was flagpole straight and pointing to the ceiling – to the kitchen to await developments.

Meantime, I pulled myself painfully off the sofa and crawled upstairs to the bathroom and stood, still bent like a staple, under the shower while the hot water did its miracle work and restored me to something resembling a normal upright human being.

Downstairs, a scalding black coffee pulled me back from the brink and allowed the cogs in my brain to re-set themselves as I glugged it down gratefully. One thought now was demanding attention. I glanced up at the wall clock while I poured out a second mug. It was very early still, but hospitals didn't have the same attitude to time as the rest of us.

I reached for the landline and stabbed in the number. No need for me to look it up. It was one of the telephone numbers that was scorched into my brain, probably for all time, the amount of use it got. After chatting up the young woman on the enquiry desk and waiting to be put through to the sister on Keith's ward, I was given some alarming news.

For once being famous had its advantages. 'Mr Radcliffe, *the*

Mr Harry Radcliffe, the gentleman who was in the horsebox at the time Mr Whellan was shot?'

'Yes, that's me. I was told late last night by Keith's mother, Mrs Dottie Whellan, that he was now conscious. And she suggested I ring.'

'I see.'

'So, would it be possible for me to drive over and visit Keith, please?'

'We would be pleased if you did, Mr Radcliffe. You see, Mr Whellan has been asking for you.'

'Oh, great. Sounds like he's more himself now.'

'Hmm . . .' Her voice had now dropped in tone. 'Yes, well, that was during the night. But, unfortunately, there has been an incident earlier this morning, I'm afraid.'

'I'm not with you. What's happened? Is Keith all right?'

'We had an unwanted intruder in the hospital. He tried to get into Mr Whellan's room and the policeman guarding him was injured himself. He is in theatre as we speak.'

I took a very deep breath. 'That's awful. Was he – or Mr Whellan – badly injured?'

'Thankfully, no. Certainly, the policeman's injuries are not life-threatening. But we obviously had to report this to the police and request a further police presence.'

'So, where does this leave us?'

'If you would like to come to the hospital and see Mr Whellan, I think it would be a good idea, Mr Radcliffe.'

'Ha, you said he was asking to see me . . . didn't you?'

'I did. And in view of what's happened, it might help to calm him.'

Despite her professionalism, she sounded as though she needed a bit of calming herself. I suppose it was the equivalent of having a violent burglar in your house. And that was a very disturbing experience, as I knew only too well.

'Would it be OK if I were to drive over now, right away?'

'Yes. I'll leave a message on the front desk to allow you access as it isn't regular visiting hours. And, of course, security has been stepped up . . .'

I bet it had.

THIRTY-ONE

I fed Leo. Then fed myself – a few mouthfuls of scrambled egg sufficed – before picking up my mobile and contacting Mike at the stables.

'Don't tell me,' he said grumpily, 'you can't get in today.'

'I wouldn't go *that* far. I might get to you later this morning, just not at the moment.'

'Am I allowed to ask why?'

'Seems Keith Whellan has surfaced.'

Mike's attitude altered immediately. 'Oh, now that really is good news. You going to see him?'

'Yes.'

'Wait a minute, you mean seeing him, like, right now?'

'Yes.'

'But it's only seven o'clock . . . They won't let you in, you know. Anyway, how come you know about him?'

'Because I've just spoken to the hospital and they've signed my pass to get past the border, or in other words, the front desk.'

There were a few moments of silence. 'I thought he was under police protection. How does that work? Does that get you past his police protection officer?'

'It doesn't, Mike. The policeman on duty got KO'd earlier this morning. I gather he's in theatre.'

'Good God!'

'Yes, I think He must be. The policeman's injuries aren't life-threatening, the ward sister tells me, and Keith has remained unharmed.'

'But I don't like the sound of this, homing in for another go at poor old Keith. I mean, why? What, or who, has he got on the wrong side of?'

'Can't answer that, Mike. But it does seem as though Keith was the target, not me.'

'Hmmm . . . that makes a change.'

I had to admit it was. 'However, I'll give you a ring when I know what's happening.'

'Oh, sure, yes, of course you must go . . . Pen's just interrupted to say pass on our love to Keith and we're glad he's getting better.'

'I will.'

I debated whether to ring Ginnie Cutler, put her in the picture as regards her ex-son-in-law. But I thought better of it. If Dottie wanted Ginnie to know, she would tell her. And thinking of the state Ginnie had been in the last time I'd seen her, the less stress she was put under the better. Hearing that a further attempt had been made on Keith's life wasn't what she needed to hear. I'd keep my own counsel for now, find out the true facts when I visited and take it from there.

Then I realized: Dottie had certainly told me about Keith's coming round but she, also, didn't know anything about this second attempt on his life. I sure as hell wasn't going to tell her right now.

I shoved the mobile in my pocket and went across to Leo's bowl, empty now the cat had demolished his breakfast. I washed and dried it and took it over to my desk. Ripping off the next sticky label from the roll in my desk drawer, I wrote on it: Queen's – 7.30 a.m., then stuck the label on the bottom of the bowl before returning it to the kitchen cupboard. Well, you never knew, did you? And Leo needed a back-up slave to ensure a continuous flow of grub.

Collecting my car keys, I went out and started the Mazda. If I looked sharp, I could just about avoid rush hour into Nottingham. Speed is hard-wired into a jockey's make-up and thirty minutes later I was pulling up at the Queen's Hospital.

Crossing the busy foyer, I went straight over to the huge half-horseshoe reception desk.

'Mr Harry Radcliffe.' I introduced myself to the stern-looking middle-aged woman in front of me. 'I think Ward Sister Mae Renton left instructions for me to be allowed in to visit Mr Keith Whellan.'

She would have been an ideal candidate for a poker game. There wasn't a flicker that would indicate she knew what had taken place earlier this morning.

'Can I see some ID, please, Mr Radcliffe?'

It was a good performance considering I'd seen her before, knew she *knew* who I was. But I took out my wallet and complied.

'Thank you, sir. I think you know the way.'

She didn't smile, but the merest twitch of her eyebrow sealed relations between us and I nodded back.

'I'll just ring and let the ward know you're on your way.'

Then I took myself off down one of the corridors that sprang like spokes in a bike wheel going off in every direction, and headed for the lifts. There was a plethora of people imitating ants, some white-clad, intent-looking hospital professionals, some worried-looking people who could possibly be relatives, and most of them, no doubt, wishing they were anywhere else but here. I shared that view as I weaved in and out doing my best to avoid cannoning into anyone. It was trickier than riding in a field of thirty at Aintree.

Arriving at the lifts, I found there was one standing open having presumably just deposited its occupants. I nipped in sharply and pressed the button.

A houseman, wearing a white coat and carrying the obligatory stethoscope around his neck, deeply immersed in studying a clip-board of notes, came scurrying out of a side corridor and just made it at the last second as the lift doors closed in front of me.

I was also deep in thought as to what I would say to Keith and all I registered was the white coat at the side of me as the lift juddered and lifted upwards. I noticed a couple of floors tick off on the screen, and just as the lift approached my floor, a sharp movement had me turning my head to the right – but not quickly enough. The last thing I remember was a white-clad arm swiftly raised before smashing down on the side of my head.

After that it was a blank.

'Well, Mr Radcliffe, it makes a change . . .'

I could hear a voice somewhere way above my head. Forcing open my eyelids, I peered blearily up at the doctor who was standing by the bedside.

'The last time I saw you, Mr Radcliffe, you'd just fallen off a horse . . . and the time before that.'

'Didn't I come off a horse this time, then?' I asked.

'Don't you remember?'

I was going to shake my head, but it hurt too much. 'No.'

'You were found spark out on the floor of the hospital lift.'

This time, I did shake my head in disbelief, and instantly regretted it.

'Your memory should return quite quickly,' the doctor continued, 'so don't worry about it. We've also put four stitches in your left tricep but the wound wasn't deep, so that too should heal quickly.'

'My arm?' I was having a job to keep my eyelids from closing.

'Hmm, seems whoever attacked you was, er . . .' He smirked down at me. 'Shall we say, he was hedging his bets? If he was aiming for your heart' – his smirk grew wider – 'he still lost.'

He walked off and the nurse who had accompanied him stepped forward. She deftly tweaked my sheet. 'Try to sleep, now,' she said. 'This time it will be a natural sleep.'

I felt like saying that was what I'd been trying to do when the doctor woke me up. But I couldn't get the words out fast enough before I fell asleep.

How long I slept, I've no idea. And it wasn't a voice that awoke me the second time. They say smell is a wonderful memory restorer. This smell certainly evoked memory strongly enough because it woke me up. It was that all-familiar, extremely penetrating smell of disinfectant. That alone told me even before I opened my eyes I was in a hospital. And I *was* lying in a bed – exactly why wasn't too clear. I'd come to visit Keith, hadn't I?

There was the rustle of a uniform and a nurse appeared. Now might be a good time to ask. 'How come I'm here?'

'You've got an abrasion on your head that has caused mild concussion, and a stab wound to your left tricep that has required four stitches.'

'Not serious then?' I said.

'Serious enough for us to keep you in overnight, Mr Radcliffe. How are you feeling this morning?'

'Overnight?' I struggled to sit up and she adjusted the bedrest and pillows. 'How long have I been here?'

'Well, you regained consciousness briefly last night and then fell into a natural healing sleep until' – she consulted her watch – 'six forty this morning.'

I made that pretty much twenty-four hours I'd been stuck in here. My mind was racing and it seemed my memory was now fully intact. 'I feel much better, thank you, nurse, but I came into hospital to visit Mr Keith Whellan. He'd been asking for me.'

'After the doctor's seen you later this morning, I expect you'll be able to go and see him. You've a very hard skull, you know.' She smiled. 'Mr Whellan is only in the next ward – and he's doing fine.'

After she'd gone, I did my own checks: she'd been a very pretty nurse and she was standing up straight, not wobbling from side to side, plus I'd only seen one of her. I wasn't feeling dizzy in the slightest, nor was I feeling sick.

Under the sheet, with my right hand out of sight, I counted two fingers on my left hand and kept a tight hold before raising both hands above the covers in front of me. I could see only two fingers being gripped. Great. Most of the pain in my head had also packed it up. But, much more telling, I was feeling damned hungry. So, even if the doctor tried to mollycoddle me, I was leaving hospital today.

As the nurse had said, I had a thick skull, but I'd been here before, on several occasions, and I'd also been told that little gem before. However, giving credence to her words, there was a bandage around my head.

Gingerly, I reached up and tentatively ran my fingers around the back of my head. Putting a slight pressure on the area behind my right ear certainly told me that wasn't a good idea. I withdrew my hand and inspected my fingers – no blood. I sniffed them – not even a smell of blood. That meant since the last dressing had been applied, even if the wound had bled to begin with – and I knew without being told that it certainly would have; head wounds always did – that it had stopped weeping and was beginning to heal. OK, I probably wouldn't be able to put on a crash helmet nor yet be passed fit to ride but for normal life, I was fit.

As regards the injury to my left arm, if it had only needed four stitches, it was pretty minor. Had it been a few inches more to the right, things wouldn't be looking good at all. Seems I'd got off lightly. But what about the policeman who had also been attacked? How was he doing? I hazarded a guess that he had been far more badly injured than I had.

After accepting a most welcome mug of tea, which unfortunately proved to be barely tepid, I cautiously eased out of bed and made my way, groggily, to the bathroom. I used the hand-held shower – no way did I want to wet the bandages – but still managed to make myself feel a good deal fresher. What I needed now was some food. It was a long time since I'd eaten anything. Then I climbed back into bed and was ready when the breakfast trolley came round.

Since I wouldn't be riding for a couple of days – at the very least – I helped myself to some cereal and toast.

By the time mid-morning arrived – yet another mug, coffee this time and black, so it was quite decently hot – I was practically back to normal. Not altogether, but I would be when I got home. Home was the place where you healed. And the place I yearned to be every time I landed in hospital.

The doctor's rounds and necessary checks a few minutes later confirmed my own findings. It wasn't necessary to order a coffin yet. And no way was he about to mollycoddle me.

'You may go home today – by taxi, or get someone to give you a lift. Can't risk you suddenly having a giddy spell, can we? But your bed is needed for someone else sicker than you are.'

'Someone with a thinner skull than mine?'

He allowed himself a slight smile. 'Possibly. No race riding for a few days. And when you do climb aboard a nag – don't fall off.' He had a sense of humour – I liked that. 'However, before you can go, there are two policemen waiting to speak to you, OK? They wanted to see you before but you weren't awake.'

'I wanted to ask if I could see my friend, Keith Whellan? I understand he was asking for me. That's why I came in.'

'Speak to the police first. There is a replacement policeman outside Mr Whellan's door – as well as your own.'

'Mine too?'

'Well, we don't want you sustaining another injury, do we?'

We certainly didn't.

But that alone told me that I was considered a threat to some lowlife. There had been three attacks now, thankfully none fatal – Keith had been first, followed by the police guard and finally myself. I hoped to goodness there would be no further assaults.

And then with a sinking feeling, I remembered that poor Ginnie Cutler had suffered grievous bodily harm. Someone was seriously worried. That meant I was on the right track.

Only one question – what track was I on?

I didn't know.

THIRTY-TWO

There was no time to collect my thoughts. Barely had the door closed behind the nurse than I heard a double knock and it swung open. Two police officers entered the room. They introduced themselves as Inspector Bradbury and Sergeant Briggs.

'Could you tell us what happened, Mr Radcliffe?' Inspector Bradbury asked.

'Well, no, I can't really.'

He raised an eyebrow. 'Start with why you were coming to the hospital in the first place, sir,' he suggested, while Sergeant Briggs fished out a notebook.

I related the events up until I'd stepped into the lift. 'And then, this person—'

'Male or female, sir?' the inspector interrupted.

'I'd say definitely male.'

He nodded. 'Go on.'

'He followed me in right at the last second before the lift closed.'

'So, it was just the two of you inside the lift, is that correct?'

I nodded. 'Yes.'

'Did the lift have departing passengers when you first arrived?'

'No, I didn't see anyone getting out when I reached it.'

'And then?'

'After I stepped into the lift, this *male* person just managed to get in as the doors closed.'

'Could you describe the person?'

'All I registered was that it was a member of the hospital staff. He was medium height, stocky build and wore a white coat, like a doctor. He had a stethoscope around his neck and carried a clipboard.'

I thought back to the moment I'd first seen him coming out of a side corridor. He'd had his head bent over the clipboard. 'Oh, yes, and he had dark hair, cut short.'

'Did he speak to you at all?'

'No.'

'And can you describe the attack?'

'No, not really. I was thinking about my friend and what to say to *him*. All I caught sight of was an arm raised and just as suddenly brought down sharply on my head.'

'Was the man left or right-handed, would you say?'

'Left, I think, because I'd just turned my head to the right as his arm was raised.'

'Was that arm still covered with a white coat?'

'Yes.'

'Hmm, seems he didn't hit you as hard as he meant to, because he then stabbed you. Did you feel him stab you?'

I shook my head and hastily stopped. 'No, I didn't even know I *had* been stabbed until the doctor told me.'

'Hmm.' The inspector rubbed his chin. 'It was your left arm that took the impact, we understand.'

'Yes.'

His next question rang alarm bells. 'Would you say it was injured enough to stop you from riding?'

We stared at each other. I knew if it was only my arm that had been injured, I wouldn't have let it stop me from riding. What the on-course doctor would decide was, of course, up to him. But what had very effectively stopped me racing was the blow to my head. Any concussion, even a blackout for ten seconds – never mind ten hours – would have seen me definitely grounded. Head injuries were taken very seriously these days.

'Have you spoken to Mr Whellan yet, sir?'

'Not yet. I haven't had the opportunity.'

'But you *will*, won't you?'

'Yes.'

'We would appreciate it, sir, should Mr Whellan throw some light on the situation, if you would inform us immediately. In particular as to whether he saw the person who fired at him whilst he was driving the horsebox.' Inspector Bradbury's dark eyes sent a laser beam into mine.

At that moment, I was very glad I was on the right side of the law. What he would have thought – and done – if he'd seen Ginnie Cutler's arm and knew I'd driven her daughter and granddaughter to a safe house up in Yorkshire to protect them, heaven alone knew.

'Yes, Officer, of course I will,' I said.

'And you, yourself, have no idea why anybody would take a shot at the horsebox? *You* didn't see anyone?'

'No, sorry. I was asleep at the time.'

'You do seem to sleep a lot of your time, don't you?'

I kept my temper with difficulty. 'No, I wouldn't say that, no more than a normal person.'

'Do you think that these three attacks are connected?'

'I'd say so, yes. How is the injured policeman?'

Both officers ignored me. I expected them to, but I'd just about had a gut full of being grilled.

'The doctor tells us you are not fit enough to resume riding yet, but fit to leave hospital today. It would be better if you go home and stay there for a few days, sir. If you *should* want to leave the area, perhaps you will be good enough to notify us first.'

'I'll do that – if I do decide to go somewhere. But I don't envisage that I will. I expect I shall be asleep most of the time.'

Inspector Bradbury gave me a smile with all the warmth of a glacier. 'Thank you, sir.'

Both men turned and went out.

I sank back against the pillows, feeling drained. The urge to sleep again was becoming overwhelming. But I could sleep as long as I liked once I was back home. And right now, I needed to speak to Keith.

However, it was a morning for seeing everybody else.

The nurse came in. 'You have another visitor, Mr Radcliffe, is that OK?'

'Who is it this time, the mad axeman?'

'No. It's a Mr Mike Grantley.'

'Oh, him, yes, show him in, thank you, nurse. He's pretty harmless.'

'You reckon?' Mike was inside the room before she could stop him.

'What do you think you're doing then, just lounging about in here, Radcliffe?'

The nurse gasped.

Before she could ask him to leave, I raised a hand. 'Ignore him, nurse. I have this abuse day in and day out. I'm used to it.'

'Really.' Her face had turned a very fetching shade of pink.

Mike laughed out loud. 'I can see he's just about recovered. Mind you, the lengths some people go to avoid work – you're grounded now for seven days.'

'Yes, sorry, you'll have to get Kip.'

'I should think he feels like Johnson did, waiting for McCoy to retire.'

'If you expect me to feel sorry for him, forget it. He's got years in front. I haven't. And he heals a lot quicker.'

Seymour Herring had disowned his parents at an early age for their choice of name – around the time he started school and became the butt of the other kids' jokes. Progressing onward through school, a discerning child had come up with yet another name: Kipper. He had immediately settled happily for Kip, much to the disgust of his parents.

I liked the young chap, despite the fact he was the bloke who would take over my job in the not-too-distant future. He'd got the talent, the skill and the indefinable 'X' factor that Mike and, I suppose, most of the other trainers had spotted. The fact that Kip had accepted Mike's offer of a job as second jockey reflected back that Mike's stables were right up there. But I had to admit to a stern pushing down of a touch of green eye regarding Kip's age and future prospects.

But life is like a horserace: you can only go forward, never back. And life is also a moving spectacle, sometimes moving at a very fast rate, and if you can't keep up the pace, stay in the race – and nobody could in the end – someone else was going to take your place, for sure.

Unfortunately, like in all sports, you were acutely aware of time going past and your own sell-by date coming up far too fast. Not a damn thing you could do about it, except accept that the ageing was inevitable, it happened to us all and railing against it wasn't going to change a thing. To do otherwise was a waste of precious energy. A commodity that grew ever shorter as you grew older.

'I really think, Mr Grantley, that you should stop upsetting my patient, because if you don't, I'll have to ask you to leave.'

I grinned up at the nurse. 'He's not upsetting me. If our roles were reversed, I'd be having a good go at him. And he knows it.'

Muttering darkly, the nurse took herself off to care for more deserving cases that needed her.

'So.' Mike was all business now. 'Have you seen Keith yet?'

'I was on my way when plods one and two turned up. I take it you know about the policeman who was attacked outside Keith's door?'

'Common knowledge now.'

'Hmm, they seemed to find me highly suspicious.'

'Well, either that or they're jealous of you.'

'Jealous?'

'Oh, yes, mate. Look at all the villains you've sent to prison. I mean, you're putting them out of business.'

'You're a first-rate trainer, Mike, but you do talk some crap.'

'Oh, nice. And this is the man who's come to take you away from all this.' He waved an encompassing hand around the room. 'Your horseless carriage is waiting outside.'

'You're going to give me a lift back home?'

'Got it.'

'That's decent of you, Mike, thanks. The doctor told me no driving yet.'

'Well, he would, wouldn't he? So, how soon can you leave?'

'Basically, all I have to do is pick up a supply of painkillers.'

'Are you in *need* of painkillers?'

'No. But the stock cupboard needs replenishing.'

We looked at each other and smiled.

Countless times at Harlequin Cottage I had been forced to raid my stock cupboard for a painkiller in order to get to work at the stables – usually following a racing fall. But these weren't the sort of painkillers you could buy over the chemist's counter – these ones did the job.

Mike had a glance at his watch. 'Look, I'll get myself a takeout coffee and wait for you in the Range Rover. I'm parked in D bay.'

I nodded. 'Be about ten minutes with Keith, I should think that's all they'll allow.'

'Don't forget you'll have to queue for your pills. That could take some time.'

'You're so right.'

'Don't sweat. I've got all afternoon.'

He ambled off, and I went to find the nurse to clear things before going to talk to Keith.

THIRTY-THREE

'Christ, am I glad to see you.'

'I hope you won't be seeing Him just yet.' I grinned down at Keith lying in his bed, feeling smugly superior that I was actually upright.

'Why didn't you come to see me before? I told them I wanted to speak to you.'

'Well, it could have had something to do with being just around the corner in the next ward.'

'Not with you.'

'I *was* on my way until a piece of lowlife laid me out in the lift on my way to see you. I've been taking up a bed for the last thirty-six hours.'

His face was a ploughed field of furrows. '*What?*'

'Oh, yes. And he also stuck a knife in my arm, but I think that was a mistake. He was probably aiming for between my ribs, but I moved at the last moment.'

His face relaxed when he twigged I was struggling to hide a smile. 'How the hell do you do it, Harry? You know something,' he continued before I had a chance to say anything else. 'You're just not safe to be let out. I mean, you attract criminals like a muck heap attracts flies.'

'Charmingly put. However, you *do* know, don't you, your tame policeman who was sitting outside your room was also attacked a short time before I was?'

'There was some scuttling about going on, but they're a cagey lot in here. They wouldn't tell me. So, what happened?'

I filled him in on what scant information I had.

'This is because I've now come round, isn't it? And what I might remember and pass on?'

I nodded. 'That's my guess, yes.'

And I told him about the two plods who had been to see me. 'They want to know if you saw who it was that took a shot at the horsebox. Did you?'

Then I waited, didn't bother breathing, just hoping Keith was going to hand me the key. But after a couple of minutes' silence, I was forced to take a deep breath.

'No,' he said, eventually.

And for the first time since I'd met him, come to know the man as brave and honourable, I didn't believe him. There had to be a sound reason why he was lying.

He changed the subject. 'Where's Sophie?'

I looked at him steadily. 'Safe.'

'Yeah, but where is she? Is she with Rosy? Is Rosy safe?'

Seeing the beads of sweat forming on his forehead and remembering his weak state, I reassured him. 'Both safe.'

'But where?' he persisted. 'Tell me, for God's sake.'

'Better if I don't. Just in case any more lowlifes come calling.'

He stared at me and shook his head. 'I'm sorry, Harry.'

'Sorry you can't help, or sorry you're not going to tell me?'

He shrugged, and had the grace to look down, plucking at his sheet in agitation. It was obvious telling lies didn't sit easy with the man.

'So, why *did* you want to see me?'

'I need to know what's going on.'

'Horses are being drugged, that's what's happening. But perhaps you already know that.'

'How the hell should I know that? I'm not clairvoyant.'

'You wouldn't need to be if you're involved. I think you have already been approached. And if you have, then you know all about what dirty little scam is going off.'

'It's you that's fishing in dirty water. Why don't you get after the shits who *are* involved, instead of having a go at me? All I wanted to see you for was to make sure Sophie was safe.'

'Yes, I know.' I gave him a hard look. 'It's obvious you're scared stiff about her. That tells me a lot, Keith. Like, Sophie is your Achilles' heel. Did they threaten her, use her as a lever to get you to agree to this business of doping horses?'

'Look, Harry, you've no idea what it's like, having your family threatened.'

'Oh, no? Come off it, Keith. Why do you think I've been forced into chasing would-be murderers – because I wanted to?' I glared at him, angry now. 'Don't tell me I don't know how it feels to have a loved one threatened, because I damned well do.'

'You claim my girls are safe, but how do you *know*? What makes you so sure?'

'Because I personally drove them to a safe house, Keith – that's why.'

His mouth dropped open. 'You did?'

'Collected them from Dottie's.'

'But they weren't supposed to be at my mother's.'

'Hmm . . . I know that as well.'

'So.' Keith's shoulders sagged. 'How much *do* you know?'

'If I level with you, are you prepared to do the same?'

'No choice, have I? It's only because I'm so damned scared for their safety, Harry. You can see the squeeze I'm in.'

I nodded, placed a hand over his wrist where it lay on top of the bed cover. 'Course I can. But I can't do anything about removing the threat without your help.'

'Yeah,' he said reluctantly and sighed heavily. 'I can see that. OK . . . The doping is carried out by the driver in the horse-boxes, on the way to the tracks, perfectly timed and always two very similar horses being transported.'

'I've already worked that out.'

'I was approached because I'm a box driver, right?'

I nodded. 'Keep talking. If I don't understand anything, I'll stop you.'

'OK.' He blew out a gusty breath and reached for the glass of water standing on the locker. He took a long swallow. 'It's so bloody hot in here, isn't it? We're not used to it. We're outdoor men. I'll be bloody glad to get out, get home. See my dog, old Tugboat. Hope he's doing all right on his own.'

'Er, he's not on his own, Keith. He's got his own bed and at least one devoted little slave, I can assure you.' I stared hard at him. 'Do you know anywhere safer?'

'You mean . . .' A smile slowly spread across his face, smoothing out the worry lines. 'Yeah, I'd call that safe . . . real safe, thanks, Harry. I owe you.'

'You owe me nothing. Look what debt I owe you. I'll still owe you when they screw down my coffin lid. But for God's sake get on and tell me all the rest. We've only got minutes before I get thrown out. The nurse said only ten minutes when I came in. She'll be back very soon.'

The words flowed now. 'They contacted me by phone, said they'd do for Sophie if I didn't do what they told me. I couldn't see a way out, thought the only way was to try and get through the lower layers, you know, find out who was masterminding this scam. But it's a lot bigger than I'd ever guessed. The drugs aren't just being used on horses; there's cocaine's being sold to users, too. If anyone gets in the way of these lowlifes, finds stuff out like, seems they're disposed of pretty sharply.'

'Like Lenny Backhouse?'

'I reckon. Can't prove a thing, though. I've still no idea who's behind all this. And to be honest, I don't think I ever will.'

'Are individual stables being targeted?'

'No. It's just where the circumstances and details marry up.'

'So, Mike's stables aren't being specifically targeted?'

'No.'

'What about Tal Hunter's place?'

'No. I think the choice is quite random. There's no set pattern, like I said, it's just dictated by the details conforming to make it possible.'

'And the man who took a pot at us in the horsebox – who was he?'

'Dunno, but it was a four by four, black.' He mused. 'It happened too damn quick to notice much. But he did have black hair.'

'So had the man who clobbered me in the lift. But that's not much to go on. What about informing the police?'

He snorted. 'Are you joking? They can't provide round-the-clock security.'

'Well, they're doing that for you, here in the hospital.'

'And look what's happened, eh? Yes, I'm all right, but the poor old policeman copped it and now you . . .'

'So, what else have you found out?'

'They're using racing as a cover, delivering cocaine in the horseboxes.'

'And Ginnie knows who two of the top men are, doesn't she?'

He nodded wryly. 'She was in the right place at the right time, except she wasn't the right person to hear what was said.'

'Do *you* know who these two men are?'

'Businessmen, obviously – must be. There's a ton of money behind this. I reckon one of them could have been the owner of the firm Dust Chasers – that's why Ginnie is in such a state.'

'Ah, her boss, then?'

'Yep.'

'Any trainers, do you think?'

'Could be, I just don't know. One of the box drivers involved is Paul Oats.'

'Yes, I know about him. Anyone else?'

'Gary Butt's uncle, Jeff Marsden, maybe. He's the one who got Lenny involved. But they were very cute. They keep the links separate – no one knows anything that links people or places further up or down the line. That's why they're successful. The boss men can't be traced back. Lenny was taken out because I reckon he knew the names of the next players. An' he wasn't afraid of them either. God knows, he must have been the only man who wasn't.'

'And that's why he was eliminated?'

We stared at each other.

'Makes sense, doesn't it?' Keith said.

Before I could answer him, there was a tap on the door. It opened and the nurse came in.

'Time to go, Mr Radcliffe. Mr Whellan needs his rest.'

I nodded. 'Thank you for letting me in to see him.'

'Yes, thanks, nurse. He's put my mind at ease. Now I've spoken to Harry, I'll be able to rest properly, get some quality kip.'

She nodded. 'Good. Now, don't forget to pick up your painkillers on the way out, Mr Radcliffe.' And she left us to say goodbye.

'Better get off, then,' I said. 'Oh, by the way, I never asked when I arrived, how are you doing?'

He held up two fingers.

I raised both eyebrows. 'No need for that, surely.'

He snorted. 'Two days, *two days*, you silly bugger.' Then realizing he was looking at his palm, turned his hand round the right way. 'Two days, OK, then I'll be out of here.'

'Got you.'

I left the hospital with the usual feelings of relief mixed with gratitude and met up with Mike in the car park.

'Got everything?'

'Everything that's needed, yes. I take it you looked under Leo's dinner bowl, then?'

'As a reliable messenger for your whereabouts, it can't be beaten.'

'And I take it you got conned into filling it with yummies for him?'

'Dead right, what a scrounger. Now, shut up and tell me where to drive. Some of us do have work to do, you know.'

'Yes, sir.' I touched the spot where on race days I would have sported a peaked crash cap.

'So, where are we headed?'

'Home, James. And don't spare the car.'

THIRTY-FOUR

Mike dropped me off at Harlequin Cottage, said goodbye to me – hello and goodbye to Leo, who had materialized out of the ether the minute he heard the car engine – and disappeared up the lane.

It had only been a couple of days, but it seemed far, far longer. And an awful lot had gone off. The speed with which I'd applied tyre rubber to tarmac leading to the Queen's, as I'd realized only this morning, had caused me to leave my mobile phone charging up on my desk, utterly useless to me bedbound and constrained within the hospital. I fell upon the phone with relief that I could now update myself on the SP of the outside world.

Whipping through my emails, I searched for news about Keith's relatives. There were plenty of work-related ones but no personal ones – except one from Annabel. She told me that because Sir Jeffrey's health had worsened suddenly, Molly, his partner and nurse, had taken the tough decision to send him to hospital. I was very sorry to hear that. Sir Jeffrey was a grand bloke and a great mate of mine. It seemed between us we were keeping the health service very busy.

I needed to contact Annabel, see if there was anything I could do. Then I realized there was probably nothing I *could* do.

Forbidden to drive, under doctor's orders to stay home and rest, I couldn't even offer to go and visit him.

Temporarily shelving that particular drama, I lifted the landline receiver and checked any messages left on that phone. Ginnie's voice came down the line full of emotion, basically regret, that because of visiting Keith I'd been struck down myself. And she was blaming herself.

Likewise, the second recorded telephone message was a similar one from Dottie. However, there was no mention of dire happenings up in Yorkshire from either woman – for which I was considerably relieved.

But there was still a third message – this time from Eliza. She'd not heard from me since Lady Willamina's party but she was sure I'd want to know the result from the sample I'd left with her that evening.

'I don't know if it's the result you were looking for, Harry, but I can confirm that it is the same as the first sample. Anything else I can help with, let me know. Bye.'

And instantly, I was reminded of attending Lady Willamina's party. She had readily answered my question about who had attended one of her previous parties just a short while before. I'd coupled that with the scant detail Ginnie Cutler had let slip. It had been a tenuous, instinctive guess. Now, it had the makings of a promising lead. I couldn't wait to follow it up.

And I should also ring Eliza back, thank her for getting the crucial result for me.

A cavernous yawn coupled with a crushing wave of exhaustion took me unawares. And suddenly I was feeling decidedly groggy. If I didn't succumb and get some sleep, I'd find myself flat out on the floor. I'd experienced this before and knew what to expect. But there was something essential to do first. Tottering back to the kitchen, I refilled Leo's water and put a generous helping of kitty kibble in his bowl. Then, locking and bolting the kitchen door, I staggered up the stairs. Very strangely, they seemed to get far steeper with every step, and surely there were more risers, ever rising, than the last time I'd gone up to bed.

I must have made it, though, because when I came round it was after nine a.m. – twenty-odd hours later – and I was actually in bed under the covers. There seemed to be a lovely hot-water bottle near my feet. Now, even in my near-comatose state, I knew you don't get the luxury of a hot-water bottle in hospital.

Most reluctantly, I opened one eye. No hospital bed, this one, but my own at Harlequin Cottage. And, no doubt having felt my stirrings, a loud purring gave the lie that I had a hot-water bottle on my toes.

'Hiya, mate,' I croaked, mouth dust-dry as the remains of last night's fire. And it certainly felt like it was full of ash and cinders, too.

Testing out my left arm in reaching down to stroke the warm fur, I realized just how long I must have been asleep. The pain-killers, even the hospital-strength ones, had completely worn off and the knife wound to my arm was giving me some stick.

Thankfully, though, when I explored the back of my head, it confirmed the doctor's opinion that my skull was a thick one. Still a bit sore, perhaps, but basically I'd had much worse concussion in the past from coming off a horse. Happily, to add to things, I'd now regained my appetite: I was starving. How long was it since I'd last eaten? I couldn't remember.

Oh, yes, the signs were looking good. Unfortunately, I was an expert on giving myself cracks to the head, and I'd had a lot of practice in getting over them. The best treatment was sleep, lots of it. It hastened the healing. But I'd been hogging it for many hours already and any more would be sheer self-indulgence and idleness. I had to tell myself this very insistently in order to swing both legs out of bed and stand upright. And then, even more importantly – after several gallons of scalding tea – get back to work. If ever man needed anything to motivate and sustain himself, it was work.

I called Eliza first. 'You're a beauty,' I told her.

She gave a gurgle of laughter. 'Well, thank you, kind sir. You make me feel like a filly about to race.'

'No greater praise,' I assured her.

'But it's not good news, is it?'

'Well, depends which way you look at it. Using the drug ille-gally, no, it's certainly not good news. Giving me the confirmation to back up my investigations, yes, it's crucial knowledge.'

'I'm glad to have justified your trust in me.'

'Trust is lovely to have, Eliza, however, it doesn't pay the Council Tax, does it? Let me have your account soonest, OK?'

'Call it my contribution to good causes.'

'Oh, now, come on, girl . . .'

'Harry, I've just landed an extremely influential client in Lady Branshawe. I'm OK, truly.'

'Hmm . . . Can I ask a leading question, one that shouldn't ever be asked . . .?'

'My charges, yes?'

'Um, yes. Don't answer if you'd rather not.'

'I'm not giving you figures, Harry, but I'm beginning to know you a little better and I *think* most, if not *all* your questions are related to what you call your investigations. Am I right?'

I sighed heavily. 'I've been rumbled.'

A gale of laughter swept down the phone. 'So, no figures, but yes, my charges are mid-range. I feel fine being paid to heal an animal in pain. It cost me years of training. As you point out, we all have unavoidable bills to deal with. But I want to sleep deep and peacefully, and if I charged exorbitant prices, like some vets, it wouldn't happen.'

'Are you talking about local vets, maybe?'

'Now, Harry.' Her tone became professional and guarded. 'You are definitely asking a question that shouldn't be asked. And I'm declining to answer.'

'I'm chastened, and rightly so. But surely you could say if it was one of the younger generation at least, couldn't you?'

'If I affirmed that, I'd probably be hauled up for breach of human rights.'

'OK, but try stretching a point here, give me the gender.'

'In today's ridiculous world? Are you kidding?'

'Fair enough. But one last question, please – it will help, I promise. And it's not just for me, but an awful lot of other people, too.'

'I suppose so . . .' It was her turn to sigh heavily.

'Did Jim Crack proposition you?'

'I'm rightly assuming you *are* talking business, yes?'

'Oh, yes.'

'He did.'

'And did he ask your prices?'

'That's two questions. But, yes, he did.'

'And I bet he smiled, didn't he?'

'He did indeed. Do you know, Harry, if you lose your present employment, I suggest you could apply for one as an investigative journalist. You'd be a wow.'

'Thank you, very much. May I take you out for dinner?'

'Harry, I'd love to have dinner with you, but you've forgotten something.'

'I have?'

'Hmm, a certain person who has your back informed me you met with an undesirable and the result was concussion, a hospital stay and now you're under house arrest – no driving allowed. Is that correct?'

'Absolutely. And I suppose the big mouth who told you was Mike Grantley, yes?'

'No less. But he insisted it was only as essential back-up because of lovely Leo and his possible needs.'

'Of course. I've just realized what a loyal band of followers I have around me.'

'I'm sorry you're injured, Harry. If you need any help, ask me.'

Far off, a doorbell rang at her end. 'Oh, that'll be Alfie.'

'Alfie?'

'Hmm, Alfie Smith, my work experience student. He's at vet training college. I have to go. Now don't forget, if you need any help, call me.'

'Yes. And thanks again. Can we have a different dinner date? When I'm mobile again?'

'You bet.'

I hung up the landline and then immediately began ringing Dottie Whellan.

'So, how're you doing, Harry? And did you manage to see Keith at the hospital?'

'I did, Dottie. And thanks, yes, I'm getting on fine. Keith would send his love if he knew I was speaking to you, so take that as read. What he did say, and this was to his nurse, was that now he'd spoken to me, he would be able to rest easy and get some decent kip. I hope that reassures you a bit.'

'Oh, it does. He trusts you, you see, Harry. Well, we all do.'

My heart dropped – a very long way. How the hell was I going to face them all if it went bottom up?

'I can only do my best, Dottie.'

'Well, we're all doing fine at the moment. It's yourself that you
need to look out for, make sure you get plenty of sleep, it's the
best thing.'

'Hmm, I know that. And believe me, I'm rivalling Rip Van
Winkle in the sleep stakes.'

She laughed. 'Keep on doin' that. Thanks for checking on Keith
for me. Bye.'

Her phone call left me feeling worse than I'd done before
speaking to her. If trust in me was the shared opinion of the others
involved in this powder keg, I'd better get my act going, never
mind going to sleep.

And as far as I could see, there was one course open that might
yield a result. But it meant I had to involve Ginnie. She held the
key to breaking this vile network. I felt sick at the thought of what
might result but I needed a breakthrough – any sort of breakthrough
right now. There was so little in the way of proof and even fewer
clues or leads to follow up on. Except the information only Ginnie
knew. And a lot of people had placed their trust in me, at least
six at the final count, could be more, all hanging on to the
slim hope that I could pull off a result. So, I had to do it – and
God help us all.

I reached for the telephone receiver, dialled her number. It rang
half-a-dozen times and I was about to replace it when the call was
answered.

'Who is it?' The voice was barely louder than a whisper, full
of anxiety and suspicion.

'Ginnie, it's me, I'm home.'

'I did know. Like, yesterday.'

Her words rocked me. No one knew, except Mike – and I was
sure he hadn't said anything – and then, of course, the hospital
staff. But there again, they were extremely tight-lipped. They
wouldn't have divulged any information. 'You knew?'

'Yes.'

'How?'

'*They* told me, said you'd left hospital yesterday.'

I took in a sharp breath. '*Who* told you?'

'Don't know. I don't know their names. But I recognized the
voice. It was that bloody swine who stubbed his fag out on me
arm.'

THIRTY-FIVE

Ginnie's words took my breath away. Whoever was behind this, it seemed they had every move taped and were using the same lowlifes to carry out their vile intimidation.

And it was also very disquieting to think my every move was being observed. That also told me something.

'What else did he say?'

'Nothing else, just told me you were being sent home. Oh, and to remind you what will happen if you don't drop it . . .'

Even as she told me, I could hear the echo in her voice craving reassurance. But I couldn't do that. Rosy and Sophie would be isolated up in Yorkshire, unable to get back home, if I ceased my investigations.

'Ginnie, we both know this man has to be stopped, the man behind all the threats and drug pushing. I'm not about to give you a false promise, OK? But what I want you to do, when you put the phone down, is to dial 1471 and make a note of the number that rang you. Most likely it will be caller withheld, but it's worth a try. We're on the same side here, Ginnie, and I *need* your help. You're the one person who saw that evil bastard . . .' I broke off.

Ginnie had begun to sob. It was heart-breaking to hear and not be able to comfort her at all. Steeling myself, I carried on. 'Promise me you'll check your phone. You can do that safely.'

She gave a shuddering sigh. 'Yes,' she quavered.

'Good woman. Now when you've done that I want you to make a cup of tea, then sit by the phone until I ring you back; it shouldn't take too long. I will definitely get back to you. Of course, if you don't want to help stop this nightmare, well, that's your choice. But I feel with your help, I *can* nail this man. I'm putting the phone down now, but I'll speak to you again in a few minutes, OK?'

'Yes.' And she put the receiver down at her end.

I could only pray she would find the nerve to help. But I had to do some spadework now and time was short.

I fired up my laptop and flipped through some racing websites. I was looking for coverage from different stables showing their actual stable yards and their racecourse wins. Making a note of stables that met my criteria, I then struck lucky because the one I was specifically interested in showed me exactly what I needed. Maybe the gods were smiling on me, because at last something was paying off.

However, the one thing I'd been banking on following through on had come to a juddering full stop. It was more than just a nuisance, it was a crucial part of what I had in mind. But looking at it sensibly, it was after all simply a logistical hiccup. There would be some way around it, had to be.

I grabbed the phone again and dialled Annabel's number. Then prayed she wouldn't be tied up with clients. She wasn't.

'Hello?' Her voice sounded concerned.

'It's me.'

'Harry, darling.' There was a smile in her voice now. 'I'm so sorry to have passed on bad news, but it's wonderful to hear from you.'

'Yes, it's a sod about Sir Jeffrey. I'm really sorry. And the trouble is, I'm not able to do anything to help.'

'Hmm. You're grounded at home now, yes?'

'That's right.'

'I phoned Mike this morning and got the news you're back from hospital, so that had to be good.'

'Well, it is – and it isn't. I was actually going to ask for *your help*, ironically, because I'm forbidden to drive.'

'You're stuck for something, is that it?'

'Yes, yes, I definitely am.'

'Well, when Molly telephoned and told me about Sir Jeffrey, I cancelled my client list today. Apart from leaving myself free to help, if I'm needed, I wouldn't have been able to give my fullest attention to my clients. And they deserve that; they're paying for it.'

'I need your help, Annabel.'

'Ask, Harry.'

I filled her in on what I hoped would happen.

'Of course I'll do it. The only question is will Ginnie agree?'

* * *

She did, eventually. We all met up at Taylors at Southwell. A garden centre, high class, genteel, complete with tearooms, peacocks and views over extensive lakes upon which swans glided regally. A beautiful place, established over sixty years ago and one that did not attract the coarser, rougher elements of society. There was nothing here for the likes of Ginnie's lowlife attackers. She should feel completely safe. And I'd taken precautions to make it so.

The taxi I'd ordered collected me from home and dropped me off at Mike's stables. Whereupon Pen, bless her, had squeezed her precious bump behind the wheel of her Audi and driven me to Southwell, passing the magnificent cathedral before parking up at Taylors. Anyone keeping tabs on Harlequin Cottage and on my movements would have drawn the logical conclusion that I'd simply obeyed rules regarding not driving anywhere myself, booked a taxi and been dropped off at the stables.

I'd then discreetly hidden inside the tack room and exited by its rear door, totally out of sight of the house and stable yard. Covered by a tartan travelling rug, I'd travelled most of the way lying flat out along the Audi's rear seat.

Annabel, meanwhile, had collected Ginnie from the rear car park of the pub in Redmile and driven them both to Southwell. I couldn't have done it without the two women's help regarding the driving. The taxi driver I discounted – he was just doing his job. Now, everything depended on Ginnie.

We were all seated at the last table on the eastern side, facing the lakes, and were served excellent coffee and a selection of freshly made cakes. Ginnie now seemed relaxed and more cheerful. She had chosen a raspberry roulade which she demolished with obvious enjoyment. I knew coming here, even in these circumstances, would be a real treat. Money was tight for her. She was on the minimum wage and had to count every penny. But I appreciated what she was doing for me and was pleased to give her a little luxury.

I waited until we'd sampled the most agreeable food and were at the refill of coffee stage before reaching down by the side of my chair. Glancing swiftly around, I saw that the nearest people were a couple of elderly ladies engrossed in discussing a knitting pattern laid out before them on the table, before putting my laptop on our table in front of us and opening it up.

'What I would like you to do, Ginnie, is take a look at these pictures of some local stables and members of their staff. They're all within a twenty-mile radius. It seems to me this is a fairly local set-up, could be wrong, but the speed things happen, it seems likely.'

She nodded. 'What am I looking for?'

'Anything that rings a bell. I'm not going to prompt you, OK?'

'Yes.'

'Here we go, then.'

I brought up the first image which was of Barbara Maguire's stables – and very impressive they were, too – plus a smiling line-up of her stable staff. The lads were all beaming at the camera on the occasion when one of their horses had won. I had no qualms whatsoever about Barbara's set-up and knew Ginnie would find nothing wrong. It was the reason I'd chosen that one to show her first.

Ginnie scrutinized the picture, then shook her head. 'Nothing, sorry.'

'That's OK. Take a look at some more.' I wasn't worried about the nil result. I knew for certain Barbara's staff were above suspicion. They were the most loyal bunch of lads I'd ever known. Although Barbara was a strong woman and an exacting boss, she was above all else fair. If any of them were in trouble, they knew that they could go to Barbara and they'd be helped. And they all held her in the greatest regard as a superb trainer. No, I hadn't expected Ginnie to react and I wasn't at all disappointed, rather it reinforced my hopes of a definite conclusion in the end.

I continued to show her several more images, including some of Tal Hunter's stables, which I'd debated about, but putting in a couple that I knew were above suspicion would assist me to see Ginnie's reaction, if any, when – if – she came to the right one. But none of these drew any recollection of anything. Then I clicked on the one stable that I was really interested in. If this, too, elicited no reaction, I'd be right back at the start with hardly any other leads to follow.

The picture, again of a stables and yard with horses looking over half-doors, appeared on the screen. Ginnie shook her head, grimacing wryly. Then a further picture appeared that was obviously a celebration of a recent win by one of the horses. It showed a gathering of the staff. They were all having a great time, joshing each other, holding aloft beer glasses, wearing wide grins . . .

'That's him!' Ginnie's cry brought us all to rapt attention. 'Look, look . . .' She pointed at one of the men. 'That's the swine who burned me.'

I felt a swift surge of elation. My calculated gamble had paid off. The stables were owned by the man I had down as the prime suspect. The man she was pointing to was one of his stable staff.

'And that one, the man next to him, he was the one who was helping him. He held my arms whilst that devil burned me. And he was the driver of their car, too.'

The picture panned out wider, showing the house and part of the grounds including the gravelled car park. 'And look there.' Ginnie pointed again in agitation. 'Do you see that car? It's the same one he came to my cottage in. It was a black four by four.'

'Wait a minute, Ginnie. How can you be sure? There are a lot of those vehicles on the roads.'

'Oh, I'm sure, Harry.' She gave a determined snort. 'Oh yes, I'd know him – and his car – because when he left after stubbing out his fag on me arm, I peeped through the curtains. I wanted to make sure those bastards had definitely gone and I made a note of the vehicle's number plate as they drove away. It's not something I'll forget, let me tell you. And that car.' She stabbed at the screen with a rigid index finger. 'That car's got the same number plate.' She flung herself back in her chair in satisfaction. 'Is that all right, Harry, have I helped you?'

'Helped, Ginnie?' I smiled at her. 'You've absolutely clinched it.'

In high spirits now, we departed from Taylors, not forgetting to leave a sizeable tip for our waitress, and headed home in our different vehicles. Annabel had already decided she was taking Ginnie back to Melton to stay with her until things calmed down. Pen, meanwhile, was doing the honours and driving me.

The smile stayed on my face all the way back to Mike's stables. Not only had Ginnie confirmed my suspicions, she'd given me a real bonus. And it was completely unexpected. With the identification of the car they had used on that occasion, it was a very good chance it was the same vehicle from which those bastards had taken a pot shot at the horsebox.

I didn't know if Keith would recognize the number or not – it was doubtful after being shot – but I was a hundred per cent sure in my own mind that it was the same one.

Talk about buy one get one free. I was most definitely in Ginnie's debt.

THIRTY-SIX

'Dead lucky. That's what you are, mate, dead lucky. I said as much to Rantby when he wished you a speedy return from hospital.' Across the kitchen table, Mike shook his head at me. 'Wish I'd got half your luck. I mean, you've got everybody helping you – I even loaned you my partner as personal taxi driver.'

I nodded. 'She's a woman and a half.'

Pen giggled and patted her bump. 'I'd certainly say so.'

I looked at the pair of them, friends through good and bad times, and knew how lucky I *really* was. 'Can I impose again?'

'You need to get home, Harry, of course.' Pen began heaving herself up.

But Mike stepped in. 'Not so fast, woman. It's my turn to drive.'

'You call my rate of progress fast?'

He held up his hand, palm down, in front of her. 'Now sit.' It was said sternly.

Sunny, the yellow Labrador, who had at that moment finished lapping water from her bowl, immediately obliged. Pen was convulsed with laughter and I leaned forward quickly and gave her a kiss on the cheek.

'I'm going, while the going's good. Don't want your man tipping me out as we go over the Smite on the way home.'

'That's tempting,' Mike said darkly.

However, by the time he dropped me off at Harlequin Cottage, he was all concern. 'You're supposed to be taking things easy, sleeping it off.'

'Yes, sir.'

'I mean it,' he stressed. 'You've made a load of progress today, more than you'd hoped for. Take a pull, eh? Get some sleep. That's

what you're supposed to be doing, not gadding about the countryside. Look, everybody's safe for the moment, grab some kip.'

'I hear you. And thanks, Mike. It's been a good team effort
today, and I'm very grateful.'

'Well, go and lie down for a bit now. Give that famous intuition
a chance to work.'

'Now, that is very good advice – and I intend to do just that.'

I raised a hand as he engaged first and pointed the vehicle
between the gate posts. Then I went into the cottage, made sure
the door was locked and bolted against any marauders, took a
couple of extra cushions through to the conservatory and arranged
them for maximum comfort on the sofa. A pen and notebook
followed and I plumped down, feet up.

I read through all my notes over the last couple of weeks then
added today's findings. The picture it showed me was illuminating.
But there were some gaps in the jigsaw. Thoughts, assumptions,
that needed confirming and turning into facts.

Oh, yes, I knew beyond doubt the name of one of the main players,
but there was someone else, a shadow at the side. I wrestled with
the facts as I knew them, the ones I'd found out plus the ones I was
guessing at right now. But nothing gelled. I was starting to feel tired
and had the makings of a good headache threatening. I pushed the
notebook to one side. Continuing to hassle at the problem would get
me nowhere right now. Mike was right. I needed some kip.

It was the insistent ringing of the landline that awoke me. Peering
blearily at my watch, I realized I'd lost three hours somewhere. I
heaved myself up and went through to the kitchen.

'I hope I didn't wake you, darling.' It was Annabel.

'No, course you didn't,' I lied. 'It's lovely to hear you.'

And it was. I realized as I shoved the kettle on to the hotplate
my head was clear now and the headache had departed, plus I was
feeling much better.

'How are things over at your end?'

'Fine.'

'And your house guest, they're doing OK?'

'Oh, yes. It was the right thing to do, Harry. I phoned the boss
at Dust Chasers and cleared it with him, said the person had gone
down with a stomach bug and was in bed.'

'Well done, you. The person is in need of a good bit of TLC at the moment.'

'That's what I thought.'

'And you gave the said person some spiritual healing, for a good guess.'

'True, but it calmed them down beautifully and, of course, it will speed up the healing.'

We didn't mention names or specifics, even though we were speaking on the landline – it was safer not to. Safety was the key word for the whole sorry business. We couldn't afford any slip-ups.

'Do you think you could ask them a couple of questions for me? I forgot earlier today.'

'Of course, fire away.'

'Ask if when they were working and overheard what they didn't want to hear, was that in the three-toilet cloakroom tiled in amber tiles?'

'Cryptic,' she murmured. 'And the second thing?'

'Do they know anything about a young chap called Alfie Smith?'

'OK, I'll ask and get back to you.'

I replaced the receiver and made a mug of tea. Annabel had not only mentioned the firm Ginnie worked for but had named the boss man of the firm she'd spoken with. It gave me a boost to know I was on the right track.

Before I had a chance to finish drinking the tea, Annabel called back.

'The answer to your first question is yes. And to the second, no.'

'Thanks, Annabel. Take care of both of you.'

I mulled the answer over. The affirming one confirmed my view of who one of the main players was – it fitted very neatly into the jigsaw and was doubly confirmed by the answer Lady Branshawe had given me – there was absolutely no doubt.

But that left me floundering as to who Alfie Smith was and just where he fitted in. Eliza's name popped into my thoughts. She would know – well, it was more than a probability. He was at her surgery on work experience today. I downed the rest of my tea and lifted the telephone receiver.

'Hello, Eliza. How're things? OK?'

'A little busy at the moment, Harry, could we speak later?'

'Of course. Just one quick question. Do you know anything about Alfie Smith's background? Or is it tricky to answer with him being there?'

'Not tricky. He's out in the recovery room at the moment. I'm doing this as a returned favour to a friend of mine who trained at the same time as I did. Alfie is her much older sister's son. He's been a couple of times before – I hope today might be the last time. Personally, he's a pain. I'm probably counting the paperclips when he's gone home.'

'Could you tell me his mother's name, anything at all really that you know about him?'

'He's Audrey Smith's son. He's the result of an ill-judged fling that was over before it started when she was little more than a kid herself.'

'And the father?'

She told me and my eyebrows went up so fast I'd lay money on them joining my hairline.

'Didn't have anything to do with the lad until a year or so ago. He was married, of course, when Audrey got herself knocked up, but his wife, Jessy, died of cancer about eighteen months ago. There were no children from his marriage.'

'But now, he's regretting ditching Alfie?'

'Something like that. The lad's pretty mixed up. Thought he wanted to be a jockey when he left school. Actually he went to work for Barbara Maguire, the trainer, for a bit. You know her?'

'Indeed I do.'

'Well, I don't think things worked out too well whilst he was there. She sacked him. Could be that his father is bank-rolling him, because it was after that he decided to go in for training to be an equine vet. Have to say, he is mad keen on horses. Oh, yes, and keen on having a bet, too.'

'I'm very obliged for the information, Eliza. You've been a big help. I'll let you get back to work, and thanks again. I haven't forgotten about taking you out to dinner – in fact, make that *two* dinners . . . bye.'

I put the receiver down and fist-pumped the air.

Yet another piece of jigsaw slid gently into place. The picture was shaping up nicely. Then, returning to the conservatory, I sat on the sofa, opened up the laptop and did some in-depth checking on Alfie's father. What I needed was proof.

The nap I'd taken – some nap, all of three hours – had been just what the doctor ordered, literally. My head was clear, my brain working overtime now. I needed it to. A little girl's safety was at stake. And although I'd thought taking her up to Yorkshire was the best place, I was beginning to doubt it.

Obviously, there was a mole of some sort in the hospital. The fact that my being sent home was known to the opposition, practically before I knew, suggested the dark-haired man in a white coat, while possibly being an employee at the Queen's, was also working for the other side.

And that meant Keith himself wasn't safe. If they realized he knew where his daughter was being hidden, they'd try and work on him to tell them. I winced. What they might stoop to doing in order to make him talk wasn't pleasant to contemplate. Well, if I couldn't drive over to see him, check he was properly protected by the policeman – indeed level with the policeman about the possible threat from a member of the staff – I could at least telephone. I made the call from the kitchen again, the only safe thing to do. Mobiles left themselves wide open to abuse. But the ward sister assured me she would personally see that there were always two members of staff attending Keith at the same time, never just one. Furthermore, she said, taking firm charge, she would instruct the policeman on guard outside his door that no single member of staff was to be allowed in – full stop.

I put the phone down feeling like I'd just been given a deep massage pummelling. She was a forceful woman. But she had reassured me about Keith's safety. I could now focus on directing the fire to myself. I'd known for some time that it was the only way to play this. No more letting the likes of Ginnie and Keith take any more flack. The drag, of course, was I couldn't drive. If I did, and anything happened – say, I had an accident – it would be disastrous.

I counted back the days since I'd been attacked. It was more than I thought. There had been long periods when I'd been completely out and time had gone past. Tomorrow would be about five days – ample time to have recovered in my book. Maybe not in the hospital's opinion, but they were going by laid-down rules

they had to follow – myself, I'd had a lot of unwanted experience
in getting concussed, some of it pretty grim, and this time it was
nowhere near as bad an injury as getting kicked in the head by a
horse galloping in excess of thirty miles an hour.

And I knew my own body very well. So I'd see what occurred
between now and tomorrow and, if necessary, I knew I could drive
safely with all memory and reactions fully working.

Closing the laptop, I stood up and stretched. Taking it easy
didn't come easy. I was used to being active most of the time. But
since I wasn't expecting anybody, I could use the time for more
sleep, hellishly boring, but sensible.

And then the horseshoe door knocker on the back door was
banged twice in quick succession.

THIRTY-SEVEN

Who was it? I had no idea. But I was about to find out.
Going through to the kitchen, I edged sideways
along the wall and took a slanted view out of the
window. The relief had my shoulders dropping and a smile finding
its way to my face. I went to the door, removed the safety chain,
drew back the bolt and unlocked it. My actions told me just how
dangerous I considered the present situation. The opposition knew
that the threats against Sophie had not stopped my investigation
and anything could be expected to kick off.

'Come on in,' I invited. 'I'm glad it's you, and not some
drug-crazed boss man.'

'Hmm, as a welcome, it's a bit back-handed, I must say. And
I don't think the boss man would be taking the drugs – he'd have
more sense.' Eliza held out a metal container. 'Is your Rayburn
operating? I anticipated it would be.'

'Oh, yes.'

'Then I'll just shove this in to heat up a bit more and we'll eat.
Is that all right?' As she spoke, Eliza opened the lid and a delicious smell of onions and herbs wafted out into the room.

'Yes, I know you promised me a dinner – or two – but you've

had several days of hospital food. Try my version of succotash. You must be starving.'

I stared at the manna from heaven she was holding and my stomach growled.

She heard. 'Thought so, you're starving. Go and sit down, get comfortable. I'll make us a drink while the meal's warming up.' She was taking charge.

For once, I was delighted to take it easy and be waited on. It was a novel experience. I took myself off to the conservatory and languished happily on the sofa. Eliza joined me a few minutes later, pushing a mug of tea into my hand. Arranging herself comfortably in the armchair opposite, she kicked off her shoes as though she were at home, closed her eyes and sipped her drink appreciatively.

'Hmm, I was in need of that. It's been a long, long day,' she murmured, circling her feet and wriggling her toes.

I took a long pull from my own mug. 'This is a very good idea, of course, but what made you think of coming over?'

'Let's face it, Harry.' She continued circling and wriggling. 'You're stuck, so no chance of dinner out tonight. But I thought you must be ready for a decent meal by now. I know I am.'

'Thank you,' I said, humbly. 'You're a lifesaver.'

'That's my line of business.' She opened her eyes. 'And it might even have included my own life this afternoon.'

I gulped more than I meant to of my tea. 'How come?'

'That little squirt, Alfie. I only caught him hunkered down about to light up a smoke in the recovery room. Of necessity, there's a lot of bedding in there, including some inflammable stuff – shavings, sawdust and hay . . . Only takes one careless action and . . . well . . . I needn't spell it out.'

'You certainly don't.' It was a golden rule in stables: no smoking. The dangers were all too obvious – flames out of control equalled terrified – or worse, dead – horses.

'Anyway.' She stood up, taking my empty mug from my hand. 'I took the lighter from him and told him to bugger off home.'

'Good for you.'

'Don't get up.' She held out her hand. 'I'll bring the chow through on a tray, keep it cosy.'

I inclined my head in agreement. She was obviously in a

hectoring mood, but I was happy to go along with her. To have a meal cooked for me at home was a very rare treat.

She was back within minutes and we ate together. The food was delicious.

'Not only a life saver, but a damn good cook,' I said, and set my tray down.

'Hmm, that wasn't a bad effort, must admit.' Eliza followed my example and put her tray down on the floor. She dipped into her handbag for a tissue. As she drew it out, something heavy fell on to the rug at her feet. 'Oh . . .' She retrieved the object. 'Here.' She held it out. 'This is what I confiscated.'

I took the cigarette lighter from her and inspected it. It had to be the most expensive one I'd come across. Very heavy, solid gold, engraved on one side with what appeared to be an image of Everest, or some other mountain. I turned it over. There were three letters inscribed, close together. The age of the lighter was uncertain, old for sure. The letters were somewhat blurred, edges softened by much use. But one thing was certain. This lighter had cost far more than Alfie boy could have afforded. As a student, he wasn't earning anything; he was also in hock for the university fees.

'You said this lad was light-fingered – I'd say he's nicked this. It's way out of his league. Plus, it's old . . . classy, not something the younger generation tend to go for.'

'Hmm . . .' Eliza nodded thoughtfully. 'I'd say it's owned by the person who has those initials.' She pointed to the three letters.

I looked at them: POR. 'Who do we know that has those three?'

She shook her head, lips pursed. 'Don't know. Can't think of anyone.'

'Well, discount the O in the middle, obviously that's the middle name. That leaves PR.'

'Only one person I can think of – Perry Rantby, the vet.'

'Yes, you're right, could well be. I think it's certainly a man's lighter, very masculine. I'll check on what his middle name is.' I moved over to where my laptop sat on the coffee table and switched it on.

Eliza was shaking her head. 'I don't think it's O. Way back his sister Claire was friends with my aunt. I'm pretty sure his middle initial is I, for Iain, after his maternal grandfather. I do know his mother came from Scotland.'

While she was trawling her memory, I was trawling the internet. 'D'you know, you're dead right. It is Iain. So, presumably this isn't his lighter.'

'So annoying though. I'm like you, dead sure that Alfie isn't the rightful owner. However, I'll have to give it back to him. If I don't that makes *me* a thief.'

'Unfortunately, yes. All the same it's very odd, having that image of a mountain on the other side. What does that represent, I wonder?'

'No idea, really. However, thinking back to when I was a teenager, my aunt told us a very sad story about Rantby's wife. She died in childbirth. I don't think she was very strong. Apparently, according to my aunt, she referred to her husband as her rock. Carried on the tradition, it seems, because her own mother called her husband the same. Do you think that could have anything to do with the engraving on the reverse of the lighter?'

'No idea. But in any case, the initials don't match. His middle name is definitely Iain.'

'Oh yes, of course, what a bummer.'

'I did know Rantby was a widower. But I've never heard that before, about his wife. What happened to the baby?'

'It died, too.'

'Poor bloke.'

'Hmm . . . afterwards, when things were being sorted following the funeral, he gave my aunt a whole pile of knitting patterns, including ones for baby clothes. Said he knew his wife would like her to have them – she was pregnant herself at the time, you see. And they had been part of a knitting circle. Funny what you remember years after, isn't it?'

'Yes. Trouble is, I'm afraid it's the more negative things that come floating up. Well, we've done our best to try and find out who the lighter really belongs to, and since neither of us know of anyone with the initials POR, it's a dead end. So, you're quite right, you'll just have to give it back to Alfie. No choice really.'

She slid the lighter back inside her handbag. 'He's in the surgery again tomorrow, last day, thank God. I'll make sure he gets it. I'll also ask him point-blank if he's nicked it – and where from. I've more than given value for the favour from my friend. We're definitely even now. I certainly don't want him back.'

*   *   *

Eliza stayed for another hour then, still in her role of dictator, instructed me to have an early night and log up more sleep.

'Are you saying that as a friend, or perhaps in your complementary medical opinion?'

'The latter. But right now I'm away . . . look after yourself.'

I replaced the chain, the bolt and relocked the door behind her. She was right, of course; there was a sudden need within me to stretch out and sleep. But before I gave in and flaked out, I needed to be sure there would be no unwanted guests gaining entry tonight.

The need to drop off had caught me unawares. I'd thought the amount of sleep I'd had was enough, but Eliza had picked up on it through her medical training, albeit not in treating humans. I'd already ear-marked tomorrow as showdown time and it dented my confidence to find I still wasn't fully fit. And I needed to be. 'You're getting old, Harry,' I chided myself, 'that's what it is.' But I obediently went upstairs to bed. Somehow, sleep was always better in your own bed than on a sofa.

I slept undisturbed until the arrival of Leo the next morning. Obviously, he'd made use of the conservatory roof before achieving the height of my windowsill. Sliding through the partially opened sash window, he'd jumped across the intervening few feet, landing on my bed.

Bellowing a greeting, he proceeded to rub his whiskery face up and down my chin. When Annabel had lived with me, my awakening had often been preceded by soft kisses, but I accepted Leo's greeting and was pleased to see him.

Downstairs in the kitchen, we ate breakfast together after which he climbed into his basket on top of the worktop, hung a 'Do not disturb' notice and signed off until further notice. I, in turn, took myself through to the conservatory and set to work on the laptop.

Running through all the bits of information Eliza had given me the previous evening, I attempted to slot them into the overall pattern I was creating. But I'd barely spent an hour on it when the landline rang. Knowing Leo was going to be in a temper at being woken up, I hastened through to kill the ring. Snatching it up, I was surprised to hear Eliza's voice.

'Hi, Harry. I have news.'

'Will I like it?'

'Seems we misjudged Alfie. Well, I certainly did. He didn't nick that lighter.'

'Oh. You believe him?'

'I do. Apparently, he was sent on an errand to Nottingham early in the morning, the day before yesterday. I think he was going to say he was sent to the hospital but changed it to hostel – I didn't believe that bit. He wasn't expecting to go and hadn't any matches with him. He had ciggies but nothing to light them. He cribbed and asked his dad for some, but he doesn't smoke. Alfie said he wasn't going all the way to Lenton without a smoke and his Dad told him to borrow the lighter from his partner who was there with them at the time.'

'Does he mean as in wife or a business partner?'

'Oh, I'm sure it was a businessman. Alfie seemed scared stiff of him. When I asked for his name he refused to say. Just said he must have the lighter back tonight because the man was going to be at his dad's place this evening. Then he seemed to realize he'd said too much and clammed up. I think he was telling the truth about handing it back tonight. Anyway, have to get back to work, earn the pennies. Just thought you ought to know. Bye.'

'Whoa, just a second, before you go, Eliza. Will Alfie be going to his father's straight from work?'

'Sorry, Harry, I've no idea. But I suppose it depends on where he lives, doesn't it? Bye.'

It didn't really matter where Alfie's father lived because her words had given me my next lead. I intended to follow it up, literally. Yes, I was breaking hospital rules, but then there were lives at stake here. And I was going to be lying low in my car in one of the lanes near the surgery tonight, monitoring Alfie when he left. Whatever vehicle he was using I was going to follow it right to the point where he stopped, whether it was to his father's place or not. But I had a gut feeling that *was* where he was going. I smiled with satisfaction – I already knew where the venue was.

And it would lead me straight into the lion's den.

I replaced the receiver. Yet again, it was an air-punching moment. I was quite sure she was right in her assumption that Alfie had been going to say hospital – the Queen's, it had to be – because he'd mentioned Lenton, which was the area close to the hospital. He could easily be the go-between, passing on the information about my movements gleaned from the lowlife who'd clobbered me in the lift. I was no closer to knowing who that was, but if Alfie knew, I was sure at some point I could persuade him to part with the man's name.

I referred to my notes earlier this morning and noted something Eliza had just told me. It married up with an idea I'd had. I couldn't wait for the evening to come.

I spent the rest of the day looking stuff up on the internet. The one thing it was really good for was checking facts – and now I had a few facts to check and it was proving very helpful indeed.

The shadowy figure was no longer simply a shadow – he was three-dimensional.

THIRTY-EIGHT

D usk had fallen early. What remained of daylight was now obscured by ominously dark purple storm clouds banking up from the west. It would be a thoroughly wet, dirty night for sure. And it suited my purpose admirably. But it wasn't time yet to start out.

Whatever the weather, Alfie's knocking-off time would depend on Eliza. I could have pressed her further, asked what time he might be leaving, but she was a sharp woman and could have guessed at what I had in mind. And I didn't want her anywhere near the action tonight. Because there *was* going to be action – how dangerous or violent could only be guessed at. This time, God help me, I didn't want any of the innocent ones getting hurt. It was probably odds-on that I would be, but like racing falls, injuries went with the territory.

Whilst I waited impatiently for the moment I could go into action I was still marvelling at the person my industrious delving on the internet had uncovered. And I even knew the make and registration number of his vehicle. And it wasn't a black four by four.

But, like so often in the past, it had come down to this because of family. Annabel had once said to me, 'It's all about families, isn't it, Harry?' And, yes, I told her, it was. Blood wasn't just thicker than water; it formed a powerful bond. You had a job getting by without them, but conversely, sometimes you had an even more difficult time dealing with them.

I sat and watched the meagre afternoon light leach away before the encroaching onset of evening. There was nothing more I needed to check on the laptop – it had done a wonderful job for me. I didn't need any more proof to convince me who was behind all this. But I knew the police would want more, a lot more, and short of catching the lowlifes in action, there was nothing more I could do – except stick my own head in the noose and bring it on.

I felt the flutter of nerves in my stomach. I'd only just come out of the Queen's; I was not keen to have a further head injury. But it was extremely likely, after tonight's escapade, I'd be back in there, either in a bed or in their morgue. Then I slammed the nerves down, hard. There was a little girl up in Yorkshire waiting to see her daddy. And her daddy was still in the Queen's. He'd taken a bullet probably meant for me.

I walked into the kitchen and picked up the telephone receiver. Mike hadn't left for evening stables yet and he answered. 'I'm setting off now, Mike—'

'*What?*' he roared. 'Did I hear you correctly?'

'Listen, just listen, OK? It's all about to kick off, and I'm driving the fire on purpose.' Before he could chip in and object, I carried on. 'I'm not sure how this will end—'

'Like most *bloody* times before,' he snarled, 'with you in hospital.'

'Yes, I think there's a fair chance of that.'

I could hear him snorting down the phone but ploughed on. I told him where I was going. And because I was damn sure there was going to be trouble, I gave him an instruction to carry out if I'd not rung back by a certain time. 'Safer this way, Mike. By the time you'd sussed out there was a problem and looked under Leo's bowl, it would be too late.'

And I knew he couldn't argue with that.

'Let me come with you, for God's sake.'

'No,' I said flatly, 'you stay where you are and do as I've asked. I'm relying on you to do that. Oh, and by the way, I know who the two ring leaders are now.'

'Are you going to let me in on who they are?'

So I told him.

Then, putting down the phone, I picked up my car keys.

It wasn't far to Eliza's surgery. I took a slow drive past, noted the lights were still on and two or three cars parked up on the small strip of concrete, before continuing on down the lane. At the first junction, I took a right turn and meandered along to the next crossroads. Pulling off the tarmac, I cut the engine and waited. Obviously Alfie was still hard at it. I checked the time. It was coming up to ten minutes to the hour. It seemed likely he'd finish then.

Counting off the minutes that seemed to stretch for hours, I retraced my way back towards Eliza's. Before I reached the surgery, I could see a wide blaze of light spill out across the concrete as the surgery door was swung open. A figure came out. Seconds later, an old beat-up Subaru came scorching off the concrete and was floored down the lane.

I was about to follow when, in my rear view, I spotted a vehicle that had just come round the bend. And I could also make out the registration number. It wasn't a black four by four, but it was the one that belonged to the shadow. Well, he had been a shadow, but now he was in my sights. Literally. Mr 3-D was either keeping tabs on me or he was following Alfie. Without waiting to find out, I spun the Mazda's wheel and took a sharp left. Hopefully he hadn't recognized my car, assuming it wasn't me in his sights.

I didn't need to know which way Alfie was going. I'd already worked that out. And if Mr 3-D was heading for the same place, and there again it looked a sure bet, it couldn't have worked out better. The whole corrupt gang would be together.

Now, all that was needed to deliver some concrete, undeniable evidence was for the horsebox coming back from Southwell Races to turn up. I was really taking one hell of a gamble here but, fingers crossed, they would be complete with a consignment of cocaine. But like skinning a cat, there was more than one way of doing this.

All I needed to do was keep my own skin intact while it all played out.

I took the scenic route. I needed to ensure the main players were all in place before I rolled up. I paused at the entrance and read the signboard 'Tralee Racing Stables'. I nodded. Yes, most appropriate, since that was where O'Brady came from. These were his stables – and Alfie was his illegitimate son. It was also where Pat had been born. His throw-away phrase – 'soap gets things clean' – was an oblique reference to the dirtiness of O'Brady and that I would find a clue somewhere there was soap. And in our business, that most likely meant saddle soap.

I drove some way further on past the entrance gates and parked on the grass verge of the lane, as close to the hedge as possible. Since there were no streetlights out here in the middle of nowhere, and no other houses in the vicinity, it was unlikely to be noticed.

I locked the car and walked quickly back to the stables.

The meeting had been orchestrated to perfection. The stable yard was quiet. The lads had obviously all finished working at evening stables and had disappeared – down the nearest pub, for a good guess. All the stable half-doors were closed against the coming storm and the coldness of the night. Inside I knew the horses would be contentedly pulling at hay-nets or standing on three legs, resting a back one and dozing. An aura of calm peacefulness spread over everything. If only it could continue.

Praying that there were no guard dogs about to give voice and betray my presence, I took advantage of the deep shadows along the drive and pressed close to the house wall. Sidling my way round to the far side, I could see there was only the one room showing a light. From the size of it, I judged it was the main lounge, and the curtains – heavy, lined jobs – were caught back with ties, the entire room fully visible.

O'Brady was knocking back what looked like a treble whisky and chatting to Alfie. Good, two of the three were safely here. But although I could see the two men, I needed to hear what was being said as well. Following the angle of the wall, I worked my way down to the back entrance. Presumably this would lead me into the kitchen, the whole door of which was a solid wood job, no glass inset at all, no chance to see if the room was unoccupied or not.

Testing, I put my index finger near to the handle and pushed very gently. For a second the heavy door stayed where it was. Then, very slowly, it moved away from the door frame, only a

couple of inches, but enough to show me the door wasn't locked.
I hesitated.

The night wind was blowing towards my face. In the last few
seconds, I'd become aware of a fresh, manly odour – aftershave.
And as my brain relayed the message where I'd last smelt this, I
felt the menacing, unyielding pressure of a gun between my
shoulder blades.

'Dead lucky, Radcliffe?' said a familiar voice. 'I don't think so.
Well, what are you waiting for? Get inside – now.'

THIRTY-NINE

Alfie was just about to light up a cigarette when I entered
the lounge. He was using the solid gold lighter.

'Mine, I think.' The man behind me kept the gun
jammed into my back and held out his left hand.

Alfie's face lost all colour. Cigarette forgotten, he meekly handed
over the lighter.

'Where did you find *him*?' O'Brady jerked his thumb
towards me.

'Outside the kitchen door, about to come in. Uninvited.'

'I knew he was trouble. He's good at playing detective. But I
didn't expect him right now.' O'Brady's face was twisted up with
a combination of fear and anger.

'Shut up.' The gun was pushed harder into my back. 'Move.
Outside.'

There was no point in arguing; he was the one holding the cards
and the gun.

'Take him to the small hay barn. We'll get him tied up before—'

'*Shut up.*' The words were aimed at O'Brady and full of
menace.

The man snapped his lips together and nodded at Alfie. 'Find
some rope and look sharp.'

I was frogmarched from the lounge into the kitchen and through
the back door. By now the cloud formations overhead had
descended, blacking out the yard. No rain was falling yet but it

was only a matter of minutes. Already there was a muted roll of thunder in the distance. The horses in the stables seemed to have picked up on the ominous heavy stillness that was preceding the coming storm. I could hear several moving about restlessly. And then into that stillness I caught the sound of an engine coming along the top road. It was a heavy vehicle.

'Stay,' the man commanded. It could have been the tone used to control a wayward dog. I stayed.

All four of us waited like statues in the yard as the noise of the engine increased. The powerful double beam of headlights ploughed across the drive in an arc, illuminating the whole house, stable yard and the four of us.

O'Brady stepped forward, waving the driver on to the far end of the yard. I caught a glimpse of two men in the cab – the two who Ginnie Cutler had pointed out on the laptop screen. Remembering the nasty red burn on her skin, I felt anger rise within me. Sometime soon, maybe even tonight, I was going to settle the score with the sewer rat. But all I was hoping for at this moment was that Mike had done what I'd asked of him.

'OK.' I felt the jab of the gun barrel biting into my flesh. 'Start walking, Radcliffe. Follow Alfie.'

Detailing the sewer rat and his sidekick to unload the returning horse from the horsebox and settle it into a stable, he took us across the yard, past the run of stables and on down a side pathway to what appeared to be a small decrepit barn.

Alfie switched on the overhead light. The place was crammed with bales of hay. There was an old worm-eaten chair in the corner beneath a wide gap in the boards forming the side.

'Sit.' The brusque order came again.

He would have made a good dog trainer. I fought down my rising temper and complied.

'Tie him up, arms and legs and jam the chair upright so he can't rock it over.'

I groaned inwardly because that was exactly what I was intending to do should they leave me even half a chance. Alfie was detailed to do the honours.

'But first, strip him naked.'

Even I goggled at the bizarre command. But I knew it was good practice for lowering confidence. It instantly put you at a massive disadvantage, creating a distraction from what you should be thinking about. In my case right now, that was escaping in one piece.

I put up a token struggle but against this number of assailants, it was useless. Indeed, the struggle only resulted in retaliation – two men immediately kicked out, one at my crotch, the other, as I doubled over, my head. After that I succumbed to being tied up by Alfie. Any further damage to my head injury now could prove catastrophic.

Securely tied to the arms, the back and the legs of the chair, there was nothing I could do.

In front of me, Mr 3-D man, aka Perry Rantby, had re-holstered his pistol under his left arm and was leaning against the side of some hay bales. 'Now talk. You know where Sophie Whellan is, don't you? And you are going to tell us where she is – otherwise . . .' He smiled nastily. 'We will have to make you talk.'

I had wondered why they hadn't gagged me – now I knew.

Sewer rat had joined us now, together with the other one, and both stood to one side manically chewing gum. They were also smiling. I'd already had sewer rat down as a sadist – he had to be to injure a small defenceless woman. But I hadn't thought Rantby could have sunk so low. Seems I was wrong – by a long way. His next words proved it.

'One last chance. Where is *she*?' He leaned forward over me, digging his fingertips into the side of my neck at strategic nerve points that had me squirming and yelling out. He stepped back. 'Well?'

I let the nerve pains ease away then smiled up at him. 'She's safe.'

'Told you so. You'll not get anythin' out of him.' Sewer rat snorted with satisfaction at his own cleverness.

Rantby swung round on the man. 'You think not?' His fists were clenching and unclenching. He pointed a finger at the sidekick. 'Go and fetch that damned horse.'

'What horse?'

'That useless bloody nag you've just brought back from Southwell.'

I had been following progress at Southwell Racecourse on and off all afternoon. Gypsy-Belle had trailed in four lengths behind as back marker. It was going nowhere as a racehorse. I knew it;

O'Brady and Rantby also knew it. Their reason for going to the racecourse was to gain convincing cover for picking up a consignment of cocaine from a lower-level link in the chain, the late Lenny Backhouse's uncle. If I had any chips to bet with right now, I'd put the lot on the cocaine still being somewhere inside the horsebox. All I needed now was a bit more time. Time for Mike to come across and do as I'd asked.

But Rantby's next words blew away any hopes I had.

'I'm not wasting my time on shits like you, Radcliffe. This is going to be on your conscience, certainly not on mine.'

There was the sound of hooves on the concrete outside. The barn door was opened by sewer rat and his mate led in a tired Gypsy-Belle.

'Tie it up somewhere.' Rantby waved a dismissive hand around the barn. Then he swung round on Alfie. The youth was sheet-white. 'Take this . . .' He dug in his pocket and produced the gold cigarette lighter. 'You were keen enough to get your mucky little hands on it earlier.'

Alfie, eyes bulging widely, shook his head and backed away. 'No, no . . . I don't want it.'

'Here, let me have it.' Sewer rat was practically jigging up and down with anticipation.

Rantby snorted at O'Brady. 'No balls, your *bastard* son. Like his father. Both of you needing bailing out all the time. Without me you'd be in the bankruptcy court. It's only my money keeps your stables and that bloody cleaning business going. Show him some guts.'

Despite the rate my heart was pounding, I was gratified to know I'd been right in one of my calculated leaps of speculation. Rantby was O'Brady's sleeping partner in Dust Chasers. That seemed about right – in the muck together.

Rantby suddenly tossed the lighter across to Alfie who involuntarily grabbed for it. 'That's right.' Rantby's voice softened menacingly. 'Now light it.'

Alfie stared at the man totally mesmerized, flicked the lighter and the flame blossomed.

The night was cold and I was stark naked, but a wave of sweat washed over me.

'You used a cigarette end last time, didn't you, Ernie?' Rantby addressed the sewer rat. 'Well.' He turned to look at me. 'This time, I can do better. Start at the bottom of his legs, burn his big toe,' he instructed Alfie. 'We'll work our way up.'

But the order only sent Alfie off into excessive trembling. His mouth opened and closed as he tried to speak. No words came out.

'For God's sake . . . Ernie, you do the job. I *know* you've got the balls.'

And the lighter was snatched out of Alfie's hand. 'Better check Radcliffe's bonds; if he jerks hard enough, they might come loose, boss.'

We waited, watching Rantby to see whether he would accept his minion's advice. Then he smiled. 'We wouldn't want him to get away, would we?' He nodded at Alfie who was still next to me on my right-hand side. 'Check the knots, tighten them.'

Inside, I felt a wave of despair. I knew – and I'm sure Alfie knew – that he'd not pulled them anywhere near as tight as he could have done. The lad bent over me, his back to the other four men. I felt him fumbling with the knots and then something cold and hard was pressed into my palm. Instinctively, I curled my fingers around it, but released my pressure a little as I felt the sharpness of the knife edge begin to cut into my skin.

I breathed deeply, sending the despair from me. I wasn't on my own against five of them. Alfie, it seemed, was on my side. It improved the odds enormously: instead of one against five it had just become two against four.

'Tell me, where is the girl? Or you're going to burn.'

Lips pressed together, I looked straight through him.

'What are you waiting for?' Rantby screamed at sewer rat. 'Burn the bastard.'

And sewer rat moved forward eagerly, a depraved grin spreading across his face.

'His big toe, burn his big toe.'

The lighter was thrust towards me. The flame moved from three inches away to one inch.

'*Where is she?*'

I kept my lips pressed tight. And then the flame was being played around on the inner side of my big toe.

FORTY

For a split second I watched the golden flame lick its way round the hallux, then glanced up. Five faces were riveted, eyes wide. All I could think was: *this is going to play hell with my race riding.*

Then sewer rat yelled: 'Told you! He's tough. You'll not get anything out of him.'

'Shut up,' O'Brady ordered. 'He'll talk, he *has* to talk.'

'Only to us,' Rantby said. 'He knows if he spills it to the police, the girl's dead.'

'Not if we don't know where she is,' put in sewer rat's mate. 'There's still her dad . . . we've got him by the balls. Soon as he's out of hospital . . .' He made a slicing motion across his throat. 'He'd do anything to keep her safe.'

And so would I, I realized. Her dad had saved my life once. Right now, it seemed fitting that if I could keep my mouth shut, I could repay that unrepayable debt.

'Try higher up his leg!' Rantby shouted. 'Go up his shin. And keep going up until he cracks.'

By now, my big toe was throbbing beautifully. But a jockey rides with the toes of his feet in the irons. The pressure exerted down to keep his balance of necessity hardens the skin around the big toe in particular. After many, many rides and years and years of race riding, mine were like horn, callused and extremely tough. I'd undoubtedly have an almighty blister, but I'd rather be hurt there than anywhere higher – and far more sensitive. Looking at the gloating, evil face of sewer rat, I felt another wave of sweat and fear flood over me.

Alfie, who had drawn closer to my chair, was also awash with sweat and fear – I could smell it as it poured down his face. Or maybe it was my own . . .

The cigarette lighter was lifted higher, the flame now held directly against my lower leg. And now the pain blossomed in my head as the flame touched me. The skin seared and there was a smell of burning as the hairs on my leg caught fire and shrivelled up.

'Higher, higher!' Rantby demanded, quite beside himself now. 'Make the bastard talk!'

Through gritted teeth, I managed to say, 'What would Porphyry Senior think to the use you're putting his lighter to now?' A long shot. The words might gain me a few seconds – and right at this moment, by God, each second counted.

But Rantby was too far gone. 'Burn the bastard!' he screamed.

And as sewer rat joyfully lifted his arm to comply with his boss's orders, overhead there was an unexpected mighty crash of thunder that seemed to shake the barn. His arm jerked as, caught off guard, he shot a quick glance upwards. In that split second, Alfie swung his arm up, connected to sewer rat's hand, and the golden instrument of torture flew high into the air, soared over the four men's heads to land on the top of one of the hay bales near the rear of the barn. The hay was dry; it caught alight instantly.

'Oh God, oh God.' O'Brady panicked and ran for the fire bucket at the back of the barn.

'No! Leave it,' Rantby shouted, going after him. 'The bastard's not going to talk, so let him burn with it. You'll get the insurance.'

Meanwhile, Gypsy-Belle, smelling the smoke, began rearing up, screaming in fear and yanking hard against the rope looped through a ring in the side of the barn.

'No, no, Dad,' Alfie was screaming as well now. 'Get them out.'

Taking advantage of the chaos, I'd been twisting the penknife Alfie had put into my hand and the thin rope snapped apart. With bloodied hands and arms free now, but still attached to the chair, I moved into a crouching position. Then I swung round violently, clouting the rotten chair hard against the barn wall. Chips and slivers of wood flew in all directions as the chair disintegrated.

Sewer rat and his mate darted for the door, dragged it open and disappeared outside into the night. The crackle of flames within the barn now rose to a strong roar as the wind rushed in to assist the flames. But as well as the noise from the fire, outside I could hear the crash of thunder mingling with the screaming of sirens and the yard was flooded with the powerful beams of headlights from police cars racing down the drive. And soon, I didn't doubt, to be joined by fire engines alerted by the police seeing the flow in the sky as they drew closer.

Thank you, Mike, I said silently. He'd not let me down; he'd telephoned the police, no doubt laid it on thick, and they'd arrived to the rescue. Ignoring the searing pain in my leg, I backed further into the barn. Gypsy-Belle was still screaming in panic, striking out with her front hooves, but Alfie had now dragged off his sweater and, as I watched, threw it over her eyes. I went to help him. Between us now the mare, calming down a little, was on all four legs. Trembling violently, nostrils flaring, she allowed us to slowly lead her forward towards the fresh air blowing in through the doorway.

Knowing Alfie could cope with the horse now, I turned back into the inferno. The heat had ratchetted up and the smoke made it impossible to see further inside, but I hadn't seen the other two men get out. I bellowed their names as I frantically waved away the smoke, trying to see where they might be, if they were stuck. They'd been prepared to roast me alive, but I hoped I wasn't down at their level. If there was a chance I could help get them out, I had to try.

And then the world imploded above my head as the main beam spanning the roof of the barn gave way.

I *think* I scrambled back just as it was coming down, but I couldn't swear to it because everything just, suddenly, went . . . black.

EPILOGUE

'How do you do it, Mr Radcliffe?' The nurse stood shaking her head at the foot of my bed. 'You've no eyelashes left, no eyebrows, no hair at the front—'

'And I look like I've been under the grill, buried alive, then dug up – yes, I know, you can't say things like this to a patient, but as a patient, I can.'

She was laughing now and wagging a finger. 'I don't know how you do it, but I do know you've got three extremely attractive ladies waiting to see you outside your bedroom door.'

'You selling tickets?'

They weren't the only visitors. Yesterday, the first day I was allowed *any* visitors, Mike had turned up – his gift to the afflicted not a bag of grapes, but a copy of the *Racing Post*. He had also used the same words.

'Dead lucky, you are. I don't know how you do it. Fallen head-first in the muck heap – again – and the RP editor wants you to write an article about it.

'Why?'

'Took place at a racing stables, in the hay barn, didn't it? In his words, "It's got legs". Made it sound like a bloody horse. *And* he's going to pay you.'

I tried a smile. It was decidedly one-sided, wonky, and it hurt.

'Always a silver lining.'

'You're bloody impossible.'

'You're probably right,' I said amicably. 'Thanks for phoning the police. Did they catch them?'

'Oh, yes. Collared the two men with the drugs cache in the horsebox. And they got O'Brady. He was running across the yard towards his house. Trying to save his own skin, of course.'

'Rantby?'

'Hmm, Rantby's body was discovered later at the back of the barn.'

'What about Alfie? He came good in the end. Without his help I don't think it would have ended so well.'

'Singing like the proverbial canary. All the names he can remember, including Paul Oats and his activities, so that lets Tal Hunter off the hook. But, I gather, he's very happy to do so. Wants nothing more to do with his biological father – says he's no father of his.'

'Yes, his face said it all when he was told to torch me.'

Mike's face twisted. Drawing a deep breath, he changed tack. 'Let's have it then, how did you figure it out? I promise not to spoil the editor's scoop.'

'I had a lot of help from other people. I spent most of that day joining up jigsaw pieces, getting a clearer and clearer picture. Watched the racing from Southwell. Made two or three phone calls – well, I wasn't supposed to be out driving to check so it was a bit restricted, really. Anyway, I took a few imaginative leaps of speculation – then checked some of them out on the internet. Amazing what you can find out using just a few clues.

'Oh, yes, and Gary Butt telephoned me back later. Not a bad boy, Gary. Told me about Lenny Backhouse's uncle shifting "goods" at Southwell.'

'But how did you get on to Perry Rantby? I'd have said he was straight, y'know. I did know Perry was a shortened version of his real name, but still, it just shows you . . .'

'Charges for services, to begin with. He made the mistake of doubling his prices. Course, he was also making the mistake of bailing out his nephew. Same with Alfie and O'Brady. Since O'Brady lost his wife, emotionally he fell back on his illegitimate son. Giles was in deep with the bookies, so was Alfie. And Jim Crack wasn't the only person who voted with his legs and changed vets.'

'He told you?'

'Well, dear Eliza was loyal to her fellows and wouldn't say. No, she gave me the biggest clue, without ever knowing. We were checking on the initials inscribed on that golden lighter. Said Rantby had been called after his maternal grandfather. So that gave the initials as PIR, not POR.'

'Hmm . . . I knew Perry was his nickname . . .'

'So, then I thought, what about his *paternal* line? It's what

families do, isn't it? And I discovered he had been christened
after his father who had been named after *his* father, Perry's
grandfather.'

'So his real name is?'

'Porphyry.'

'Eh?'

'It's really a rock, means solid, dependable. Both Perry's wife
and his mother referred to the men as Por – their rock. The three
letters on the lighter.'

'A certain eminent person also used that description. My rock,'
Mike murmured.

'Yes, so I understand. But that was for a gentleman who
deserved it.'

We were silent for a minute or two in reflection.

'They, the nurses and doctors, said it was a good job you've
got a thick skull, Harry. Apparently that fiery beam caught you
across the side of your head, scorched off a lot of your hairy
bits . . . the ones at the top of your body, that is, not . . .
er . . . the lower ones.'

'Careful, Mike.' I could hear the nurse's footsteps approaching.
'You don't want to embarrass the lady, do you?'

The door opened. 'Time's up, Mr Grantley,' said the uniformed
nurse. 'Mr Radcliffe needs rest.'

And Mike dutifully took himself off.

That had been yesterday.

Today, it seemed, it was the turn of the females. With a warning
not to tire me, the nurse showed in the three of them: Annabel,
my darling Annabel, Eliza – and, most surprisingly, Dame Isabella
Pullbright.

'Ten minutes only,' the nurse exhorted.

Their gasps of dismay at the sight of me, followed by their
solicitous concern, was most gratifying to a grounded man. I
thanked them sincerely for coming, and I meant it.

Dame Isabella wrung her hands, widened her eyes and blew
me a kiss. Well, she was an actress.

'Wouldn't have missed it for the world,' said Eliza and
gave me a half wink.

Annabel, bending over to kiss me, having found a spot that
wasn't charred, was very grounding herself.

'It'll keep you out of the saddle for a while.'

Our eyes met at a distance of a few inches. The old familiar current plugged us both in, instantly, as always. It hadn't gone away. And I knew it never would. It was pure electricity, sizzling hot. But it was the one type of heat I didn't mind if it burnt me forever.

'And, of course,' she continued, 'you can't stay here much longer, I mean, Leo's waiting for you at home.'

'Is he on his own?'

'Would I let him be? No, we're both there . . . waiting . . .'